ONE
FALSE
STEP

ONE
FALSE
STEP

CLIVE WOOLLISCROFT

The Book Guild Ltd

First published in Great Britain in 2024 by
The Book Guild Ltd
Unit E2 Airfield Business Park,
Harrison Road, Market Harborough,
Leicestershire. LE16 7UL
Tel: 0116 2792299
www.bookguild.co.uk
Email: info@bookguild.co.uk
X @bookguild

Typeset in 12pt Adobe Jenson Pro

Printed and bound by CPI Group (UK) Ltd, Croydon, CR0 4YY

ISBN 978 1916668 928

British Library Cataloguing in Publication Data.
A catalogue record for this book is available from the British Library.

As always –
for Sue, Kirsty, Karen, Ian, Ben, Luke, and Bonnie.

Man, the lawless libertine, may rove,
Free and unquestion'd, thro' the paths of love:
But woman, sense and nature's easy fool
If poor weak woman swerve from virtue's easy rule
If, strongly charm'd, she tempt the flow'ry way,
And in the softer paths of pleasure stray
Ruin ensues, remorse, and endless shame,
And one false step entirely damns her fame:
In vain with tears the loss she may deplore,
In vain look back to what she was before;
She sets, like stars that fall, to rise no more.

The Tragedy of Jane Shore
Nicholas Rowe

WILLIAM DUNBAR

ONE

I almost held my breath as I stood and watched a sunrise of singular beauty and splendour. The stars that had twinkled far and near gradually faded and disappeared. Heavy masses of white clouds hung in the east, through which poured incandescent shafts of the sun's morning glory, revealing a flood of changing shades of delicate colours, spreading upwards from the horizon. It was magical.

By now, the waters of the River Scheldt shimmered in the golden light. I could see a small boat heading along the river, breaking the smooth surface into multiple rippling waves of light. For that moment, it seemed that nothing would despoil the splendour of the scene, especially as I was about to begin a journey back from Flanders to my beloved Scotland. However, whilst I relished returning home, my head was a maelstrom of conflicting thoughts.

I was excited by the prospect of my return – my cousin, Robert Campbell, and I had been serving on the Continent as lieutenants with the Royal North British Fusiliers for several years – but I also felt disappointment, hurt and bitterness. I had entertained such high hopes for my future when I arrived in

Flanders, but those hopes had been dashed at almost every stage of my time away from home.

'How?' I hear you ask, dear reader.

Well, let me explain. Ever since I can remember, my sole ambition has been to become a rich man. Life has taught me that a full purse never lacks friends; castle gates always open for gold-laden waggons. My difficulty, though, has been to find the way to achieve my ambition, especially since the most straightforward way – to inherit wealth – is not available to me. Whilst my father was a wealthy Scottish nobleman, I was his fifth-born son, and even though three of my older brothers died while they were young, my eldest brother, James, survived. Accordingly, when my father died, James inherited his title, lands and virtually all his money.

My father can't have liked me or, if he did, he had a funny way of showing it, since all I received under his will was an annuity of £150, which James pays me out of his inheritance. Of course, such an income is ample for some, but for me, it is a mere bagatelle in the greater scheme of things – it inevitably falls far below my hopes, aspirations and actual annual expenditure.

As a solution to my predicament, I decided to follow a military career, especially when my great-uncle, Mark, a general in the Dragoons, offered to loan me the money, interest-free, to purchase a commission as a lieutenant in the Royal North British Fusiliers. That gave me two incomes, and I additionally had the prospect of profiting from a share of any booty taken during a successful campaign. Thus, and with apologies to William Shakespeare, there was a tide in my affairs, which, taken at the flood, could lead to my fortune. However, things hadn't worked out for me as I had hoped.

I took part in the victory at the Battle of Dettingen and had expected to accumulate substantial and much-needed booty in its aftermath. Unfortunately, however, my expectations went unrealised. What is more, I soon exhausted what little share of booty that was awarded to me; several unsuccessful evenings at the card table or in the company of ladies of little or no virtue saw to that. In addition, I was steadily incurring debt to fund my lifestyle.

Now, any hopes of mitigating my circumstances had disappeared. There was no subsequent battle – no further opportunity of gaining booty. Instead, all we had done was to advance in stages to Ghent, where we had been encamped until now, leaving me with the feeling that my life's voyage had become bound in shallows and miseries.

Then as I stood there, increasingly in danger of allowing myself to slip into a mire of self-pity, my train of thought was broken.

'A penny for your thoughts,' a familiar voice called behind me.

'Good morning, dear boy,' I replied, facing my cousin, Robert Campbell.

As usual, he looked immaculate – every inch the officer and gentleman he was. His dark blue eyes sparkled as he smiled at me.

'Everything has gone so well this morning,' Robert said, raising his tricorn hat above his powdered wig. 'I awoke from a deep and restful sleep. I'm in excellent health and spirits and can't wait to return to Scotland. Before that, though, I need a substantial breakfast. Will you join me in the dining tent, William?'

For a moment, I looked at Robert blankly.

'You go on ahead of me,' I eventually replied. 'I'll join you shortly... I just need a moment or two... of reflection and all that.'

'Suit yourself.' Robert chuckled. 'But don't complain if I've left you nothing to eat before you arrive.'

'That's a chance I'll have to take,' I retorted somewhat glumly as Robert headed on towards the dining tent.

Then, fully realising I had become unduly morose and feeling needful of his counsel, I hurried after Robert. 'Hold there, cousin!' I called out. 'If I know you, you *really* will leave nothing for me if I don't come with you now... in any event, I would like your advice about something that has been bothering me a great deal of late.'

With that, Robert and I made our way to the dining tent, which to my surprise, was far less populated than I had anticipated.

'Where is everyone?' I asked, looking all around me.

'I don't know... and I don't care.' Robert laughed. 'All the more for us.' He sat down and turned to look at me, his face now showing genuine concern. 'Come, William, sit down and tell me what has been bothering you.'

I sat down slowly and took a deep breath.

'I'm not sure where to begin,' I mumbled slightly, looking down at the dining table. 'This is all so difficult for me... so embarrassing...'

Robert reached out and touched me on my arm. 'Steady there, cousin, just tell me what ails you... I can't hope to help you unless and until you do,' he said softly.

I looked somewhat vacantly around me. 'Are you content with your life?' I eventually asked.

A quizzical look crossed Robert's face. 'What a strange question,' he replied. 'I can only assume that you ask it because you are not content with your own.'

'In some ways, I am, but in others, I am not.' I sighed.

'Meaning?'

I looked at Robert and smiled. 'Well, cousin, some men have a pleasing physical appearance – some wealth. You are lucky enough to have both, and you will eventually inherit your father's title and his estate. Sadly, life has dealt me a less fortunate hand on those attributes. I am not so concerned about my looks – after all, appearance is just smoke in the wind, and mine has never challenged my becoming a man of pleasure. However, I did not inherit my father's title or any meaningful portion of his estate. So, instead of taking my place among the hereditary lawmakers and wealthy men of the nation, I have had to seek employment to augment my income. I became a soldier to do just that. I had hoped... indeed expected... that I would accumulate substantial and much-needed booty during our time in Flanders... but that expectation was never met. Now, my lack of wealth is increasingly becoming a barrier to me. I must... I must somehow ensure that I rapidly become truly wealthy and have resolved to do just that, whether by hook or crook.'

Robert looked at me somewhat painedly, shaking his head slightly.

'But, William, remember the saying: *a greedy desire for money and the willingness to gain it by almost any means is the root of all sorts of evil.*'

I looked away from Robert briefly and then back at him. 'Well, that's as it may be, Robert, but I intend to become wealthy as soon as possible, and unlike Macbeth, I am not *too full o' th' milk of human kindness to catch the nearest way.*'

'Come now, William, by longing for wealth as you do, you will ultimately bring sorrow upon yourself,' Robert chided.

I released a deep sigh. It pained me to hear Robert speaking like that. He didn't seem to grasp my predicament.

'My dear cousin, a lack of wealth *is* what brings me sorrow.'

At that moment, a servant arrived to serve our breakfast, and silence fell between Robert and me, broken only by the clatter of our cutlery on our plates as we ate. Eventually, Robert looked at me, finished chewing the slice of buttered bread he had been eating, swallowed and then chuckled.

'William, have you ever thought of marriage?' he asked.

'Marriage...' I gasped, raising my eyebrows questioningly.

'Only insofar as it can serve just two purposes: to continue a man's name and to preserve inheritance within his family. Neither of these purposes is relevant to me; there is no pressing need for me to continue my name, and I have no inheritance to preserve.'

Robert leant forward, both elbows on the table, resting his head on interlinked fingers. 'You are wrong, dear cousin,' he replied, smiling somewhat impishly. 'Marriage can also serve a third purpose. It can offer a path to riches. I am all too familiar with the old saying: *he wha marries for love without money hath merry nights and sorry days*, but I have no love match in mind for you. I am contemplating an arranged marriage whereby you acquire a rich wife. Such a wife would bring wealth through a tocher. On top of that, since a husband has the right to acquire his wife's personal property upon marriage – *jus mariti* in lawyer speak – you would gain unfettered access to the assets owned by any wife you may take.'

I looked at Robert and grinned. 'I'd never thought of you as someone so subtly artful.' I chuckled. 'But I like your train of thought. What is more, life as a soldier will offer me plenty of opportunities to find a suitably wealthy woman to marry, with the added advantage that my duties will provide me with a legitimate escape from the shackles and confines of the marriage. I can have my cake and eat it.'

Robert looked at me, a beaming smile across his face. 'And you also have the considerable advantage of your title and connections. Doubtless, plenty of wealthy fathers are willing to put up a large tocher to match their daughters to someone like you and, through you, to our family,' he guffawed. 'Let's not forget that we are both related to most of the great Scottish houses. Let's also not forget that several marriage prospects are close to home.'

'I'm not sure I'm quite with you there,' I replied.

'Why, we have several unattached cousins in Edinburgh, and better marry among those you know rather than strangers, don't you think?'

'Absolutely!' I enthused. 'Does that mean you've already been studying the runners and riders among our cousins?'

'Good God, no, William, why would I buy a horse when I can easily hire one from a reputable stable?' Robert laughed. 'Unlike you, I do not need to consider taking a wife just yet, but I may be able to help you with any quest of *yours* to do so.'

'How?'

'Well… do you know Ann Macclesfield, the niece of Janet Bruce, who married our great-uncle, Charles?'

I paused, trying to picture the Ann Macclesfield in question. 'No, I do not,' I finally admitted.

'Then permit me to arrange a meeting with her mother, Frances Macclesfield, once we return to Scotland. I think it may help you with your quest to find a wife, but there are caveats.'

TWO

The morning had promised so much at first. The sun shone brightly; the azure sky was clear apart from a few white, fluffy clouds drifting on a light south-westerly breeze. Then, gradually, the cloud blocked out the sun as it thickened and turned a dirty grey. Finally, a drizzle began to fall that soon gave way to a steady downpour, bringing my cousin Robert and me an ever more challenging obstacle course of puddles as we hurried to meet Mrs Frances Macclesfield, Ann's mother.

We walked up to the front door, and Robert rang the bell. A liveried footman opened the door.

'Good morning,' Robert announced. 'The Master of Lothian and the Honourable William Dunbar to see Mrs Macclesfield.'

The footman showed us through a hallway into a parlour facing the street. 'I'll inform my mistress that you are here,' he said.

He left, and I looked around the room. I noted the luxurious wall coverings, a gold watch and a group of four miniature portraits on the wall, a porcelain figurine and tea service on a hanging *étagère* and bric-a-brac on pedestals and mantels. But I also noted crumpled papers on a small side table, a ball of yarn on the floor and a cloth tossed on a footstool.

Mrs Macclesfield seems to be a lady of some wealth but not concerned with tidiness.

At that moment, Mrs Macclesfield swept into the room, followed by the footman. She was a short, grey-haired woman with piercing blue eyes. I guessed she was probably the same age as my mother, and they also looked alike in some ways.

'Good morning, gentlemen,' she gushed. 'My apologies if I have kept you waiting.'

'A lady's privilege,' Robert replied with a smile. 'Permit me to introduce my cousin, William Dunbar. You and I have, of course, spoken about him before.'

'Of course,' Mrs Macclesfield said, turning to look at me.

I bowed.

'I am delighted to meet you, William. Robert has told me a great deal about you. Please do be seated.'

'Thank you, Mrs Macclesfield,' I replied and sat on a high-backed leather armchair. Robert sat in the chair next to me.

'Some coffee, perhaps?' asked Mrs Macclesfield.

'Yes, please,' Robert and I both replied.

Mrs Macclesfield turned to the footman. 'A pot of coffee, and then we are not to be disturbed further,' she ordered before looking back at me. 'It's such a shame the weather's turned out as it has.' She sighed. 'It would have been much nicer to take coffee in the garden.'

'Indeed,' I replied before leaning towards Mrs Macclesfield. 'Thank you for agreeing to meet with us,' I began, somewhat nervously. 'Robert will doubtless have explained that I am seeking a wife. He has suggested that your daughter Ann would make a good match for me.'

Mrs Macclesfield smiled and looked at me, her eyes twinkling.

'I hope so,' she replied. 'But first…'

At that moment, the footman appeared with a tray. He placed a pot of coffee, a jug of cream, a sugar bowl, cups, saucers and spoons on a table.

'Thank you. Off you go, man. I will take it from here,' said Mrs Macclesfield somewhat sharply.

The footman left, and Mrs Macclesfield poured coffee for Robert, me and herself and sat down.

'Now, where was I… ah, yes… I was about to provide you with some background information. My husband was a successful merchant here in Leith. His father was the baronet, Sir David Macclesfield. When he died, the title passed to my brother-in-law, Alexander. My husband died a dozen or so years later, and Alexander in the following year. Whilst Alexander had married, he died without issue, and so, on his death, the baronetcy passed to my son, David.' Mrs Macclesfield paused to take a sip of her coffee. 'My son was only sixteen when Alexander died,' she continued. 'He was then, and is still, a minor. My husband made provision in his will for Ann, our only other child. He bequeathed her the sum of £5,000, which will vest in her when she reaches the age of twenty-one—'

'And how old is Ann now?' I interrupted, simultaneously feeling ashamed of myself for having done so. Mrs Macclesfield looked at me, and I glimpsed her annoyance at my rudeness. 'My apologies, madam,' I mumbled.

'Since you ask,' replied Mrs Macclesfield curtly, 'she is twenty. However, my late husband's will provides that the £5,000 will pass to her when she marries if she has not reached twenty-one years of age by then.' Mrs Macclesfield paused, looking me fair and square in the eyes. 'So you see, Ann will become a woman of some wealth sooner or later.'

I looked away from Mrs Macclesfield to Robert, who smiled at me, and then back to Mrs Macclesfield.

'You will forgive me for asking, madam,' I said. 'I appreciate that looks aren't everything, but is Ann at all fair of face, and does she have a friendly and cheerful disposition?'

Mrs Macclesfield looked at me and chuckled. Then, she stood

up, went over to the group of miniature portraits on the wall and took down one before returning to where I was sitting. 'Well, William,' she replied, handing me the picture, 'I am, of course, Ann's mother, but here is a portrait of her painted about a year before her father died. I hope that it answers your first question. As to your second question, yes, I would say that she has a friendly and cheerful disposition. She also projects a general air of wisdom, although she can occasionally be somewhat naïve, so much so that she might be considered simple.'

I took the painting and looked at it closely. It showed a very comely young woman. She seemed thoughtful; her eyes, soft and forgiving, were gazing into the distance to her left; her hair was light brown and worn "up". Her thin lips formed into a half-smile; her face unblemished and without any unseemly marks or scars.

So, looks as well as wealth.

'You have a lovely daughter,' I said, looking up at Mrs Macclesfield. 'And she certainly has a look of her mother.'

Mrs Macclesfield looked slightly embarrassed, and her face momentarily reddened, the slightest hint of a blush.

'Oh, what a flatterer you are, William,' she replied. 'I don't know about that... but... let's return to the business at hand. We're here to discuss the possibility of a marriage between you and Ann. As you have said, Robert has suggested that Ann would be a good match for you – I can see how you would be a good match for her.'

I looked at Mrs Macclesfield and smiled. 'I am pleased to hear you say that, Mrs Macclesfield, but may I ask why you think so?'

Mrs Macclesfield left the portrait with me and returned to her seat before replying. 'Now that my dearest husband, and Ann's father, is no longer with us, I feel Ann's best interests lie in her marrying into a family of impeccable standing – a family such as yours. As you will know, my sister-in-law, Ann's aunt, is married to your great-uncle, Charles. Through her, I know all I need to know about your family. It is undoubtedly one of impeccable standing. Ann's marriage to you, and through you, affords her a place among so many of the great Scottish houses.'

When I heard those words, I smiled inwardly. It seemed clear that Robert had blown my trumpet for me. He had made the same point to me before we left Flanders.

'That's very kind of you to say so,' I replied. 'But I'm sure you will be aware that I have no great fortune of my own, although, hopefully, that situation will change through my soldiering.'

Mrs Macclesfield looked at me wistfully. 'I respect your honesty, dear William. It speaks volumes about you,' she said. 'And I may well have the solution for you there.'

'In what way?' I asked somewhat quizzically.

'I am the sole executrix of my late husband's will and, as such, control my son's legacy while he remains a minor. That said, I have discussed Ann's position – and yours for that matter – with him, and he agrees with what I am about to propose.'

My ears pricked, and I leant forward. I was trying to repress the smile that was forming on my lips. *This is beginning to sound promising.*

'If you and Ann marry,' Mrs Macclesfield continued, 'you will receive £250 per annum from my late husband's estate while David remains a minor. Then, when David reaches his majority, he will continue to pay the annuity to you for as long as you and Ann are married.' She looked me straight in the eye with her eyebrows raised. 'How does that sound to you?'

At first, I could think of nothing to say. What had been proposed seemed almost too good to be true. If I married Ann, I would receive the annuity of £250 and acquire the right to the £5,000 by operation of *jus mariti*. Heads I would win, tails I could not lose.

'But what about Ann?' I eventually asked. 'How does she feel about the prospect of marriage to me? After all, she and I have never met.'

'Ann will do as I bid – and without question. She knows I always have her best interests at heart and will always act in those best interests.'

'If you're sure,' I said.

'Oh, absolutely,' she replied. 'Well, what say you?'

I looked at Robert, remembering the caveat he had mentioned whilst on our return to Scotland.

'Now you mention it,' I said, 'I am happy to marry Ann. But some difficulties need to be thought through very carefully.'

Mrs Macclesfield gave me a curious look. 'Pray, what difficulties?' she asked.

I leant forward towards her, lacing my fingers before me on the top of my knees as I did. 'It's like this, Mrs Macclesfield – Ann and I have important differences. She is Roman Catholic, as are you and the rest of your family; I am a Presbyterian, as is my family. Your family are Jacobites. My family are loyal to His Majesty King George. There are rumours that King Louis of France is helping Prince Charles and that an army will soon sail for Scotland. If those rumours prove true, it will place both Ann and me in an invidious position. For those reasons, I fear I must protect my position in the longer term and, in turn, Ann's. I would need the marriage between Ann and me to remain a secret.'

Mrs Macclesfield scowled. 'A secret,' she exclaimed. 'Are you proposing that Ann should enter into marriage like a thief in the night?'

I fumbled for a response. 'I fear my chances of promotion…' I started to say, but my words petered out when I saw Mrs Macclesfield's expression. Lines of anger were showing on her face. Her eyebrows grew closer together. Her face reddened. I looked down and, not knowing what else to do, picked up my cup of coffee and took a sip. This action provided a short period of acceptable silence, but eventually, I would have to set my cup down and continue my explanation. Then, Robert came to my rescue.

'Forgive my dear cousin,' he jumped in. 'He has understandable concerns, but there is a way around them – one that allays them. It is unavoidable that some people will know of the marriage, but only a few outside the three of us – and Ann. So far as Ann is concerned, she and William will share an exclusive private ceremony conducted late on a summer's evening in a quiet family chapel on the outskirts of Leith. Not even you and I will be there. Those elements will add to the excitement of the marriage.'

'But why can't you and I be there?'

'It may seem alien to you, even harsh for you, but one who shares a secret with a friend invariably forgets that the friend has a friend – and that friend has a friend – and so on. Best to keep the circle as small and as tight as possible at all times.'

A look of realisation flashed across Mrs Macclesfield's face, and she seemed to relax. She stood up and ambled over to a window. My gaze followed hers, where it had wandered to watch what was happening outside.

'Of course, you are right, Robert.' She sighed after a short pause. 'Leave this with me, then. I'll appraise Ann of our discussion, speak with my lawyers and instruct them to draw up a suitable contract.'

*

The day of the wedding was rather gloomy. Dark clouds hid the sky, but it did not rain, and the evening was warm. I had persuaded a young woman to attend and act as the single witness to the marriage, someone connected to neither Ann nor me. In truth, I had made her acquaintance in a tavern only the previous evening. I also procured the services of a minister known only to me to conduct the ceremony. A half-merk minister, as such men are known.

The minister, witness and I travelled together to a remote chapel in a carriage I had hired. Ann was waiting outside the chapel in a carriage Robert had hired to take her there. I have to say that she looked radiant. She was wearing a pink silk satin robe *à la française*. Pearls and other jewels adorned her stomacher. Bands of bobbin lace almost covered the pleats of her bodice front and embellished the edges of her wing-sleeve cuffs. Around her neck, she wore a white silk lace choker, in the centre of which sparkled an oval-shaped emerald and diamond brooch. On her head was a small lace cap decorated with lappets, tied with white silk ribbons matching those at her elbows. On her feet, she wore gold-fronted, ivory, high-heeled mules. Her eyes sparkled, and a beaming smile lit her pale face.

I walked over to Ann, took her hand and drew her towards me. I kissed her lightly on her cheek and then her brow. Neither of us said anything. We then wandered into the chapel, hand in hand, preceded by the minister and followed by the witness.

Ann and I stood together in front of the altar. The minister prayed before he commenced the wedding ceremony, placing Ann's hand in mine. Soon afterwards, he pronounced the words that made us man and wife.

I paid the minister and the witness for their services. They climbed into the carriage that had brought them and me to the chapel and returned to the city. After that, I never saw either of them again.

Ann and I watched until the carriage disappeared. Once it had, we linked arms and made our way to the carriage that had taken Ann to the chapel, climbed inside and drove to a house I had rented in Edinburgh.

When we arrived, I led Ann into a parlour.

'Some wine?' I asked.

'Thank you, yes,' she replied.

'Sit yourself down,' I said before crossing the room to a table on which stood a decanter of what was sure to be a fine wine – a gift from Robert – and two glasses. I half-filled both and returned to Ann, handing her one of them.

'Here's to us,' I said softly, lifting my glass towards her before taking a sip.

'To us,' Ann replied.

I sat down on an armchair opposite Ann.

'It seems strange, Ann,' I said. 'Only a few hours ago, we had never met – now we sit here, man and wife.'

Ann looked at me and smiled. 'But my mother had told me all about your family. I also met your cousin, Robert, when he visited my home. He told me so much about you that I feel I know you already.'

'Yes, Robert's been a good friend – oh, and he has arranged with your mother for your clothes and other belongings to be brought to the house. You should find them upstairs in the dressing room.'

We continued to drink our wine in silence.

'May I offer you some more wine?' I asked when Ann had emptied her glass.

'No, thank you,' she replied. 'I'm feeling rather tired after all of today's excitement.'

'Then shall we go up to bed?'

Ann looked at me and nodded.

'Yes,' she whispered.

*

Ann and I continued to live at the house after our marriage. I cannot honestly say that it was an idyllic time for me, but that said, it was no great hardship either. Then, eight weeks into our marriage, I received a visit from Robert.

My footman showed him into the front parlour, where Ann and I joined him.

'Hello, Robert,' I greeted him, shaking his hand firmly. 'It's so good to see you. Ann and I were only saying yesterday evening that we hadn't seen enough of you since we came here.'

Robert turned to Ann and embraced her.

'You will appreciate…' He chuckled. '…that I had to leave you two to get to know one another without any interference from me.'

'Dear cousin, you should know that you are always guaranteed a warm welcome from us,' I replied. 'Now, how about a glass of brandy? You can tell us what you've been up to these past few weeks while we drink.'

'That's kind of you, William; a brandy would be most welcome.'

'Then sit yourself down, and I will get us both one,' I said, crossing the room to the brandy bottle. I poured two large measures and returned to where Robert was sitting. I handed him a glass and sat down. 'So, is this a social visit?' I asked.

'I only wish it was,' Robert replied a little wistfully. 'I'm afraid that we have orders to march south to London and thence return to Flanders.'

Ann gasped audibly and started to cry.

'I always knew that you would have to return to your soldiering, William.' She sobbed. 'But not as soon as this.'

I looked at Robert. 'When must we report back, cousin?' I asked.

'Next Wednesday.'

'But that's only five days away,' spluttered Ann.

THREE

We had struck camp and were underway by five o'clock in the morning. The weather was foul, with an icy gale and a mix of rain and hail, but this did not bother us. On the contrary, we were confident and determined. We had returned from Flanders and joined the rest of the army under the Duke of Cumberland. Our objective was to deal with the Pretender – Bonnie Prince Charlie – once and for all.

We had been on the march for about five and a half hours when we were ordered to form a line and march forward in full battle order. Like a deep, sullen river, we progressed across Drumossie Muir, a bleak, long, boggy morass overlooking the Moray Firth about two miles south-east of Inverness.

Ahead of us, I could see the rebel force drawn up in two lines across the moor. Surprisingly, they had taken up a stretch of open moorland between the stone-walled Culloden enclosures to the north and the walls of Culloden Park to the south. This seemed rather odd to us on several counts. Firstly, they appeared to have insufficient troops to fill the enclosures, leaving themselves vulnerable to being outflanked. Secondly, deciding to fight on a boggy moor rather than on higher and firmer ground made little sense. It did not favour the tactic of the so-called "Highland Charge" that had brought them such success in previous battles. Thirdly, it played to one of our main strengths: we possessed powerful artillery.

The way the duke formed us into three lines belied the generally held view that he was no soldier – after all, he had been lucky at Dettingen and soundly beaten at Fontenay. A combination of overmastering brutality on his part and disciplined troops like ours enabled him to arrange us in no time so that the centres of the regiments in the second line covered the gaps in the first line. My regiment was positioned in the centre of the first line.

Once the duke was satisfied that we were all correctly positioned, he rode out in front of us. An overweight, jowly man, he looked older than his twenty-five years. Nevertheless, he cut a dashing figure as he sat astride his chestnut charger in his red tunic edged and adorned with gold braid.

'Gentlemen,' he shouted out, 'the time has come for us to end the shenanigans of these rebels. However, I have one thing to say to you. If there is any man of you who, for whatever reason, would prefer to retire, I beg him in God's name to do so immediately. I would rather face the rebels with one thousand determined men at my back than have ten thousand with a tithe of them lukewarm. Is there any such man?'

The question was met with silence.

'As I had thought and hoped,' announced the duke triumphantly. 'Time then, for battle. Godspeed!'

The duke turned his horse away to take up his position. As he did, the air filled with cries of 'Huzza!' and 'Flanders! Flanders!'.

We advanced in line closer to the rebels and halted. Ahead of me, I could see the first line of the Jacobite army. A storm of snow and hail set in, blowing full in the face of the rebels. Notwithstanding this, I could hear cheering, whoops and cries floating through that storm towards us. I could faintly see the Pretender riding along his front line to rouse his men.

Immediately, a storm of a different kind poured forward. Our cannons belched cannonballs, and our sharpshooters opened fire with their muskets. I saw several of the Pretender's escort crumple to the ground. Somehow, though, he escaped unharmed.

As the Pretender disappeared behind his front line, the Jacobite pipers began to play. We took this as a sign that their army was about to commence their anticipated attack on us. I felt my heartbeat quicken and my stomach began to knot. I took several deep breaths and readied myself. However, nothing happened. There was no immediate rebel advance towards us.

Then the weather changed for the better, which acted as the signal for the Jacobite artillery to open fire on us, using two pieces of cannon. Our artillery began to shower the rebels in retaliation. Death flew wholesale across the ravine towards them; grapeshot swept through them like a hailstorm. The noise was deafening as our cannons belched out their deadly fire. Smoke filled the air. Meanwhile, all the men were ready for anything, standing with muskets loaded and bayonets fixed.

Suddenly, the right and centre of the rebel front line emerged, ghost-like, through the smoke. They briefly stood facing us, banging their targes and yelling battle cries at the top of their voices. Then, they began to move forward. Slowly. As they got closer, they opened fire. Rather than reload, they threw their muskets down and sprinted towards us.

As the rebels advanced, they faced the fiercest response from our first line. A deluge of bullets and grapeshot swept them as they charged, scything wide gaps in their ranks. Two of them disintegrated into unrecognisable fragments before my eyes.

The noise of battle formed one relentless wall of sound. The smoke was dense. Cannonballs sent up plumes of mud as they crashed into the soggy moor. Mud, limbs and heather were constantly in the air somewhere. A white cloud of smoke hung over the battlefield as a storm of grapeshot with whistling and terrible rattling spewed relentlessly onto the advancing force, delivering continuous death and destruction.

The charge of the Jacobites, though, pressed on undeterred. So furious was the onslaught that they broke through part of our first line. We counter-attacked, trapping the rebels on three sides. We opened a rolling fire at close range so sustained and heavy that the rebel attack disintegrated into complete disorder. Men were dropping like leaves in a final autumn flourish. There were sights almost too terrible to contemplate or take in properly. Men fell backwards, some doubled over, while others danced like marionettes as they were pulled hither and thither by the rain of musket fire. A carpet of bodies lay motionless all around.

Before the Jacobites could recover, our cavalry and foot soldiers charged them on both flanks, driving them together until they became a confused mass. Then, swept by continuous brutal gunfire and faced with deadly bayonets, the rebels were forced to retreat. There was nothing more they could do. They turned, scrambled into the dense smoke and headed for their lines. Hardly an hour had passed between the first shots and the final flight of the rebel army.

After the fighting had ceased, my regiment marched towards Inverness. I could see Cumberland, his sword drawn in a menacing and symbolic gesture ahead of us. As soon as we reached the town, we were ordered to empty the gaols of all English prisoners. After that, we were ordered to round up as many known Jacobite sympathisers as possible and incarcerate them in the emptied cells.

While this was happening, I was aware of a convoy of waggons rolling into the town loaded with wounded Jacobite survivors of the battle. These were huddled together cheek by jowl in their shared misery. Other waggons were loaded with women and children. Unwounded prisoners were handcuffed in pairs. They trailed behind the waggons, as did a few of their officers who were mounted on horseback, bound hand and foot.

'I just wish we could pull that rabble from the waggons long before they ever start for their ultimate destination and deal with them summarily,' I hissed.

My wish was soon granted. Cumberland gave the order to execute all the Jacobite wounded and prisoners brought to Inverness. I went about my work with relish – as I did the following day when I joined a party searching for rebel stragglers or fugitives in or near the battlefield.

There was an added attraction for me in returning to Culloden. It allowed me to line my pockets, albeit I had to exercise extreme care for fear of being discovered peculating. I surreptitiously slipped into my pockets all the cash and valuables I could find when searching the bodies of the slain.

We picked our way through the dead, lying in heaps on and around the battlefield, sometimes two or three bodies piled one on top of the other, sometimes their bodies mangled by our grapeshot. In one case, all that remained of his face was a bloody pulp.

As we worked our way back and forth, we found wounded men lying alone or in groups. Some were writhing on the ground. Some were trying to walk or crawl back to where they had started. My men beat several to death with the stocks of their muskets; other rebels were shot or bayoneted. Men with the recent defeats at Falkirk and Prestonpans still fresh in their minds gave little thought to mercy. For sure, I was not in any mood to show any clemency.

Jacobites were dragged from their hiding places one by one and summarily executed. Some wounded had crawled into a farm building.

'Look what we've found, sir,' shouted one of my men upon discovering the rebels. 'What do we do with them?'

'Very simple,' I replied. 'We can't waste time trying to bring them out – close the doors and set fire to the building.'

The door was shut fast with them still inside it and set ablaze. I watched as the building burned to the ground, deaf to the screams of the terrified men inside.

We found around twenty wounded rebels who were too seriously injured to join the retreat and had taken refuge in a small copse. These were herded together at Culloden House, where they lay without care until the following day. After that, they were tossed into carts and taken to the park wall. There they were lined up and shot dead. I happily discharged my musket at the head of one.

'This one's for all my fallen comrades,' I shouted as I did.

I felt a sense of joy like I had never experienced before as I returned to Inverness and went to a coaching inn to meet up with Robert. As I approached the great gateway of the inn with its deeply reeded oaken posts and heavy double doors, my heart was racing; my breathing rate was unusually fast. I was almost overwhelmed by a sense of invulnerability, of increased energy and strength. Almost superhuman. But I was soon brought back down to earth.

I went through the gateway into a spacious courtyard, partly surrounded by a gallery supported on stout oaken pillars, and reached a staircase. Robert stood about halfway inside the courtyard. As I approached, he looked up and raised his hand in welcome.

'Welcome back, cousin,' he greeted me cheerfully. 'I trust that you had a fruitful day yesterday.'

'Aye, cousin,' I replied, grinning. 'In more ways than one – I'm in the mood for celebration.'

Robert looked at me, frowning. 'Perhaps in a moment or two,

William. But first, I need to have a chat with you. So, let's go into the garden.'

Somewhat puzzled, I followed Robert as he moved towards the end of the courtyard into the inn's extensive gardens bordered by large elms, at least 150 years old and further screened by dense shrubberies.

'Is something wrong?' I asked once we were in the garden.

'I fear so,' replied Robert, somewhat dolefully. 'It's David Macclesfield—'

'David?' I interrupted.

'Yes. He fought against us at Culloden.'

'Is he dead, or has he been taken a prisoner?'

'Neither. He is on the run.'

'But, how do you know?'

'While you were away, I was tasked with interrogating rebel officers. One of those told me that David had been appointed as aide-de-camp to the Pretender and fled Culloden with him.'

'David!' I gasped, slightly open-mouthed. 'But he is a mere boy.'

'That's as may be, but an uncle of David raised a troop in Edinburgh, officered by David along with other Lothian traitors.'

My heart sank. Mentally, the annuity I was receiving evaporated at a stroke. More importantly, I feared my professional reputation would be tarred with the same brush as David and his uncle. I was married to their sister and niece, respectively.

'I think I need to speak with a lawyer,' I spluttered.

FOUR

Several weeks had flowed from the rivers of time into the ocean of eternity since we had defeated the Jacobites at Culloden. I was standing at a crossroads, knowing that, whichever path I chose, I would ruin someone's life, but I also knew that the someone in question was not going to be me. I needed legal advice about my dilemma, however much I resented the cost I would incur. Accordingly, I made the journey into Edinburgh and was shown to the office of John Balfour, Attorney-at-Law.

As I entered the room, I saw Balfour sitting on a high-backed carver chair. He was hunched over a rectangular walnut table on which several documents were strewn. Quill pen in hand, he was seemingly lost in studying a manuscript before him. His white hair was swept back from his forehead, away from his somewhat elongated, ruddy face. A pair of spectacles was perched precariously on the top of his head. Two other quill pens were sat in an ink pot to his right. To his left was a wide bookcase stacked with leather-bound law books in varying degrees of disarray. A mass of papers littered the floor under the table.

I coughed – not the subtlest way of attracting Balfour's attention, but it worked. He looked up at me for the first time since I had entered the office.

'Forgive me,' he said, standing up and offering his hand. 'You must think me very rude. It's Lieutenant Dunbar, isn't it?'

'Yes,' I replied, shaking Balfour's hand.

'Please sit yourself down,' Balfour invited. I sat on a carved walnut ribbon-backed side chair with a lumpy padded seat that had seen better days, and which I soon discovered was decidedly uncomfortable. Balfour also sat down. 'How may I help you?' he continued.

I looked at Balfour, then away and then back at him. 'This may sound very strange, but without wishing to put too fine a point on it, I need your advice on how I might unpick a marriage I entered into about a year or so ago,' I replied.

Balfour looked at me quizzically. 'Unpick a marriage?' he asked in a somewhat surprised tone.

'Yes,' I replied. 'But perhaps I should begin by explaining the circumstances of the marriage in question.'

Balfour looked at me and smiled. Then, he reached into his desk drawer and took out a sheet of paper. 'Well, as they say, it's always best to start at the beginning,' he said.

I leant forward towards Balfour, feeling just a little embarrassed. At first, I said nothing. 'I… umm… I… needed money,' I began eventually. 'Marriage seemed to be the quickest and easiest way to meet that need… by way of a tocher, you understand. Such a… marriage was then negotiated through the good auspices of a cousin of mine.'

Balfour picked up a quill, dipped it into an ink pot and wrote on the paper – notes of my response, I assumed. He continued to write after each of my answers to his subsequent questions.

'And who was the bride-to-be?' Balfour asked.

'Ann, the daughter of David Macclesfield – a wealthy Edinburgh merchant who had not long since died.'

'Ah, yes, I know of Mr Macclesfield, although I never acted for him,' Balfour chipped in. 'Please continue.'

'The negotiations were conducted with Ann's mother, who agreed that in consideration of my marrying Ann, I would receive the tocher I needed – by way of an annuity to be paid out of the estate of the late Mr Macclesfield for as long as Ann and I remained man and wife. However, matters were not entirely straightforward. Certain difficulties needed to be thought through carefully during the negotiation. Not the least of these was that Ann's family were Jacobites, which stood completely at odds with my family—'

'And presumably, those difficulties were resolved,' Balfour interjected.

'Yes… eventually. Ann's mother agreed that the marriage could take place in a private ceremony under cover of darkness in a quiet family chapel on the outskirts of Leith. It was also agreed that the marriage should remain as near a secret as possible.'

'And, presumably, such a ceremony took place?'

'Yes.'

'Who attended?' he asked.

'There were four of us,' I replied. 'Ann, a clergyman, a woman witness and, of course, me. The clergyman and witness travelled with me to the chapel. Neither was known in any way to Ann.'

'What happened to them after the ceremony?'

'They returned to the city. I have not seen either since.'

'Is there any marriage record, a certificate or something similar?'

'None at all,' I replied, shaking my head.

'What happened after the marriage?'

'Eight weeks or so later, I received a visit from my cousin with the news that we had orders to march without delay to London and thence to travel to Flanders.'

'And you left for London, did you?'

'Yes.'

'Have you cohabited with Ann since you left for London?'

'No. I have not seen her since then.'

After making a further note, Balfour paused, gazing up at the ceiling as if in thought, before looking back at me. 'I appreciate that you spent only a short time with Ann, but did your union result in any children?'

'Yes, a daughter whom I have never seen. Ann returned to her mother's home when she learned she was pregnant, and the child was born there seven months after I had left for London.'

'Did anyone other than you, Ann or her family know about the child's birth?'

'Not that I am aware of.'

'Now for the obvious question… perhaps a question I should have asked at the outset,' he said. 'Why are you now looking to "unpick" the marriage, as you put it?'

I leant forward towards Balfour again. 'There are two reasons,' I answered. 'Firstly, when Bonnie Prince Charlie returned to Scotland, Ann's brother, David, threw in his lot with him, like the rest of his family. They are traitors. I can have nothing further to do with them, including Ann and my daughter.'

'And the second reason?'

'Without putting too fine a point on it, Mr Balfour… money – the very reason I married in the first place,' I replied. 'I have maintained unfettered access to Ann's inheritance, but this has dwindled at an alarming rate since I first got my hands on it. I have had heavy losses at the gaming tables and have lived at a higher rate than prudent. I desperately need to find a way to replenish my coffers, especially since I am now certain to lose the annuity promised to me by Mrs Macclesfield. That will disappear because my brother-in-law fought with the Pretender at Culloden. For sure, his title and estate will be forfeited. The fact is that I will be stuck with a wife and a child and little more to my name other than my army pay and an annuity I receive from my late father's estate. My marriage to Ann has proved to be a false dawn. I need to find a new wife and, with it, a new tocher, but first, of course, I need to become a single man again.'

'I see,' said Balfour, who then made further notes. I sat watching in silence as he did. Then, when he had finished, he looked up slowly. 'Well, Lieutenant Dunbar,' he said, 'you will appreciate that the law is like a multicoloured candle whose dribbles intertwine at the base in a swirl of colours. Generations of legislators and courts with different aims and desires add their farthing's worth, tweaking and changing the corpus over time. So, we are left with a sometimes-confusing and less-than-uniform result. Sometimes, one can take advantage of such confusion and lack of uniformity. However, in this case, I fear not. Regrettably for you, I believe there are real difficulties that you will face if you go ahead with your plan to deny any marriage between you and Ann.'

If I am honest, I can't say that I was entirely surprised by what Balfour had just told me, but I was disappointed, nevertheless. I briefly looked up at the ceiling and exhaled audibly before returning to Balfour.

'I had hoped you would tell me differently.' I sighed. 'Please, set those difficulties out to me.'

'I will try and put things in as simple terms as possible,' he said. 'The fact that there is no record of the marriage is to your advantage – as is the fact that it is highly improbable that either the witness or the clergyman will be found. However, I fear Ann will inevitably be able to persuade a court that she and you are married under Scottish Law.'

'But, how, if she cannot show that any marriage ceremony took place?' I asked, almost pleading with Balfour.

'There are two ways she can do this. Firstly, she can claim

marriage to you based on cohabitation while you both resided in Scotland – you and she are married by repute, as we lawyers say—'

'But what if I claimed that, in reality, we did not cohabit?' I interrupted.

'Then, as I was about to say,' Balfour replied, 'Ann would claim that you and she had intercourse in Scotland and that such intercourse followed a promise of marriage. If the court accepted her word on that, a marriage would be deemed to have occurred on the date of such intercourse. Now, given that Ann's mother was a party to the arrangement between Ann and you and that she has given birth to a daughter, I cannot see how her claim will fail.'

'But, what if—' I blurted out.

'Forgive me for interrupting,' interjected Balfour. 'We could pursue several avenues – you and Ann did not have intercourse – the child is not yours – and so on, but I cannot see any court preferring your version of events to Ann's in any of those.'

I felt frustrated. Angry. My mind was racing.

'Well, here's one you may not have thought of,' I ejaculated. 'What if Ann herself denied any marriage between us... or denied that there was any promise to marry?'

Balfour put his quill down, looked at me and smiled. 'Well, that would put an entirely different complexion on the situation,' he replied.

I looked back at Balfour, paused momentarily and slowly rose. 'Thank you, Mr Balfour. All you have told me gives me ample food for thought.'

Balfour also stood up, offering me his hand. 'Thank you,' he said. 'I will very shortly post a detailed letter of advice to you. In the meantime, please do not hesitate to make another appointment if you have any further thoughts.'

I took Balfour's hand, shook it and left his office.

*

Once I received Balfour's written advice, I thought long and hard to find an answer to my problem. In the end, though, I could think of nothing better than to persuade Ann to disown me as her husband – to say that she had been my mistress and nothing more than that.

Balfour advised that any denial of our marriage had to be given in writing, so I began to draft an explanatory letter to Ann and a letter to be written by her to disown me as her husband. Eventually, I was satisfied with the wording of these letters and wrote to Ann.

My dear Ann,

I hope this letter finds you and our dear daughter, Margaret, well. I am sorry that such a considerable time has passed since I last contacted you. I can offer no excuse for the delay.

The proposal I will suggest to you in this letter may come as a great surprise – and may even shock you. However, I trust that the reason for making it will resonate favourably with you – and that you will agree with what I am proposing.

You will know that my current income amounts to a mere pittance – one that scarcely allows me to live up to the expectations people have of a man of my noble birth or procure for you, my wife, and Margaret, our dear daughter, those pleasures and luxuries that you both have every reason to expect from me.

I have given great thought and consideration to these matters and have concluded that only one thing can be done to rectify this situation. In short, I have to obtain advancement in the army.

I have insufficient capital to purchase a captaincy or higher rank – and cannot go cap in hand once more to Uncle Mark. So, I can only advance my career through my efforts. But here lies the problem. I have little hope of advancement while it is known that I am burdened with a wife and child. However, if I could once again be considered a single man, I do not doubt that I would soon gain promotion and find myself in a position where I could maintain you in the style you richly deserve.

At that point, I would make a great show of wooing you, make you my wife again and resume our life together.

My plan is a simple one. Just send me a letter in the form set out in the enclosed document.

There is the risk, of course, that I might be accused of acting fraudulently to serve my ends. But the risk is small. It is not beyond the wit of man for people to suppose that fate subsequently intervened once my circumstances improved and we came together again.

We would publicly celebrate such a reunion with a glorious wedding that truly reflects our love.

Your most affectionate husband

William Henry Dunbar

Encl. Draft of a letter to be sent by you to me.

NB – You must sign the letter as Ann Macclesfield, not Ann Dunbar. You must also keep this letter and the draft strictly between us. Therefore, you should destroy both once you send your letter to me.

I sent the letter off and waited for a reply. None came, so I wrote to Ann again, imploring her to send me the requested letter. In the strongest possible terms, I assured her she had nothing to fear from me. All we were doing was setting up a temporary smoke screen so that I might better myself for the benefit of her and Margaret.

To my disappointment and growing frustration, I wrote again to Ann, having still received no reply from her.

My dear Ann,

I had hoped that you would have replied to my letters setting out my plan to improve our mutual circumstances and those of our dear daughter, Margaret.

I know there would have been no hesitation in replying unless you had real concerns about my proposal. In this regard, it occurs to me that you may be fearful that I or my family and friends will abandon you when I receive your letter and withdraw all kindness and support. If that is so, my love, please put aside any such fears.

Our future financial well-being and my entire future happiness hang on a single letter from you purporting to deny our marriage – but which we both know will ultimately enable us to resume our lives together in total happiness and security. It would seem as if there had been no interruption to our lives together.

Your most affectionate husband

William Henry Dunbar

Suddenly, and just when I lost all hope, I received a reply from Ann. Filled with trepidation, I broke the seal and unfolded the letter. I could scarcely believe my eyes as I read it.

Dear William,

In the period that has elapsed since you left Edinburgh, it has been suggested that we are married – that I am your wife.

I realise the damage to your career that suggestions such as those might cause you, and I have no wish to cause any threat to your prospects. *For this reason, I write this letter to declare that, whilst we lived under the same roof and became lovers in the short time before you were ordered to rejoin your regiment, our relationship never progressed beyond that state of affairs. In short, you and I were not then, nor are we now, nor have we ever been, married.*

We did speak of marriage from time to time. You said you wished to marry me, but only if I converted to the Presbyterian faith. At first, I agreed with your condition, but soon afterwards, I realised I could never abandon the Roman Catholic faith.

By not converting to Presbyterianism, I fully accept that you were immediately and wholly released from any obligation that may have somehow come into being when we were lovers. I also confirm that you never made any promise of marriage to me.

Yours affectionately

Ann Macclesfield

Relieved and ecstatic, it was time to visit Balfour once more.

*

The chair in Balfour's office was just as uncomfortable as when I first met him. The office itself was just as untidy. At that moment, though, I would have been just as happy to be sitting on a pile of thistles in the corner of the foulest of cowsheds.

Balfour looked up at me and smiled.

'Good morning, Lieutenant Dunbar,' he greeted. 'How may I help you this time?'

Almost triumphantly, I reached inside my coat, took Ann's letter to me, handed it to Balfour, sat back in the chair and watched expectantly as he read it. Then, having done so, he looked at me.

'Well, as I indicated when we last met, a letter such as this puts an entirely different complexion on your situation,' he said.

I leant forward towards Balfour.

'My brother has always told me that there is nothing as powerful as a letter from an Attorney-at-Law,' I said. 'I'm sure he is right. So, I need you to draft a letter to Ann stating that in the light of her letter to me, I regard myself as henceforward released from any financial obligations to her and her daughter.'

Balfour looked at me, frowning.

'I will send Ann such a letter, but I fear that it might prompt an action to be brought against you.'

'An action!' I exclaimed. 'What sort of action, may I ask?'

'I suspect Ann may be advised to raise an action of declarator of marriage against you in the Commissary Court.'

'Let her,' I pooh-poohed. 'The letter she sent me will be sufficient to ensure any such action fails.'

'Let us hope so, Lieutenant Dunbar. Let us hope so, but *whit's fur ye'll no go by ye* – what's meant to be, will be.'

FIVE

My cousin Robert and I transferred to the Tenth Regiment of Marines shortly after I met with Balfour. We and several other officers and a party of soldiers were ordered to conduct a recruitment exercise in the counties of Berkshire and Oxfordshire in England. I could scarcely believe my ears when I learned of this. It offered the new opportunities I needed. In combination with the letter from Ann, I felt a real sense of freedom from the shackles and confines that otherwise might have hampered me. A sense of freedom that, in my mind, justified a resumption of a search for a suitably wealthy woman who would enable me to achieve my ambition to become a rich man.

In the meantime, my uncle, Mark, had decided to take the lease on a rather large house in Henley. Of course, it would be nice to believe that he did so to be close to Robert and me, but his move was a coincidence, albeit a fortunate coincidence for me as it transpired.

My recruitment duties took me as far as Reading to the south-east and Oxford to the north-west, but they also took me to many of the towns in between. A vast area for me to pursue my quest – I think you will agree, dear reader.

We began our recruiting exercise in Wallingford, in Berkshire, with some minor success, and then, travelled to Henley, where on our first morning there we set off along Hart Street. Robert and I led the parade. With swords drawn, which glinted in the morning sunshine, we smiled and nodded at spectators lining the street as we passed them. Drums that beat loudly and shrill-toned fifes heralded our advance. Hordes of excited children and bemused locals followed in our wake.

After a circuit of the town, we halted outside the White Hart. Robert and I went inside with the recruiting sergeant and mingled with a group of rustics scattered around the noisy, smoke-filled bar. I watched as the recruiting sergeant moved from table to table, looking into the faces of the men sitting around them.

'You'll make fine soldiers,' he said. 'Yes, to be sure, any man with it in him, who is steady and doesn't drink too much, is certain to get on in the army.' He paused and looked around the room, nodding towards each man standing there as he did. 'And you all look just like such men,' he continued.

He took a shilling coin from his pocket and spun it on the table before them.

'Who's willing to take the King's shilling?' he asked before regaling the men with a silken tongue as he recounted tales of the glories and splendours of a soldier's life – of Culloden and Dettingen – while hiding every dark spot.

His audience's faces conveyed a variety of responses as he painted a pretty picture of the prospect of riotous living, adventure and glory to the men. One or two, including the serving girl, seemed to hang on every word, but others appeared more sceptical. Finally, however, his words struck home in one instance as a man accepted the shilling. One step closer to reaching our recruitment target. Meanwhile, the recruiting sergeant's oratory continued unchecked albeit without further success.

Eventually, we all fell in outside the inn with the remainder of the recruiting party and marched back to our quarters situated outside the town. There, Robert and I handed matters over to the recruiting sergeant and headed back into Henley for a meal and a few glasses of whisky.

We found what seemed to be a respectable inn and entered a picturesque long, low room, its ceiling supported by blackened oak beams. Polished wainscoting adorned the walls. Latticed windows, filled with grime-covered glass, appeared to be almost covered outside with ivy. We worked our way through a choking fog of thick pipe smoke. The room bustled with constant activity. It resonated with the sound of the gentle chattering or, sometimes, the noisy bickering of its occupants. Some of these sat on benches on either side of rectangular wooden tables, others on single chairs on either end of the tables.

The landlord stood behind a bar that took up much of one side of the room. A dark-haired, comely serving woman stood to his left. Another worked her way from table to table, taking orders for food and drink. Most of the seats were already occupied, but we managed to find two that were empty. So, we sat down, ordered food and whisky to be brought over and began chatting about the recent events, specifically about Ann's family.

'I must confess that I was somewhat concerned after Ann's brother was convicted of high treason,' I told Robert. 'The immediate fallout from that was the loss of an annuity paid out of his father's estate. One of the purposes of the marriage in the first place vanished almost overnight. On top of that, I feared his misdeeds might adversely affect my military career.'

Robert reached over the table and gently placed his hand on my arm. 'That will not be the case,' he said reassuringly. 'Mark my words – he will soon be forgotten, dear boy. So you have nothing to fear.'

'That was not a chance I could take, though,' I replied with a sigh. 'Fortunately, I persuaded Ann to deny the marriage and allay my fears. And, in so doing, I've been able to return to the state of affairs that existed before the wedding.'

'So, you're back in the hunt for a rich wife-to-be,' Robert guffawed. 'Didn't anyone tell you that getting married for a second time represents the triumph of optimism over experience?'

'Oh, no, Robert.' I chuckled. 'In my case, the experience of what happened with Ann will ensure that I will ultimately triumph and achieve my goal of marrying a wealthy woman. Moreover, since I have been here in England, I have also learned that the title which courtesy permits me to bear is a commercial asset south of the Tweed, enabling me to sell myself in a far better market.'

At that moment, our food arrived.

'Frae witches an' warlocks an' langnebbed creatures an' poor or Jacobite wenches, guid Lord deliver us,' said Robert as grace as we set about eating our supper.

'Amen to that,' I replied, lifting my glass in a toast. 'In the meantime, here's to a successful visit to Wallingford when we return there in the morning.'

The last rays of the summer sun tinged the surface of the unruffled Thames with crimson and gold as Robert and I crossed the bridge spanning the Thames. We had been invited to a ball at Priory House, the home of the local member of parliament. As things turned out, he was a friend of Uncle Mark, who would also be in attendance. While Robert and I were unaware of it, this friendship prompted our invitation.

We walked together along the elm-lined avenue towards the house, the boscage of the trees diffusing the lingering shafts of evening light. Their pinnate light-green leaves fluttered in the breeze.

'Goodness me, what a magnificent building!' Robert exclaimed.

He was right. The house, with a front of Bath stone to a brick building with a hipped slate roof, had six wide bays with a central pediment supported by two columns and pilasters to the other bays. Lawns, dotted with isolated groups of trees and on which a few sheep were grazing, swept up towards the house. Knot gardens lay to either side of the front of the house, each in-filled with herbs and flowers. A majestic cedar of Lebanon, with its several trunks and clear horizontal layers in its structure, stood in the centre of a lawn to the right of the house. Its blackish-brown bark contrasted the dark grey-green needles with transparent tips, arranged in spirals around side shoots in rosettes or clusters.

We joined other newly arriving guests and were shown through a grand entrance hall into a large room, beautifully decorated in white and gold and crimson and with an area dedicated to dancing. Every door and window was open.

At first, I stood slightly in awe of the motley crowd scattered around the room's edges, looking for any familiar face. Not many ladies were present when we arrived, but several were very pleasing to the eye among those we could see. All of them were exquisitely dressed and adorned with sparkling jewellery.

'What do you reckon, Robert?' I asked.

'Well, William, I think that we shall meet three types of people here: first, the local *nouveau riche*, all as wealthy as Croesus; second, those who belong to the local "establishment" – landowners, bankers, merchants and lawyers; and thirdly, younger people like us, who are here essentially because they are thought to be able to dance dextrously.'

'Well, let's not disappoint them on that score,' I said cheerfully. 'Let's mingle, and let's dance!'

I soon became acquainted with all the principal people in the room, either by tripping almost seamlessly and unreservedly from one group to the next and engaging in polite conversation or dancing with every unattached young lady I encountered. Then I saw my uncle, Mark, chatting away amongst a group of obviously very well-heeled guests.

'Come and let's say hello to Uncle Mark,' I said as I guided Robert across the room.

'Good evening, dear uncle,' I greeted as we reached Uncle Mark. 'What a pleasant surprise to find you here.'

'Good evening, uncle,' said Robert, his hand outstretched.

'Good evening, nephews,' beamed my uncle. 'I hope you are both enjoying the hospitality of my good friend, the local member of parliament.'

'Indeed,' I replied. 'Do I take it from what you say that we owe our presence here to you?'

'That I could not say,' he replied, smiling broadly. 'But it would come as no surprise if it did. Let me introduce you to another good friend: Mrs Elizabeth McCleod.'

Standing by his side was a handsome, tall, slim woman, probably in her late fifties but looking considerably younger.

'My dear Elizabeth, may I introduce my great-nephews, William Dunbar and Robert Campbell,' he said. He turned towards her. 'You and I are old friends, eh? Many a minuet we have danced together over the years.'

Mrs McCleod blushed. 'I'm delighted to meet you both,' she said. 'I hope that you are enjoying your evening—'

'Will you please excuse me,' interrupted Uncle Mark. 'There's someone I need to speak to: the proprietor of the house I have taken in Henley. But, doubtless, you will take good care of Mrs McCleod until I return.'

Uncle Mark was gone long enough for Robert and me to dance with Mrs McCleod and explain the purpose and nature of our visit to Berkshire and Oxfordshire.

'I'm sure that you both would prefer to find people of your own age so that we will take our leave of you,' said Uncle Mark when he returned. 'I am having a dinner party at my home a week on Friday and would be delighted if you would join me.'

'Thank you, uncle,' I replied. 'It would be a great pleasure.'

'I agree, and thank you,' said Robert. 'I shall look forward very much to it.'

With that, Uncle Mark and Mrs McLeod left us, spent a few minutes taking their leave from our host and went on their way.

Robert and I continued where we had left off, alternating between mixing with other guests of our host, eating his food and drinking an abundance of fine wine.

All too soon, in some respects, the ball was breaking up. A few dancers floated on the floor, but most chairs were empty. I went to a window and looked out. The moon was rising, a wan, waxing gibbous moon about two-thirds illuminated.

'Time to go, I fear,' I said to Robert.

'I think so,' he replied. 'Especially as we have to go to Reading tomorrow on the next stage of our recruitment drive.'

We approached our host.

'Sir, we have had a wonderful evening,' I enthused. 'I never imagined I would enjoy myself so much. I fear we may have overstayed our welcome, but we found the attractions of the ball so irresistible that we could not tear ourselves away until now.'

'Have no fear of that, my boy,' he replied. 'Thank you for coming. Please pass on my best wishes to your uncle when you next see him.'

'That I will, sir. Goodnight – and again, many thanks.'

After that, Robert and I headed back towards our quarters.

*

It was a great relief to find myself back in Henley after a week or so of marching around Reading, drumming up recruits for the Tenth Regiment of Marines. It had not been easy. It had also been a tedious exercise. At least, though, we had exceeded our targeted number of men needed to swell our ranks.

We were quartered just outside Remenham, and I was looking forward to meeting up again with Uncle Mark at the dinner he had invited Robert and me to attend.

We walked from Remenham, crossed the bridge and headed along Hart Street. We continued past the White Hart before making our way to Uncle Mark's house, a square, yellowish-brick, three-storied building with a parapet front.

Five windows stretched across each of the top two floors. In addition, a pair of windows sat on either side of the main entrance. I opened the gate set in low railings that ran the width of the house, walked the short distance to the door and rang the bell.

I must confess that I was a little taken aback when Uncle Mark opened the door to us.

'Good evening, nephews,' he said with a beaming smile. 'So good to see you. Come in, please – both of you.'

Robert and I followed Uncle Mark into a hallway that I could see led to an open-well stair with turned balusters and then into a reception room, richly furnished with mahogany tables and chairs, gilt-wood oval pier glasses, mahogany tea caddies on a sideboard, cut-glass decanters, dinner plates and a complete long set of tea china.

Mrs McCleod was standing in the middle of the room chatting to a young lady about eighteen years of age; her noble features were bright and fair like the morning sunlight. Her dark brown hair was gathered on her brow in tight curls. Her light blue eyes sparkled brightly, especially whenever she smiled.

'You have already met Elizabeth McCleod,' said Uncle Mark. 'With her is her daughter, Caroline. They are staying with me for a few weeks. We are just waiting now for my other guests. Hopefully, they will join us shortly. But, in the meantime, some wine, I think.'

Uncle Mark beckoned a servant carrying a silver salver on which stood several glasses of fine white wine. Robert and I took a glass each.

'Here's to your very good health,' I said, raising my glass towards Uncle Mark, Mrs McCleod and Caroline.

At that moment, the doorbell rang and, shortly afterwards, Uncle Mark's expected guests were shown into the room.

'Good evening, Mr, Mrs and Miss Grundy,' greeted Uncle Mark. 'Come and meet my nephews, William and Robert.'

'Gentlemen,' Uncle Mark said as the Grundys approached Robert and me. 'Permit me to introduce Mr Francis and Mrs Ann Grundy and their daughter, Miss Mercy Grundy. Mr Grundy is both my friend and Attorney-at-Law.'

Once the introductions had been completed, the dinner party split briefly into two groups. Mercy, Robert, Caroline and I formed one, and Mr and Mrs Grundy, Mrs McCleod and Uncle Mark the other.

My first impression of Mercy was that she was no great beauty. If truth be told, she appeared at first blush to be somewhat plain. Apart from anything else, her face, like mine, bore the marks of smallpox. But first impressions can often prove misleading. Whilst it may be true that a woman without beauty is deprived of her most potent influence over men, such a woman will often possess the perhaps more enduring powers of fascination of manner, strength of will and sweetness of disposition. After all, dear reader, is it not true to say that many of the women who have made the greatest mark in the world have been plain women?

As Mercy, Robert, Caroline and I stood talking, I became increasingly intrigued by Mercy. She was taller than me, slender and exquisitely well proportioned. I guessed her to be in her mid-twenties. Her prolonged oval eyes of full and rich hazel, generally seeming half shut and shaded with dark eyelashes, opened out beneath her arching brows and danced whenever she laughed. She was a veritable picture of youth, health and happiness. However, before I could engage her in deeper conversation, Uncle Mark's servant appeared to announce that dinner was to be served.

With that, we all moved slowly into the dining room and took our places around a magnificent mahogany triple-pedestal extension dining table. Uncle Mark sat at the head of the table, with Mrs McCleod opposite him. Mr Grundy was to his right, Mrs Grundy to his left. I sat to the right of Mrs McLeod, Robert to her left. Mercy sat between her father and me, and Caroline between Mrs Grundy and Robert.

As the evening progressed, I gradually learned more and more about the Grundys. Mercy was an only child and, clearly, the much-loved daughter of devoted parents who would do anything for her. Mr Grundy had a very successful law practice in Henley and had acted on numerous occasions for Uncle Mark. Indeed, it was through Mr Grundy that Uncle Mark had come to take the lease on the house we were sitting in on very favourable terms.

'I am not the wealthiest man you will ever meet, Lieutenant Dunbar, but I possess wealth,' he announced, but not boastfully. 'As long as I can afford it, Mercy will have everything she wants.'

Mrs Grundy firmly believed that the greatest gift she could give her daughter was the best education possible. To this end, she had taken personal responsibility to ensure that Mercy was well educated by tutoring her daughter herself.

'You and I have similar beliefs on that score, Mrs Grundy, I also took it upon myself to educate Caroline,' Mrs McCleod concurred, looking at her daughter, smiling at her as she did. Caroline smiled back at her mother, nodding gently, prompting the look of satisfaction that crossed Mrs McLeod's face. A brief silence ensued as Mrs McCleod took a sip of wine before looking back to Mrs Grundy. 'Do you have a teaching philosophy that you have put into practice?' she asked.

'Indeed, yes, and a very simple one,' Mrs Grundy replied almost immediately. 'I learned that the word "philosophy" means "love of wisdom" – I just want Mercy to aspire to a love of wisdom. I prided myself on being fully aware of the educational defects, too often visible in men and women, that are sure signs of an incapable or impatient teacher in the earliest days of home or school teaching. You know what I mean, I'm sure, Mrs McLeod. Too shallow a knowledge of literature, the wrong emphasis in reading, incorrect spelling, indistinct pronunciation of words, a monotony of tone, inaccuracy and inexactness of quotation, insufficient knowledge of the multiplication table, together with a confused and vague idea of history and elementary geography.'

For a moment, Mrs McCleod looked at Mrs Grundy in a way that suggested that she had just found herself somewhat out of her depth intellectually.

'Absolutely, Mrs Grundy, you are so right,' was her hushed reply.

Mercy leant forward towards Mrs McCleod. 'To my mama, a love of wisdom encompasses three elements,' she said with a smile. 'First, fostering a love of reading and an appreciation for different types of literature. Second, developing writing to entertain, convey information and express opinions to others. Finally, to delve into people, places and times throughout history and gain the background needed to give context to present-day events.' Mercy paused, looking firstly at Robert and then at me. 'A tall order, you might say. However, I am a willing pupil, particularly when it involves reading. My mama's ambition has been for me to become omnilegent in both senses of the word: someone extremely well read, having great knowledge of literature and addicted to reading everything that came their way. I do not think I disappointed her; I soon developed an insatiable appetite for books. I became an unquestionable *helluo liborum*, a "book glutton". Not only did I read by day but also by night; a veritable *elucubrator* or, as Shakespeare preferred, "a candle-waster".'

'I wish I could say the same about reading,' said Caroline, somewhat dolefully at first. 'I like to read sometimes.' She paused as if deep in thought. Then her eyes twinkled, and her face lit up. 'But my passion is music. In particular, I love the music of Domenico Scarlatti,' she enthused.

'I, too, like Scarlatti,' replied Mercy. 'But as far as I am concerned, Handel is undoubtedly the greatest musician ever. I've thought so ever since Mama and Papa took me to the Sheldonian Theatre in Oxford to see the performance of his three oratorios, *Esther*, *Deborah* and *Athalia* when I was thirteen. Then, to cap it all, they took me to see the premiere of the *Messiah* at the National Concert Hall in Dublin when we visited there four years ago.'

'Oh, how I envy you,' exclaimed Caroline. 'On two counts. Firstly, going to Dublin. Secondly, seeing a performance of the *Messiah*. Have you been anywhere else exciting?'

Mercy looked at her father and then at her mother before turning back to look at Caroline.

'Well, yes. Papa took several months away from work some years ago and accompanied Mama and me to Bath for the season.'

'Bath?' queried Caroline. 'Isn't Bath Britain's leading matrimonial shopping centre?'

'Yes.' Mercy giggled. 'I think Mama and Papa were hoping for me to find a suitable match.'

'And did you?' I asked.

'Well, William... I met several young men who seemed interested in me but soon lost that interest for reasons I won't bore you with.'

'And since your time in Bath, has there been no one else?' I pressed gently.

'Well, there was another, but that came to nothing also.

Finally, after a short while, I realised he was not the one for me, and I sent him packing. He then accused me of being a flirt.'

'A flirt?' I gasped.

Mercy laughed.

'Yes, William – a flirt.'

'But you don't strike me as someone who might be described as a flirt.'

Mercy shrugged her shoulders. 'I am no flirt, I assure you,' she replied. 'Since the accusation, I have asked myself what a flirt is. Is she someone who does not know her mind? Is she someone who has no mind of her own to know? Is she neither of these? Or is she merely someone who plays a game that should be played with great care or, preferably, not at all? Well… I have a mind of my own. I know that mind, and I don't play games. The truth is that my accuser could not have made a suitable match. His accusation was proof enough to me that I was right.'

The more Mercy spoke, the more intrigued I became with her.

'All's well that ends well, I guess,' I returned.

'Yes, William, especially when I met the man of my dreams soon afterwards. Ironically, it was here in Henley that I found him. Never before had I experienced such joy. It felt as though I was in Heaven. We fell in love and recently became engaged to be married.'

My heart sank. This revelation came as a hammer blow to me. Suddenly, all hopes of my pursuing a young lady I was becoming attracted to, but more importantly for me, who was the daughter of a wealthy man, had evaporated.

'Was he not able to be with you here this evening?' I asked.

'Sadly, no,' replied Mercy. 'Like you and Robert, he is a soldier. He was recently ordered abroad with his regiment and now serves in Flanders.'

At that moment, I sensed a ray of hope.

Maybe he won't return.

SIX

It was a cold, gusty March morning. Grey clouds drifted across the sky, and trees swayed and creaked ominously. The snowdrops and crocuses now peeping above the dark brown earth in the nearby churchyard seemed in danger of being terminally battered by the chilly blasts of wind that continually pulled them this way and blew them that.

Head down and fearing that my hat would be blown from my head at any moment, I was on my way to meet up with Mr Grundy once again – a meeting that had been arranged when a letter arrived from him out of the blue. At that time, I was on a further recruitment exercise in Newbury. Mr Grundy was to be staying in Reading at his cousin's home. Leaving aside the weather, my main problem was that my horse had thrown a shoe, and I needed to find a blacksmith quickly to avoid being late for my meeting.

I led my horse by the bridle for what seemed like an eternity. I could feel my anxiety rising. During my years of military service, the strict discipline of arriving at least five minutes before the appointed time for any parade or meeting was instilled in me. So if, on the face of it, a parade was to start at eight o'clock in the morning, what was meant was that it was to begin at seven fifty-five, and I needed to be ready to go on parade by no later than seven-fifty.

As luck would have it, a village came into sight as I rounded a bend after walking for less than twenty minutes. With a massive sigh of relief, I could see a smithy and hurried towards it.

'Good morning, sir,' I said to the blacksmith as I handed him the rein. 'There's an extra two shillings if you can replace my horse's shoe in less than thirty minutes.'

'I'll do my best,' he replied as I moved inside the forge to warm myself by the fire.

The forge was pitch dark except for the red glow of the open fire. A boy crouching beside the fire was fanning the flame with bellows. I watched as the blacksmith, a vast, round-faced man girded in a leather apron, pulled a red-hot shoe from the fire embers with a pair of tongs and hammered it up on the anvil, sparks flying everywhere. As I stood by the hearth watching, I looked around the forge at the detritus lying about everywhere: metalwork, ploughshares, spades, sickles, domestic pots and pans, all waiting to be mended. A lead cistern took up a great deal of space. Behind it stood a fire back, and beyond that again, half lost in shadows, was a pair of wrought iron gates. It was clear that this blacksmith could turn his hand to anything.

Almost before I knew it, I thanked and paid the blacksmith for his handiwork along with the extra two shillings I had promised him to replace the shoe in thirty minutes or less, remounted my horse and headed off again towards Reading and my meeting there with Mr Grundy at the Boar's Head in New Street.

On my arrival in Reading, I stabled my horse and made the short walk to the Boar's Head, which was attached to a brewery that reached back to Merchant's Place, where I had left my horse.

Guided by the massive carved boar's head that hung above the doorway, I soon found the inn where I was to meet Mr Grundy. I went through a hall into a low, dim room with a beamed ceiling. A log fire crackled in a great chimney place. Travellers rested their pewter tankards upon a great bulbous-legged oak table while chattering among themselves and drinking.

I thought how charming and warm the room looked as I scanned it looking for Mr Grundy. Then I saw him sitting at the end of a long table close to the fire. He stood up and beckoned me over.

'Lieutenant Dunbar, I'm so delighted to see you again,' he said in greeting. He stretched out his hand towards me.

'I hope you are keeping well, especially in this rather cold and windy weather.'

I shook his hand, surprised by the strength and firmness of his grip.

'Good morning, sir,' I replied. 'Or good afternoon, should I now say. It's been a while since I met you, your good wife and your daughter in Henley. I am very well, thank you. I hope the same can be said for you and your family.'

'Thank you, yes, we are all well. Please sit down and warm yourself by the fire while I order some mulled ale to warm your inner self.' With that, Grundy called a serving maid over and ordered mulled ale and food for both of us.

'Well, Lieutenant Dunbar,' said Grundy once he had finished ordering. 'I expect you've been wondering why I contacted you.'

'Yes, sir, I was,' I replied. 'Especially since we had only met briefly over a dinner a few months ago.'

'Well, let me explain,' he said. But before he began, the maid reappeared with two wooden bowls of steaming soup and a wooden platter stacked with bread, which she placed in front of us and left. As she did, the landlord emerged from the taproom with tankards of mulled ale.

'Before I start,' said Mr Grundy as he lifted his tankard. 'Let's drink to our reacquaintance and enjoy this ale... and the soup while it's still hot. Your excellent health, Lieutenant Dunbar.'

'Thank you, sir. Good health to you and your family,' I replied, lifting my tankard.

As we finished our soup, the maid reappeared. Bustling around, she cleared our soup bowls before piling the table with various plates of food: a pair of capons, a large ham, a leg of mutton and more.

'Now, where was I before the soup and ale arrived?' said Mr Grundy. 'Ah, yes. I was going to explain why I contacted you. Bit of a long story, but bear with me.'

Grundy then recounted how he and Mrs Grundy had dedicated their lives to ensuring that Mercy lacked for nothing; that she had the best possible start in life that they could provide. When the time was right, that included helping her find a suitor who could offer her a station of life befitting an heiress.

'An heiress?' I interjected.

'Yes, in the event of my death – but also a young lady who would take a dowry of £20,000 into her marriage.'

I must confess that my heart skipped a beat at that revelation. In that instant, I saw Mercy in an even more favourable light. She became an even more attractive prospect for me.

'The problem was that I made little secret of that dowry,' Mr Grundy continued. 'Once it became public knowledge, Mercy was inundated with suitors. They flocked to her like bees to a honeypot. The first of these was a young apothecary, but I quickly made it plain that whilst he was a charming young man, he was not of sufficient standing in my view for my Mercy. She was above someone "in trade", as they say. In his case, there would be no £20,000 – not even £1. That he disappeared back to his gallipots and purportedly soothing ointments so rapidly after I broke that news to him was all the proof necessary that he was merely a "chancer". His place was taken by another charming young man, a local parish clerk who had once worked for me, but he also had no pedigree and insufficient means for my liking. I told him as nicely as I could that there would be no dowry from me for him if he and Mercy married. He, too, scurried off with his tail between his legs.'

Where's this all going? I wondered. *Have I come all this way only to hear a history of Grundy's carrot-and-stick approach to finding a match for his daughter? If so, why am I his chosen audience?*

I tried to look suitably interested as Grundy continued.

'Mercy's next suitor was a soldier. Mercy liked him greatly, and he found great favour with Mrs Grundy. For me, though, he was rather lightweight – and too much of a dandy for my liking. But, like the apothecary, he showed his true colours as soon as the question of settlements was broached. I told him in no uncertain terms that he would have no £20,000 dowry; he disappeared, showing more than a little resentment. Not long afterwards, Mercy met Charles Dunster. You may recall from our previous meeting that they became engaged.'

'Yes,' I replied. 'He had been unable to join us as he had been ordered abroad with his regiment. If I remember correctly, he was serving in Flanders.'

'That's right,' replied Grundy. 'However, when he eventually returned from abroad, he did not attempt to contact Mercy. Faced with this unfortunate turn of events, my wife and I, together with other members of both of our families, repeatedly approached him on Mercy's behalf. Unfortunately, he had no wish to renew the relationship, and the engagement was ended. As you can imagine, Mercy was distraught. She now fears that she is in danger of never finding a husband and destined for a life of spinsterhood.'

'I'm sure she faces no such destiny,' I said.

'I hope that you are right,' Grundy replied. 'It is hard to face the truth publicly, but I must confess that if Mercy's fate is to be one of spinsterhood, it will be entirely my fault. I fear that the truth is that I have imposed my wishes on Mercy, trying to engineer a match that meets my ambition and not her wishes and needs.'

'Has no one else appeared in Mercy's life?' I asked, hoping above all else that none had.

'No, Lieutenant Dunbar, sadly not,' Grundy replied. 'That leads neatly to why I asked to meet with you.'

About time, I thought to myself. *Talk about beating about the bush thus far!*

'Mrs Grundy and I have become well acquainted with your great-uncle over the time he has been in Henley, and he has become a very valued client of my practice. He has often spoken about you and his – and your – family. I had never imagined just how well connected and respected they were. I also know that Mercy enjoyed meeting with you. She has spoken well of you since.'

'I enjoyed meeting her,' I replied. 'She made an impression on me that will not easily be effaced. She is a knowledgeable, well-read, well-rounded and articulate young lady – a great credit to you and Mrs Grundy.'

'Thank you for saying so, and please forgive an older man rambling about his daughter, Lieutenant Dunbar. Tell me a little about yourself. Do you have anyone in your life?'

'None that I would regard as serious – or permanent.'

Well, I wasn't lying entirely. Ann had initially been a means to an end – a financial resource – but that resource had since vanished and, with it, her usefulness to me. The annuity ended after Culloden, and her legacy had dwindled to almost nothing to finance my lifestyle. And there was always the letter she had sent me, leaving aside how it had been obtained.

'Forgive me if what I am about to suggest offends you. It is a suggestion made only with Mercy's best interests at heart.'

'Rest assured,' I said, 'I could not be offended by anything a father says or does for his daughter's sake.'

'Could you see Mercy as a suitable match for you?'

I could scarcely believe my ears.

Is he offering Mercy to me on a plate?

'Most certainly, sir,' I replied, trying as hard as I could to tone down my reply.

The palpable look of relief on Grundy's face had to be seen to be believed. Suddenly, my route to the wealth I needed to indulge myself had reopened with a straightforward question.

'But what about Mercy?' I asked. 'Have you talked to her about me? After all, we have met on one occasion only.'

'No, Lieutenant Dunbar,' Grundy replied. 'I have not, and to ensure that I do not seem to her to be trying to meddle in her life again, I do not envisage doing so yet. But I have a further suggestion if you were minded to court Mercy.'

'What might that be?' I asked, almost incredulous at the way things were unfolding.

'Arrange to visit your great-uncle in Henley,' he replied. 'Let me know when, and I will arrange to hold a dinner at my house with you, him and Mrs McCleod as the guests of me, Mrs Grundy and Mercy. What develops between you and Mercy will be in your hands from then onwards.'

SEVEN

It was spring at last. The warm touch of the late-April sun gently released the grip of a long, dreary, seemingly never-ending winter. As I rode over Henley Bridge, I glimpsed the budding trees bursting into new life. Golden cowslip bells and yellow buttercups permeated the myriad tints of green meadows that swept up to the riverbanks edged with marsh marigolds. A mantle of spring splendour bedecked them all. I was in high spirits. I was on my way to stay with Uncle Mark – pursuing the plan I had discussed with Mr Grundy in Reading when we met.

I slowly made my way to Uncle Mark's house and reached the stable block behind it, where I dismounted. I unstrapped my small leather portmanteau containing a change of linen, besides other bits and pieces, from behind my saddle and left my horse with a stable boy. Having done so, and shouldering the portmanteau, I walked back to the front of the house, opened the gate, walked up to the door and rang the bell.

Uncle Mark's footman opened the door. 'Good afternoon, sir,' he said. 'Come in, please.'

I followed the footman into a hallway and into the back parlour, a smaller, more intimate room than the front parlour I had been in on my previous visit to the house. It was furnished with similar furniture to that room, but, in addition, it contained a bureau desk, two bird cages, jars of pickles and a sugar loaf.

'I will inform His Lordship that you have arrived.'

I set down my portmanteau and waited for Uncle Mark. He came into the room a few minutes later, accompanied by Mrs McCleod.

'Good afternoon, nephew,' he greeted. 'It's so good to see you again.'

'Good afternoon, uncle. Good afternoon, Mrs McCleod,' I replied.

'Please make yourself comfortable,' invited Uncle Mark.

'Thank you,' I replied, picked up my portmanteau, crossed to a chair and sat down, placing the portmanteau down next to me.

'Some tea?' asked Mrs McCleod.

'Thank you, yes, please,' I replied.

Mrs McCleod rang for the maid and ordered tea when she arrived. She also instructed the maid to tell the footman to take my portmanteau to the room where I would stay during my visit.

After we had tea, Uncle Mark showed me to my room. 'I hope this is comfortable enough for you, nephew,' he said.

'I'm sure it will be, uncle,' I replied.

'I'll leave you to settle in, and we shall be dining with Mr and Mrs Grundy this evening. Mr Grundy insisted that you did,' he said, grinning broadly. 'You must have made an especially good impression on him when he dined here last year.'

'That's very civil of him. I shall look forward to seeing him and Mrs Grundy again.'

And his daughter!

'We'll leave here at seven-thirty, William.'

'Thank you, uncle. I'll be good and ready well before then,' I replied.

I looked around the room as Uncle Mark shut the door behind him. It was a splendid room – far grander than those I'd become accustomed to. It had matching window curtains and bed hangings. There was a small needlepoint carpet on the floor. A fine mirror, with a moulded edge to its serpentine-fronted box base and fitted with small drawers below a swing, serpentine-topped frame, stood on the dressing table. Elsewhere, a walnut dressing glass with a moulded border, a concave moulded base with a pair of drawers and bracket feet stood on a mahogany chest of drawers.

I lay down on the bed. *Firm but not too firm*, I thought as I drifted into a deep sleep.

I woke with a start. I could hear my name being called.

'William, William, get yourself ready. We leave for the Grundys' in twenty minutes.'

It was Uncle Mark. He was standing in the doorway, dressed in all his finery, looking every inch the general he was.

'Sorry, uncle,' I spluttered. 'I fear that I dozed off.'

'So it would seem,' chuckled Uncle Mark.

'I can't think why. It's not as if I've travelled far. I rode here from Hurley, where I stayed last night.'

'Perhaps a few too many glasses of brandy at the Bell Inn last evening may have had something to do with that,' joked Uncle Mark.

'Perhaps,' I replied, knowing he was right on that score.

'Either way, young man, we'll see you downstairs shortly, won't we?'

'Of course, uncle,' I replied, feeling slightly embarrassed.

He left the room, and I hastily washed and tidied myself, using the washbasin I found in the room. It had been placed there while I had been sleeping.

Afterwards, I went downstairs and joined Uncle Mark and Mrs McCleod.

'Enter the sleeping beauty,' Mrs McCleod greeted me, laughing.

'Right, then,' said Uncle Mark, 'let's not tease young William. Instead, let's go and meet our hosts – I have to say, I'm looking forward to sampling Grundy's hospitality once more. He keeps a well-stocked cellar and larder.'

We left the house and strolled the short distance between Uncle Mark's house and the Grundys' home on Hart Street. At that moment, I was a little nervous, even though I knew only too well that Mr Grundy had contrived the evening.

Uncle Mark was right. Mr Grundy was most hospitable. We dined royally and sampled the finest claret and an excellent brandy. He also engineered the evening so that Mercy and I were left talking together as he ushered Mrs Grundy, Uncle Mark and Mrs Grundy into the front parlour of the house after we had finished dinner.

I took my opportunity to ask the question to which I already knew the answer.

'If I recall correctly,' I began, 'you had recently become engaged when I last visited your home. Has the happy day been decided yet?'

Mercy's face blanched. Tears began to well in her eyes.

'I'm afraid not,' she whispered. 'Nor will it be.'

I paused before answering. 'But why?' I asked softly.

Mercy began to sob.

'I'm so sorry,' I continued before she could say anything. 'I didn't mean to upset you.'

Mercy looked up at me and sighed. 'It's not you,' she finally said. 'It happened a few months ago. Unbeknownst to me, my fiancé had returned from Flanders. My parents had come to learn of this and approached him on my behalf after he had made no contact with me. He told them that he had no wish to renew our relationship, that our engagement was ended. He gave no reason for his decision.'

'He must be mad,' I said as sincerely as I could fashion. Mercy looked at me and smiled weakly. 'But there will be others only too willing to take the fool's place,' I continued.

'It's nice of you to say so, William. But I feel all romance is now dead within me,' she whispered. 'When Mama and Papa broke the news, I went to the desk in my room and took out a dried rose I kept in there. The sight of the rose caused my heart to fill with a pain that had its element of sweetness. It carried me back to the past. I was standing in the garden. It was summer, and the roses were in full bloom. My fiancé was with me. He had just proposed to me. I had long been conscious of his love. I was aware of it – a sort of golden, sweet sunshine which filled my life with joy and beauty. I never thought that, ultimately, mine was a hopeless love.'

I leant across the dining table, for Mr Grundy had sat her opposite me, and gently placed my hand on hers.

Mercy looked at me and smiled weakly.

'All I know is that I'm left wondering whether I am in danger of never finding a husband. I regard marriage now as a mere possibility rather than a certainty,' she said dolefully.

I took my hand from Mercy's and laced my hands under my chin, looking at her directly.

'I'm sure there is no such danger,' I said.

Mercy sighed once more.

'But don't you see, William? I'm now approaching my thirtieth year. I fear I am destined for a life of spinsterhood.'

'Dear Mercy, I'm sure you face no such destiny,' I replied softly.

'But, William, you probably don't know that others have sought my hand. Each failed. Inevitably, they were lacking in means. My father holds a high societal position and is a man of great personal pride. He is too ready to disregard any insignificant, fortuneless individual who dares to sue for my hand. I cannot set myself in opposition to his will. My former fiancé was the only suitor who found favour with Papa – now he is gone. I surely cannot expect to find another.'

'And I am sure you are wrong in thinking that way,' I reassured her. 'I shall remain in Henley for a while yet. I shall make it my mission while I am here to help you find your happiness.'

The evening flew by, and all too soon for me, I stood outside Mercy's house looking at her, about to take my leave. I had already thanked Mr and Mrs Grundy for their hospitality, and they had insisted that Mercy see me to the door.

I smiled at her and bowed my head.

'Thank you for a lovely evening, Mercy,' I said. 'I hope I can see you again before too long.'

I turned and took a half-step before turning back to face Mercy again. A shiver of excitement passed through my whole body. 'This may seem a bizarre question… but tell me, Mercy, do you prefer mutual love to the grandeur of life?'

Mercy looked at me quizzically. 'Yes, a bizarre question indeed,' she replied after a seemingly endless pause, 'but I think I can… and will answer. The grandeur of life must always give way to mutual love, for it is only through mutual love that one can find true happiness.'

I looked into Mercy's eyes and smiled.

'I said earlier that I shall make it my mission while I am here to help you find your happiness. I meant it. I can and will,' I replied softly, taking her hand. 'I hope that, in time, you can see in me someone with whom you can share a mutual love.'

Mercy lowered her head, an increasing blush colouring her face, but she uttered no word, nor did she immediately withdraw the hand I had taken.

*

With Mercy's parents' blessing, I was a regular visitor at their home in the following weeks. I became increasingly attracted to Mercy as a person – and not just the means of obtaining the £20,000 tocher promised by her father upon her marriage. She exhibited more than the skills and acquirements associated with a young woman from a good family. I found her to be articulate, gregarious and sometimes flirtatious (despite her contention to the contrary when I first met her). She was equally at home with her superiors, with whom she was reverential and respectful; her equals, with whom she was free and candid; and her inferiors, with whom she was always courteous and considerate. I had discovered a delightful freshness and originality of manner and character about her. That said, I would be less than honest if I said that I was falling in love with her. I was, though, constantly seeking the opportunity to draw Mercy ever close to me, driven by the almost irresistible pull of the prospect of receiving the £20,000 tocher.

Finally, that opportunity presented itself as Mercy and I returned to her home after taking a leisurely walk along the riverbank. I took Mercy's hand as we approached the house's front door. I faced her. She stared at me. A gentle evening breeze swept softly over our faces as I slowly bent my head towards her. I smiled faintly. My heart was beating, half in trepidation, half in anticipation. My brain started to fizzle.

I gazed upon her with a growing feeling of delight, and when I spoke again, the music rang in so captivating a strain that the polish of my language itself was scarcely more attractive. My theme was love, and my words were so winning, so ardent, so wild and passionate that before Mercy had time for reflection, she whispered, 'I love you, William.'

I took her in my arms and gently guided her towards me. She lay her head on my shoulder and turned her face towards mine. I felt her breath on my cheek. Barely able to sustain the delirium of joy which fired every fibre of my frame, I sighed, a sigh of contentment.

'That's all I dared hope for, Mercy,' I whispered.

My plan was working far better than I had ever dared hope for. However, unbeknown to me then, life was threatening to get in the way of that plan.

EIGHT

I lifted my head slowly, gazed at the ceiling and heaved an
impatient, bitter sigh. It seemed so strange to me to find
myself so worried and perplexed.

How could Ann do this to me?

I looked again at the document I was holding, which
I had received earlier that morning. I had only now had the
opportunity to read it in private. I reread it, half hoping I
had mistaken its contents. I hadn't. It was a libel prepared by
Ann's lawyer and forwarded to me by John Balfour. She had
raised a declarator of marriage action against me before the
Commissary Court.

At that moment, I remembered all too clearly that I had
pooh-poohed Balfour's warning that the letter he was to send to
Ann might prompt an action to be brought against me, but the
reality of that warning had only now hit home. My brain flooded
with questions. With doubts. I was arguing internally.

What should I do?

I had to defend the action. After all, I had a cast-iron defence
– I had Ann's letter.

Do I tell anyone?

At that moment, I should tell no one and keep the libel to myself.

Not even Mercy?

But if I told Mercy, I could lose her. That's as may be, but if I didn't, and she later found out, I was sure I *would* lose her. So, on reflection, I had no choice but to tell her.

But what should I say to her? How would I break the news to her?

I put the libel down, walked across the room and looked out the window at the garden below. I was hoping for some inspiration, but that inspiration would not be forthcoming from the weather. The skies were heavy with ominous black clouds, and the rain fell steadily. To make matters worse, there seemed little prospect of any change for the better. Notwithstanding, I felt I had to get some fresh air. Hopefully, that would help clear my mind and help me focus better on the task.

I left Uncle Mark's house and struck away from it with little thought as to the direction in which my steps carried me. No sound reached my ear save for the moan of the wind and the pitter-patter of rain falling all around me.

Before I realised it, I walked along Hart Street and past Mercy's house. As I did, a plan of action began to form. Then I stopped in my tracks.

I can introduce the libel's existence – within a marriage proposal – or the precursor to one.

After Mercy had expressed her love for me, I was almost certain that she would accept a marriage proposal from me, but I had remained content to make slow and steady progress towards my goal until now. The reality of receiving the libel dictated that I must act immediately.

I spun round on my heels and headed back along Hart Street until I reached Mercy's house. Then, with some trepidation, I rang the front doorbell and waited. Shortly afterwards, a footman opened the door.

'Good afternoon, sir,' he greeted me.

'Good afternoon,' I replied. 'Is Miss Mercy at home?'

'Yes, sir. Please come inside. I will let her know you're here.'

I stepped into the hallway, and the footman left to find Mercy.

Moments later, Mercy rushed towards me, her face lit by the broadest smile.

'William,' she gushed. 'What a wonderful surprise. Let's…' She stopped short as she saw me. 'Good grief,' she cried. 'You're soaked. What on earth were you doing out in this rain? Wait there while I get something to dry you.'

I did as Mercy bade me, somewhat conscious now that I was extremely wet. I stood inside the hall until Mercy returned, clutching a linen towel. She handed it to me, and I used it to dry my face and hands before rubbing down my clothing as best I could.

'Now, we'd better go into the kitchen, and you can continue to dry yourself and warm yourself in front of the fire. I've sent the servants away so that we can be alone.'

With that, Mercy headed into the kitchen, and I followed.

'Draw a chair to the fire,' she instructed. 'Then sit yourself down and get dry.'

I complied dutifully, basking in the warmth thrown out by the fire. Mercy pulled up another chair and sat beside me. Neither of us said anything. I don't know about Mercy, but at that moment, I could not think of how to start the conversation I needed to. Eventually, though, I knew I had to say something.

'To answer your question, when I arrived,' I said tentatively, 'I received some disturbing news this morning and needed to get out and try and collect my thoughts.'

Mercy looked at me with a slightly surprised look on her face. 'Disturbing news?' she said quizzically.

I stood up and walked several paces from where I had been sitting. I could feel my heartbeat quicken. I caught my breath before beginning to spin my web of lies. 'Mercy, dearest,' I said in a hushed tone, 'since we first met last year, I have come to love you above everything on earth. I know that I always will.' I moved slowly back towards Mercy with my face lowered, my hands fidgeting behind me. My manner seemed to disturb Mercy.

'What is wrong?' she enquired perplexedly, standing up as she did.

'Mercy, I am in some trouble. I need to tell you about it,' I said softly. I paused and cleared my throat. Mercy seemed deep in thought. 'What I am about to tell you will come as a surprise, even a shock, I'm sure,' I continued. 'My affairs have turned out very differently from what I expected.'

A look of pained yearning crossed Mercy's face as if she wanted badly to speak but couldn't.

I reached across to her and placed my hand on her shoulder. 'Several years ago, I became involved with the niece of the wife of one of my uncles. Her name is Ann Macclesfield. We became lovers. I later learned that she was with child – my child. I felt obliged to do the honourable thing. I offered to marry her, subject to her changing her religion from Catholicism to my Presbyterian faith, to avoid any future difficulties we might face after marriage. She agreed, promising me that she would. However, she did not ultimately wish to convert to Presbyterianism and released me from any obligation to marry her. I took her release at face value, but now she has issued a libel against me, falsely claiming that she and I are married under Scottish Law.'

Mercy pulled away from me, a look of horror on her face. Tears welled in her eyes. She stood there speechless for what seemed an eternity. I reached towards her again. A sigh came to my strained ears. My outstretched hands came in contact with Mercy's face. Pushing back her hair, I stroked her face and hands.

'Calm yourself, Mercy,' I said gently. 'I won't trouble you with all the circumstances, but my lawyer in Edinburgh holds a letter I left with him for safe-keeping – a letter sent to me by Ann in which she denies that there was ever marriage between us. My lawyer assures me that the libel issued by her is doomed to fail. The court will find that I am not now, nor was I ever, married to Ann.'

Upon this, Mercy gave a shriek of joy, and lifting her arms, she caught me about my neck.

'I ought to have told you sooner, sweet love,' I said.

'But you have told me,' she replied. 'I cannot pretend that I am happy about what you have told me, but I am thankful that you have done so.'

'Oh, my dearest Mercy!' I cried. I drew her ever close to me, calling her by every pet name I could think of. Mercy sighed again, or was it a sob instead? 'Mercy, my sweet love,' I whispered. 'I am always thinking of you, what you do and say, how you look and what pleases you.' I stroked her hands and face, covering them with kisses. 'Tell me you love me,' I pleaded.

'You know I love you, William,' she answered, drawing me to her and kissing me repeatedly.

'Words cannot describe how happy I am to hear you say you love me.' I sighed. 'Happy beyond my wildest dreams.'

We stood there holding one another, neither one saying anything further. I could feel a sense of triumph beginning to build inside me. I had so far managed to negotiate one of the hurdles facing me. Now, anxious to press home the advantage, I lifted my head and looked into Mercy's eyes.

'Sweet Mercy, it scarcely seems possible that you could do so, but will you make me even happier?' I asked gently.

Mercy looked at me questioningly, lines forming on her forehead as she lifted her eyebrows. 'How, William?'

Time to move to the next stage of my plan.

I kissed her on the cheek. 'I have long wanted to ask you something,' I replied, 'but my honour would not permit me to before I have resolved my present difficulty.'

A look of slight exasperation crossed Mercy's face. 'Stop teasing me, William,' she scolded. 'What is it you want to ask me?'

This was my moment. Looking straight into her eyes, I stepped back from Mercy and took hold of both her hands. 'It will be some time before I can extricate myself from my present predicament, but when I do, do you think you might love me well enough to honour me by becoming my wife?'

Mercy gasped. Her eyes opened wide. At first, she looked at me almost in disbelief. Then the broadest of smiles lit up her face. Yet, she did not reply. I stood looking at her, waiting for her to say something.

Have I made the wrong move? Have I taken things too quickly?

'Oh, yes, William,' she finally replied. 'I do love you enough. I could think of nothing better than to be your wife.'

I wrapped my arms around Mercy's neck and pulled her gently towards me. 'You don't know how happy you've made me,' I whispered before kissing her. I could feel Mercy's heart pounding. Mine was also.

Then, she pulled her head away from me. 'Have you spoken with my papa about—'

'Not yet,' I interrupted, 'but I will perhaps later today, but first...'

I kissed her again. Passionately.

I made my way from Uncle Mark's house towards Hart Street. I had a distinct spring in my step. I was on my way to see Mr Grundy – on my way to formally ask for Mercy's hand in marriage, or should I say to observe the formality of doing so? After all, *he* had invited me to court Mercy when we had met in the Boar's Head in Reading.

Mercy and I had agreed that nothing should be said about Ann and the legal proceedings she had issued against me.

'There's no point in alarming Papa,' Mercy had told me. 'Least said soonest mended. After all, you have the letter Ann sent you. She will soon be sent packing by the court in Scotland and become a distant memory for each of us.'

I reached Mercy's house, rang the front doorbell and waited. Shortly afterwards, Mr Grundy opened the door.

'William, dear boy,' he gushed, holding his hand out to me.

I shook his hand enthusiastically.

'Good evening, sir,' I greeted.

'Come in,' he invited me. 'We'll go into the parlour.'

I followed Grundy.

'Sit yourself down and make yourself comfortable,' he said once we were inside the parlour. 'A glass of port, perhaps?'

'Thank you, yes,' I replied, moving to an armchair and sitting down.

Grundy poured two glasses of port and handed one to me before he sat down on a chair beside me.

'I hope I have correctly anticipated the reason for your visit,' he said.

I looked across to Grundy and grinned. 'I've come to ask for Mercy's hand in marriage, sir. Is that what you thought I might do?'

Grundy chuckled. 'You've made me – and Mrs Grundy, I know – very happy. After what Dunster did to Mercy, I know how right I was to meet you in Reading and suggest you visit Henley.' He raised his glass. 'Here's to you and my dearest daughter,' he continued. 'May you both always be happy.'

I raised my glass. 'And here's to you, sir, with my eternal gratitude.'

At that moment, Mrs Grundy burst into the room. 'Well, dear husband? Is our daughter to be the daughter-in-law of My Lady Dunbar then?' she gushed.

Grundy seemed to puff out his chest. 'Yes – William has asked me for Mercy's hand in marriage, and I am only too pleased to give my consent and our blessing.'

Mrs Grundy turned and rushed to the door. 'Mercy, Mercy!' she called out. 'Mercy, where are you?'

At that moment, I felt elated. My plan had worked. The £20,000 tocher now seemed within touching distance. However, I should have known better. Even the best-laid plans can go astray, but in this case, not in a way I could have imagined.

NINE

It was a pleasant day, warm but not too warm. White cumulus clouds drifted across the deep blue sky, occasionally obscuring the sun. Now and then, I lifted my head to allow the sun's warmth to caress my cheeks as I finally made my way towards Mercy's home. I had just returned from Southampton, where my regiment was based, ultimately bound for a long-awaited reunion with Mercy. I had decided to travel to Henley on short notice, prompted by my financial position, which was becoming increasingly dire. An imminent marriage to Mercy was becoming an absolute necessity.

First, though, I needed to stable my horse and pay my respects to Uncle Mark in the hope that he would offer me accommodation at his home as he had done previously. But that hope was soon to be dashed in no uncertain terms.

Uncle Mark's footman answered the door and showed me into the front parlour. I placed my portmanteau down on the floor and awaited my uncle. He appeared shortly afterwards. To my surprise, he had a thunderous look on his face.

'Hello, unc—' I began to say.

'Don't "hello" me, nephew,' Uncle Mark barked, immediately

extinguishing my greeting. 'What the hell do you think you've been playing at?'

'What do you mean?' I sputtered.

Uncle Mark stood staring at me for a moment, snarling. 'You know full well, boy,' he hissed.

'I don't, sir,' I replied hoarsely.

At that moment, I saw that he had a document in his hand – a letter. He thrust it forward towards me.

'Don't come the innocent with me,' he shouted. 'This is a letter from my sister-in-law, Janet Campbell, the aunt of Ann Dunbar, Ann Macclesfield – your wife and the mother of your daughter, Margaret.'

Taken completely off guard, I tried to speak. 'But—'

'Don't interrupt me, boy,' Uncle Mark cut across me. 'I learnt from Mr Grundy only shortly after receiving this letter that you had sought his daughter's hand in marriage – that she and you were betrothed. How might that be remotely possible when you are already married – and a father to boot?'

At first, I could not find words to reply to that question. All I could feel was a sense of self-righteousness and indignation inside me – inexplicably. After all, I knew Uncle Mark was right. I was already married; I was a father. But what he didn't know – what I couldn't tell him – was why I was pursuing Mercy.

'But I am not married,' I eventually mumbled, looking down while avoiding Uncle Mark's gaze.

'So, my sister-in-law is a liar then, is she?' Uncle Mark thundered. 'She tells me that the marriage to her niece was arranged by Ann's mother. Why would she lie about that?'

'I am not saying that Lady Campbell is lying, sir. It is the case that a marriage was to take place between Ann and me, but no marriage ever took place. I have a letter from Ann confirming that she and I were not, and are not, married under Scottish Law.'

Uncle Mark glared at me. All colour had drained from his face. 'If it is the case, then why has Ann raised a declarator of marriage action against you before the Commissary Court?'

'That is nothing more than an act of malice on Ann's part… for reasons only she knows. Her action is bound to fail.'

Uncle Mark shook his head in seeming disbelief. 'So, according to you, Ann and you are not married?' he asked.

'Sir, we are not, nor have we ever been.'

'Then why did Mrs Macclesfield make payment to you of £250 per annum by way of a tocher – a tocher she and Ann's brother agreed should be paid to you for so long as you and Ann were man and wife?'

'That can only be a result of her mistaken belief that… that Ann and I were… were married,' I replied, my voice trailing off somewhat.

'And did you refuse the payment at any time?'

'N–n–no, sir,' I stuttered, my heart clogged with guilt.

'That's for sure,' was the barbed reply. 'And did you ever tell Mrs Macclesfield you were not entitled to receive any tocher?' he continued.

'No, sir.'

'No, sir,' Uncle Mark retorted. 'Why not, sir?' he asked, but he didn't give me a chance to reply. 'I'll tell you why not – you didn't because you knew only too well that you and Ann *are* married.'

I was lost for words. My mind was a whirling jumble of thoughts. My lips moved, but I uttered no sound.

'There's nothing you *can* say,' Uncle Mark hissed resentfully. 'You're a disgrace: a disgrace to yourself, a disgrace to me and to our family. Now, get out of my sight – out of my house – and stay away from me until you have put things right! Get round to Mr Grundy and his daughter, apologise to them both and then take yourself to Edinburgh and make amends with Mrs Macclesfield and, more particularly, with Ann.'

With that, my uncle got up from his chair, strode across the room, picked up my portmanteau and hurled it into the hallway before storming off towards the kitchen. I followed, picked up the portmanteau and left the house sheepishly before retrieving my horse and heading towards the nearby Red Lion Inn.

Once I had stabled my horse, I entered the inn and approached the landlady. She was a comely, comfortable-looking, shortish woman, round-faced and rosy-cheeked, with brown hair flecked with grey, and her eyes were a light, bright blue.

'Good afternoon, madam,' I greeted her. 'Permit me to introduce myself. My name is Dunbar – Lieutenant Dunbar. Do you have a room free for this evening and the next few days?'

The landlady looked at me and smiled.

'And I am Mrs Dawes,' she replied. 'You're in luck, sir. I have just one room left for tonight – not our largest one, but it is comfortable enough. I have other, larger rooms from tomorrow, though.'

'Thank you,' I said. 'I'll take your remaining room this evening – beggars can't be choosers. I can move into a larger room from tomorrow. In the meantime, do you have someone to deliver a message for me in Henley?'

*

To my delight, I received a letter from Mercy the day after I sent my message to her, inviting me to visit her at her home that afternoon. Upon my arrival, I had a distinct spring in my step as I was led into the front parlour of the Grundys' home. However, to my surprise and consternation, I soon discovered that Mercy was not alone. Her parents accompanied her.

Mr and Mrs Grundy sat on a walnut love settee upholstered with a floral-patterned green and charcoal fabric. Both were stern-faced and appeared distinctly unhappy. Mercy was seated on a wing-back armchair placed to the side of her parents.

Mr Grundy stood up as I entered. At first, no words were exchanged between us other than a brief exchange of 'good afternoons' and an invitation for me to sit down.

Feeling decidedly uncomfortable, I sat down in an armchair opposite Mercy. Mr Grundy also sat down again. I looked at Mercy, at her parents and back at her, not knowing what, if anything, I should say. Then Mrs Grundy broke the silence.

'Mr Grundy and I have received disturbing news about you from Lord Campbell,' she said rather thoughtfully. 'When Mr Grundy broke the news to Lord Campbell of your and Mercy's betrothal, a shocked Lord Campbell told Mr Grundy that no marriage between you and Mercy was permissible. He had recently discovered from his sister-in-law that you are already a married man... and the father of a daughter as well.'

Mr Grundy immediately followed with his own verbal salvo. 'And have you not lied to me also – betrayed the trust I had placed in you – both in Reading and my home? How could you do this to Mrs Grundy, me and Mercy?'

I sat there open-mouthed. Silenced.

Then Mercy came to my aid. 'But, Mama, Papa, William has previously explained this woman and her child and her false claims.'

I finally found my voice. 'As God is my witness, and I have a soul to be saved,' I said as convincingly as I could muster, looking at Mr and Mrs Grundy as I did, 'I am not a married man. Nor have I ever been married.'

A look of incredulity flashed across the face of Mercy's father. 'Why on earth would Lord Campbell say what he did? Why would he tell me you were married? There is no reason I could conceive of why he should do so.'

At that moment, I began to recover my poise. 'Sir, what you are not aware of is that Lord Campbell and I had an altercation some years ago,' I lied as convincingly as possible. 'You know, the sort of alteration that families sometimes experience. I had long since believed that this had been resolved and forgotten, but it would seem not. So it would seem, my uncle still bears me a grudge.'

Mr Grundy stood up, walked across the room and looked out the window for a minute before returning to sit next to Mrs Grundy again.

'I fully appreciate that families fall out occasionally,' he said, 'but it seems inconceivable to me that Lord Campbell *actually* holds any grudge against you, especially one that would cause him to deliberately lie to me about your marital status.'

I had to think fast, to move the conversation to one that offered some credible explanation that the Grundys would accept. My present course was leading nowhere with them.

'Perhaps my belief is somewhat unreasonable,' I eventually replied. 'Perhaps he holds no grudge but is simply misguided.'

Grundy looked at me somewhat aghast. 'Misguided?' he queried sceptically.

'Yes, but understandably so,' I replied, shifting uneasily in my chair. 'He will not, cannot, know that the lady in question – Ann Macclesfield – is crafty, manipulative and capable of twisting circumstances to suit her ends. Undoubtedly, she has wilfully misrepresented our relationship. The proceedings in the Scottish courts are nothing more than an attempt by her to blackmail me, but the facts are quite plain for all to see. The action she has instigated must be decided in my favour and, after that, nothing more will be heard of Miss Macclesfield and her fraudulent claims against me.'

'Heaven be praised if that is the case,' gasped Mrs Grundy.

'I can assure you that it is,' I replied.

A look of relief spread across Mrs Grundy's face. She looked straight at me and smiled. 'Very well, Mr Dunbar,' she said softly. 'I will take your word as to that, and I am certain that Mr Grundy does also.' She looked at her husband. 'That is right, is it not, dear husband?' she continued.

Mr Grundy looked at his wife but did not reply at first. Instead, he looked up at the ceiling, seemingly deep in thought. Then he looked at me, squinting slightly and frowning as he did. 'I will accept our guest's word – for now,' Grundy finally grunted, nodding as he did.

'What do you mean by "for now", Papa?' asked Mercy, her voice edged with panic.

'What I mean is that, for your and your mama's sake, I will give Mr Dunbar the benefit of the doubt at present,' Grundy replied. 'Hopefully, the legal proceedings will confirm that I am right to do so.' With that, he got up and headed towards the parlour door. 'Please excuse me for a short while,' he continued. 'I had forgotten that I must send an important document to a client in town – one that must be delivered this afternoon.'

Mrs Grundy stood up also, a look of astonishment crossing her face. 'Now, husband?' she gasped. 'Can't it wait? Surely what we are discussing is far more important than any client?'

Grundy glared at his wife. 'No, it cannot wait, I'm afraid,' he snapped. 'Sometimes my business must take priority over family matters. Rest assured… I will be back in just a few moments.'

I watched as Grundy left the room.

Then, Mrs Grundy leant forward towards me. 'You mustn't mind my husband,' she said softly. 'You must understand, William, that Mercy has been brought up with great care and tenderness. Mr Grundy and I have only two things in mind: Mercy's future well-being and her happiness. I fully accept what you have told us. Still, I fear that Mr Grundy suspects that your intentions towards Mercy jeopardise those hopes and wishes – that your sole motivation for pursuing Mercy is the acquisition of the dowry he has promised to provide upon her marriage. I suspect he left us, not for anything to do with his business, but to think things through on his own.'

I looked at Mrs Grundy, forcing a smile. 'Rest assured, Mrs Grundy...' I sighed. 'I, too, have only two things in mind: your daughter's future well-being and happiness. My sole motivation for pursuing Mercy is my deep love for her. I have no interest in any dowry – be it one of a shilling or one equal to a king's ransom.'

If I say so myself, I lied so convincingly to Mrs Grundy that I almost had myself believing what I was saying. At that moment, Mr Grundy returned and sat beside his wife. Mercy looked at him pleadingly and began to cry.

'Oh, Papa.' She sobbed. 'Please believe William. He would never lie to me, I know.'

Mr Grundy stood up, walked across to Mercy, leant down and kissed the top of her head.

'Hush, hush, dearest daughter,' he whispered. 'I am a father who only wants the best for your future happiness.' He lifted his head and looked at me. 'I will accept your word regarding Ann Macclesfield. You shall have my trust – until you lose it.'

Mr Grundy's thinly veiled threat was not lost on me. I knew I would have to play my cards carefully in the coming days and weeks.

'Have no fear, sir,' I replied, looking him straight in the eye. 'I shall give you no reason ever to doubt me.'

Grundy looked at me, and a faint smile flickered across his lips. 'For Mercy's sake, let's hope not,' he said. He moved back towards Mrs Grundy. 'Come, dear,' he continued. 'Let's leave this young couple together for a while.'

Mrs Grundy rose from the settee and took her husband's hand. 'You'll join us shortly in the back parlour, won't you?' she asked Mercy and me. 'I'll get the maid to serve afternoon tea.'

With that, they both left the room.

I crossed to Mercy and kissed her gently on the cheek. 'Will you wait for me until his unhappy affair with Ann Macclesfield is finally resolved?' I asked.

'What a silly question, William!' she exclaimed. 'Of course, I will – however long it takes.'

A sense of relief powered through me. 'It should not take long,' I assured her. 'My attorney in Edinburgh is fully confident that I will be vindicated. Hopefully, I shall receive confirmation from him before too long.'

'Amen to that,' Mercy replied before taking my hand. 'And now, let's rejoin my parents.'

Things had most definitely not worked out as I had hoped they might. I was desperately short of money, and Uncle Mark had dashed any hope I had held of free accommodation in Henley. On top of that, I was possessed with a nagging fear that Mr Grundy would withdraw his consent to my marriage to his daughter. Still, Mercy had committed herself to me, and Mrs Grundy appeared to be my ally insofar as her husband was concerned.

*

I had not long since finished my breakfast and had returned to my room to contemplate an immediate return to Southampton as I had insufficient money to pay for my keep at the inn for more than an additional day or two when there was a knock on my door.

'Who is it?' I called out.

'It's me, Lieutenant Dunbar – Mrs Dawes,' came the reply. 'You have a lady visitor.'

My heart almost skipped a beat. A visitor? A lady? And so early in the day?

As further thoughts flashed through my mind, I crossed the room with a mounting curiosity tinged with hope and excitement. *It must be Mercy, surely?*

I opened my room door and stepped outside. Mrs Dawes beckoned me to follow her and eventually took me into her neat, well-furnished parlour, with its low ceiling and large casement windows looking out on the lawn. One window stood open, and the dimity curtains fluttered out and in with the draught. Mrs Grundy was sitting on a large couch upholstered in green velvet.

'Mrs Grundy,' I greeted. 'What a pleasant surprise.'

'Make yourself comfortable, Lieutenant Dunbar,' Mrs Dawes invited. 'I'll leave you in peace.' With that, she left the room, closing the door quietly behind her.

With some trepidation, I sat down in an armchair to the side of Mrs Grundy, smiling weakly. 'To what do I owe this honour?' I asked.

'William,' Mrs Grundy replied in a rather businesslike tone. 'I have spoken at some length with Mr Grundy since you left yesterday. Mercy was not a party to that discussion, which only began after she had retired for the night, although I spoke with her about it briefly just before I left the house to come here.'

I looked at Mrs Grundy, feeling very uneasy. At first, she avoided my gaze, looking down, but then she looked at me directly.

'I think it is true to say that, notwithstanding what he may have said yesterday evening, my husband has lingering concerns about you and your intentions towards our daughter. He remains unsettled by what Lord Campbell told him and the existence of the proceedings brought against you in the Scottish courts. For my part, please be assured that I no longer share those concerns, although I understand them. Like Mercy, I fully accept your explanation and believe in your eventual exoneration—'

'You do me a great honour,' I interrupted, looking at Mrs Grundy with all the earnestness I could muster. 'And I do take on board Mr Grundy's concerns. What my great-uncle, Mark, told him must have come as a great shock to you both—'

'It did, William, it did, I can assure you, and I can assure you also that would still be of concern to me if you hadn't told Mercy of Ann Macclesfield's action before Mr Grundy and I learned of it. But you did tell Mercy, which says more about you than I can say. You are a man I can trust; your honour for me is undoubted.'

I breathed a huge inwards sigh of relief. I recognised that Mrs Grundy would prove a valuable ally where Mr Grundy was concerned. I knew she and Mercy would provide me with the support I needed to succeed in my quest to get my hands on Grundy's £20,000.

I looked across to Mrs Grundy and smiled. Then I was brought down to earth with a bump.

'The problem for you, William,' Mrs Grundy continued, 'is that, whilst my husband is still content for you to marry Mercy, he is seriously contemplating reducing or withholding the dowry he had been minded to settle on you upon the marriage. "That'll separate the wheat from the chaff if I did," he told me.'

I caught my smile and swallowed it. I felt my insides tighten. My mind was a jumble of thoughts, but I could say nothing. Do nothing.

'I can assure you, Mr Dunbar,' she breathed, turning her eyes upon me with a look of real tenderness and taking my hand in hers for a moment, 'had I got £20,000 myself, I would gladly give it to you and Mercy with the greatest pleasure, but, sadly, I do not. However, I will do everything I can to assure Mr Grundy that he has nothing to fear so far as you are concerned.'

Finally, I found my voice again. 'Dear Mrs Grundy,' I said, 'as I told you yesterday evening – and repeat now – my sole motivation for pursuing Mercy is my deep love for her, not any prospective dowry. So, all I hope is that Ann Macclesfield's speculative action will be dismissed soon and that Mercy and I are married as soon as possible after it is.'

'As a mother, I know with absolute certainty of your feelings for Mercy – and hers for you,' Mrs Grundy replied reassuringly. 'And I think we are as one in hoping that Ann Macclesfield and her action are soon confined to a distant memory as you and Mercy share your future lives.' With that, she rose from her chair. 'Well,' she continued, 'I'd best be on my way. I am to visit my brother, who has a house nearby. He's a lawyer, like Mr Grundy, and is a member of a society of lawyers in London known as Doctors' Commons. If I may, I will mention your predicament to him. He may be able to help you – or know someone who can.'

I escorted Mrs Grundy to the inn's entrance, bade her farewell and watched as she headed towards her brother's house, feeling chastened and crestfallen. My visit to Henley had proved to be an unmitigated disaster. Things just could not have become much worse for me. Any hope of getting my hands on Grundy's tocher any time soon seemed to have vanished. I could not afford to wait for any potential white knight to come to my aid, be that Mrs Grundy's brother or anyone else. My financial circumstances demanded that I do something myself – and soon.

I was sure my original thought and plan remained as valid as ever. I would return to Southampton and continue to seek a wife. It mattered not whether she was sweet-tempered, witty or pretty, just so long as she was of a wealthy family.

TEN

Shortly after my return to Southampton, I learned of a lady, the eldest daughter of a wealthy landowner from Winchester. She was said to be endowed with few good qualities – the reason why she remained a spinster, unlike her three younger sisters. She would, though, come with a dowry similar to that promised by Mr Grundy. Seizing upon the opportunity, I obtained an introduction to her father. He, like Grundy, was attracted to my pedigree and received me well as a potential suitor for his daughter. After several discussions, he arranged a ball at his house to bring his daughter and me together.

On the appointed day of the ball, I set out for Winchester. As I made my way, I was surprisingly anxious, feeling untypically ill at ease. I slowed the horse's pace and brought it to a halt as I reached a bridleway leading up a hill towards a small wood I could see on the horizon. I detoured and followed the bridleway until I arrived at the wood.

Once there, I dismounted to reflect upon what I should do at the ball. I sat down on the trunk of a fallen tree. I reached inside my coat and took out my flask of brandy. I unscrewed the cap and took a large swig. Then, without thinking of it, I varied my reflections with sips of brandy.

What had I to worry about? After all, I was sure to cut a dash, I reasoned with the astuteness of a scholar. I had packed my finest clothes into my portmanteau: a coat of rich shot green and black silk, a waistcoat of yellow silk brocaded with coloured silk and silver threads and featuring large flowers and leaves, breeches of black velvet, silk stockings with silver trees and buckle shoes.

These thoughts – or the brandy – somewhat enlivened me and gave me confidence, so much so that I began to discover several virtues and excellences in myself which could not fail to ensure my success once I met the young lady. But then, doubts flooded my mind once more. Would I encounter the same problem that I had with Mercy? Would the situation between Ann and me return to haunt me yet again?

As I started to think about Ann, my mind flashed back to my conversation in Edinburgh with John Balfour and his parting words: *whit's fur ye'll no go by ye.* Those words were as relevant to me now as they were then. *What's meant to be, will be.*

Still holding that thought, I remounted my horse and pressed on towards Winchester, conscious that the ball took place that evening and I had to find the inn where I was to stay that night and then change into my finery, ready to meet the lady I hoped would become my intended. Already, the sun was beginning to edge down towards the horizon. The light was fading, trees becoming silhouettes against the darkening skies. Then, unexpectedly, the bridle path dipped suddenly and sloped downwards steeply. I instinctively leant back and gently pulled on the reins to check my horse's forward momentum before pressing my legs against his sides while lifting my seat out of the saddle. Then, keeping my centre of gravity directly above the middle of my horse's back and always giving him enough head, I picked my way down the slope until I rejoined the road to Winchester.

I had travelled no more than a mile or two along the road when I heard a sound in front of me – the creaks and groans of a coach a little distance away. A short while afterwards, I could see the light of the coach's lanterns. Then, not one hundred yards or so in front of me, I heard the sound of a horse snorting.

'Hello! Who goes there!' a voice rang out clearly through the evening air.

The next moment, a horse and rider came into view.

'Stand, and let's see what you've got to deliver!' the rider called out to the coach.

He had a pistol in each hand. He moved slowly towards the now halted carriage. As he did, the coachman started to reach for a blunderbuss, only to pitch forward and fall to the ground as the rider shot him.

I brought my horse to a standstill, dismounted and quickly and silently made my way to within about twenty yards of the rider. I drew one of the pistols in the holsters on either side of my waist, cocked it, took aim and fired. The rider's horse screamed and fell, taking the rider down and trapping him. I pressed forward again and quickly reached the fallen rider, a heavily cloaked figure with a black mask covering his face below his eyes.

'Help me, sir,' he called out.

I walked and stood over him, drawing my other pistol and cocking it.

'Mercy, noble sir!' pleaded the rider.

I looked down at him.

'Mercy, noble sir!' I hissed, venom dripping from every word. 'I'll show you mercy, sir. I'll spare you the hangman's noose.'

I pointed my pistol at him and cold-heartedly put a ball through his head before replacing both pistols in their holsters. Then, I started to walk over to the carriage. As I did, a man emerged from one of the carriage doors – a man of some wealth, judging by his clothes.

'Thank you, sir,' he called to me. 'Thank you on behalf of my daughter and me.'

'Yes, thank you, sir,' echoed the man's daughter, whose face fleetingly appeared at the carriage window before disappearing in its darkness.

'I'm glad to have been of service,' I replied, kneeling beside the coachman lying face down. 'May I assume that you were headed for Winchester?'

'Yes – more or less. Our home is a mile or so outside the city,' the man replied.

I turned the coachman over. He was dead, blood oozing from a wound in his neck.

'Your coachman is dead, sir, I regret,' I reported. 'I will lift him back onto the driver's seat of the coach and drive you to your home before making my way back into the city.'

'Of course, of course,' the man replied. 'I'll help lift him into the coach. Leave the highwayman where he lies. I will arrange for someone to be sent from Winchester to deal with him in due course.'

'Thank you, sir, but first, permit me to introduce myself. I am William Dunbar, Lieutenant in the Tenth Regiment of Marines.'

'And I, Sir Richard Archer. My daughter, Eleanor, travels with me.'

After a struggle, Sir Richard and I managed to lift the coachman onto the driver's seat. After that, I hitched my horse to the back of the coach, and we headed off towards Winchester.

At length, we reached Sir Richard's home, Chilcombe Hall, a magnificent building in the Palladian style perched on the banks of the River Itchen a mile or two to the north-east of the city walls, as I was later to discover. I brought the coach to a halt outside the house and climbed down just as servants emerged to greet their master and his daughter, lanterns in hand.

By now, it was pretty late in the evening. There was no chance

I could return to Winchester or attend the ball. It suddenly seemed that my journey from Southampton had been a fruitless one. That was until Sir Richard approached me, reached out and took me firmly by the hand, saying: 'You'll join us for supper this evening, won't you – and stay with us overnight?'

'Oh, please say you will,' said Sir Richard's daughter as she appeared from behind him, looking up at me, a bright smile lighting up her face. I gasped, and my heart beat faster than it ever had at Dettingen or Culloden. At that moment, I faced a petite lady of about thirty years of age whose beauty seemed to me to be too dazzling for any mortal pen to describe. I took off my hat.

'How could I refuse?' I answered with a soft laugh, brushing my hand over my head.

'Then that's settled,' beamed Sir Richard. 'But first, permit me to introduce you to my daughter, Mrs Eleanor Corbishly.'

I came to attention, bowed and extended my hand.

'I'm delighted to meet you, Mrs Corbishly,' I said. 'I am William Dunbar.'

'Yes,' she replied a little coyly, 'and a Scotsman, if I'm not mistaken.'

'No, you are not mistaken.' I laughed. 'A Scotsman all the way from Edinburgh.'

'Well, you can tell us all about yourself during the evening,' Sir Richard chipped in. 'In the meantime, I'll get one of my men to look after your horse and bring in any luggage you have with you.'

'Thank you, Sir Richard. I have brought a portmanteau with me.'

'Follow me, then.'

I followed Sir Richard and Eleanor as they led me through an anteroom into a parlour so fine and delicate that, in all appearance, it seemed to me that its sole purpose was to be seen, not occupied. I almost felt intimidated by the luxury displayed everywhere. The chairs and couches were carved, gilt and covered with cream silk damask, so smooth and slick that they looked as if they had never been sat upon. In the centre of the room, a rug in shades of blue and gold lay upon a floor, the boards of which were rubbed and waxed in such a manner that I could imagine that one was obliged to slide along rather than walk on them.

'Make yourself comfortable, Lieutenant Dunbar,' invited Sir Richard.

'Thank you, Sir Richard,' I replied, 'but I will remain standing if I may. I fear my travelling clothes are scarcely fitting for such fine furniture.'

Sir Richard chuckled. 'Well, bless you for that, Lieutenant. I appreciate your consideration,' he said. 'I can offer you a change of clothing if you wish. You are, I believe, the same size as me – there must be something in my wardrobe that suits you.'

'Thank you, but I have a change of clothes in my portmanteau.'

'In that case, may I suggest I show you to your room for tonight, where you may change your clothes.'

I followed Sir Richard as we ascended a wide marble staircase and passed through a large, extravagantly furnished anteroom until we reached the bedroom door.

'I hope you will find this room to your liking,' said Sir Richard.

I quickly looked around the room. There was a high bed with curtains, a wardrobe, chairs, a hand washstand, a chest of drawers, a dressing table with a couple of drawers and a mirror and a night commode.

'I'm sure I will,' I replied.

'I'll leave you to ready yourself for supper then,' said Sir Richard. 'We eat at nine o'clock, so you should have plenty of time for your purpose. My servant will call for you in good time beforehand and escort you back to the parlour before we go into the dining room.'

With that, Sir Richard turned away from me and headed back in the direction he had brought me. I watched him go before carefully opening my portmanteau, which had been placed near the bed. I took out my coat, waistcoat and breaches and put these on one of the chairs. Then I laid out the articles for my toilet on the washstand by the side of which I found a pitcher of hot water and towels.

After this, I stripped off my travelling clothes, washed thoroughly and donned the clothes I had placed on the chair. No sooner had I done this, and was admiring myself in a mirror and making my final preparations, when there was a knock on the door.

'Supper will be served in half an hour,' came a voice.

'One moment,' I called back. 'I'm almost ready. Please wait a moment, and then you can show me downstairs.'

Moments later, I crossed the room and opened the door. 'Thank you,' I said. 'Please lead on.'

When we reached the parlour, Sir Richard was standing alone, with his back to the fireplace. As I entered the room, he seemed genuinely pleased to see me. He held up his hand in greeting, a beaming smile lighting up his face.

'Would you join me in a glass of Madeira wine while we wait for Eleanor?' he asked resignedly.

'Yes, thank you,' I replied.

Sir Richard crossed to a mulberry gilt-wood drinks cabinet, which he opened. He took out a bottle of Madeira and two glasses. He filled the glasses, returned with them to where I was standing and handed one to me.

'Now that you have changed out of your travelling clothes,' he said with a chuckle, 'I hope you will sit down and make yourself comfortable.'

I nodded appreciatively, mouthing words of thanks.

I sat on a sofa and leant back amongst its cushions, closed one eye and looked abstractedly at the light through my glass of

Verdelho Solera with the other. As I did, Sir Richard raised his glass towards me.

'Your very good health, Lieutenant Dunbar,' he said. 'I am so pleased to welcome you to my home.'

'And to your good health, sir,' I reciprocated. 'I am delighted to be here with you.'

I had scarcely finished speaking when Eleanor swept elegantly into the room. I stood up and bowed towards her.

'Please sit down,' she said, shaping her lips into a beaming smile.

'Can I get you a glass of Madeira?' asked Sir Richard.

'No, thank you, Papa,' Eleanor replied.

She crossed in front of me, sat on a fauteuil and leant back, burying one hand in the rich masses of her hair, resting the other on the arm of the chair. Then, saying nothing, she stretched out one foot on a small ottoman, her eyes, with a thoughtful expression, riveted on mine.

I was at a loss for words. Something that had not happened to me for many years. Something was captivating about Eleanor. Something I just couldn't put my finger on. At that moment, Sir Richard's servant appeared to announce that supper was ready to be served.

With that, we all moved slowly into the dining room and took our places around a magnificent oval mahogany drop-leaf dining table with its cabriole legs headed by pointed-eared satyr masks and with claw-and-ball feet. Sir Richard sat at the head of the table, with Eleanor and me on either side of him.

As the evening progressed, I gradually learned more and more about my host and Eleanor. Sir Richard was an architect who had studied in Rome under Carlo Fontana, and also Pietro Francesco Garoli, before returning from Italy to work in London. He moved to Chilcombe Hall upon his father's death, at which time he succeeded to his father's baronetcy, giving up his practice as an architect to run the family lands and estate. Eleanor was a widow. Her husband, a captain serving with the Twenty-Third Regiment of Foot, had been killed at the Battle of Fontenoy.

'Do you have children?' I asked Eleanor.

'My husband and I were not blessed with children.' She sighed.

'I'm sorry,' I said, a lump seeming to rise in my throat as I did. Then, perhaps for the first time in many a long year, I felt compassion for someone – for Eleanor.

Eleanor looked at me. There were tears in her eyes. 'Sometimes life plays its cards in a way that no one can comprehend,' she whispered without bitterness, only a heavy sadness.

'That's true,' I replied, 'but, from my experience, it's not the hand of cards you are dealt that matters but how you choose to play them – the holder of the best hand is not necessarily the winner.'

'I agree,' Sir Richard added, reaching over to Eleanor and taking her hand. 'And every occurrence in life, whether good or bad, is not the full story but merely a single chapter in that story.'

'You're both right,' Eleanor murmured, wiping the tears from her eyes. Then a smile spread over her face. She picked up her wine glass. 'Lieutenant Dunbar,' she said affably, touching the glass with her lips, 'you haven't told us how you came to rescue us or why you were heading for Winchester.'

At first, I was a little taken aback; a straightforward request – on the face of it – but in my case, not so straightforward, perhaps.

'I was on my way from Southampton to attend a social function in Winchester – a ball. I had taken a brief detour and stopped en route for some refreshments. When I rejoined the road to Winchester, I saw the attempt to rob you. The rest, as they say, is history,' I replied somewhat elusively.

Sir Richard reached over to me and put his hand on my shoulder. 'Well, thank Heaven that you did stop for refreshments on your journey, or else you would not have arrived when you did to save us from the highwayman,' he said.

'Thank Heaven indeed,' echoed Eleanor. She paused, taking a sip of her wine. 'Now you've heard about Papa and me, it's your turn to tell us about William Dunbar, Lieutenant in His Majesty's Tenth Regiment of Marines.' Her teeth flashed in a further smile.

Feeling just a little bit awkward, I swallowed a nervous dryness from my throat. Then I drained my wine glass before giving a brief, albeit adroitly Machiavellian, account of myself before quickly moving the conversation on.

Sir Richard and Eleanor proved themselves to be excellent company. We engaged in genial conversation, jests and laughter, and, for me, more than all these, I realised that the proximity of Eleanor so warmed my blood that I felt increasingly attracted to her. In that moment of realisation began the dread of the necessity of separation. In the morning, I would be returning to Southampton.

Will I see Eleanor again when I do?

ELEVEN

Almost before I could comprehend it, summer began giving way to autumn. It had been a summer like no other I had experienced before. I had seen Eleanor as often as my military duties permitted. We became closer to one another with each of our meetings. Mercy was becoming a rapidly fading memory. Ann had vanished from my mind completely. For the first time, I had fallen head over heels in love with someone – in love with Eleanor.

For good measure, my financial circumstances had changed beyond my wildest dreams, thanks to a sustained run of good fortune at the gaming tables. Additionally, with the help of Sir Richard and his contacts in Winchester and Southampton, I set up a lucrative business acting as a financial intermediary between them and London business associates of my family. For a suitable commission, I received and paid money in London on their behalf when banking facilities were inadequate to cope with the growing number of business transactions as markets and intermediaries proliferated. All of this saw me more prosperous than I had ever been before.

I was feeling euphoric. The weather matched my mood. The

sun shone brightly in a cloudless blue sky. I was on my way to Chilcombe Hall. I was to be the guest of Sir Richard at a ball and a supper he was hosting to celebrate Eleanor's birthday.

Undoubtedly this is a day when it's so good to be alive.

I reached the entrance gates of the hall and turned my horse up the long driveway leading to the house. Once there, I dismounted and handed the reins to a waiting servant. I knocked on the door, and somewhat to my surprise, Eleanor pulled the door open.

'Come in, dearest William,' she gushed and, slipping her hand into the crook of my elbow, she led me into the hallway. 'Wait here a while,' she whispered. 'I'll close the door.'

I stood and watched in awe as Eleanor glided across the hallway, closed the door and returned to me. Her white satin dress flowed gracefully down her slender body, and her natural dark brown hair had been powdered blue-grey and supplemented with delicate, artificial hair extensions and pieces.

She drew me to her breast and kissed me passionately. I could not speak. I could not think. Everything was drowned out in an ocean of unimagined bliss. We stood there together for what seemed an eternity.

'Come on, William,' Eleanor finally whispered. 'We'd best join the others in the ballroom.'

'If we must.' I sighed.

'We must,' Eleanor replied with a chuckle.

Pressing her to my beating heart, I kissed her on the forehead and then looked down into her eyes. Our breath mingled in a single stream.

'Then let's go,' I said, my arms slackening from around her.

Hand in hand, we entered the ballroom, and music greeted our arrival. I floated through the assembly with Eleanor and joined several other couples dancing the minuet. Our bodies swayed to the rhythmic breeze of the dance.

Then, after several dances, I exchanged glances with Eleanor.

'I don't know about you,' I said, 'but I'm feeling the need to take some fresh air. So why don't we take a stroll down in the garden.'

'Sounds good to me,' replied Eleanor, taking my hand.

We strolled down through the garden to the banks of the River Itchen.

'It's so beautiful here,' said Eleanor as she sat down. 'Sit by me, William.'

I did as I was asked. Eleanor slowly eased backwards until she was lying down, looking up at the clear night sky. I stretched out next to her and took her hand. We lay there briefly, not moving until I lifted my upper body, turned, leant down and gently kissed Eleanor.

An hour or so later, intoxicated with pleasure, we returned to the house – this time to throw ourselves into the country dancing, which was in full flow by then. When the music finally stopped, we glided to a finish near an alcove where Sir Richard was conversing with a man and a woman who seemed vaguely familiar to me.

Sir Richard looked up as Eleanor and I reached the alcove. He waved at me and beckoned before saying something to the couple, leaving them and crossing the room towards Eleanor and me.

'I hope you are both enjoying yourselves.' He beamed, thrusting his hand towards me and grabbing mine. I winced. His handshake was the strongest I had ever experienced, as I inevitably forgot each time before shaking hands with him. 'I've been looking out for you all evening, but you've eluded me until now,' he continued. 'Apart from anything else, I wanted to invite you to stay with us. There's some business I want to discuss with you – but not tonight. Tonight is Eleanor's night. In any event, supper will be served in the dining room before too long, and eating a fine meal of an evening with you and Eleanor is my preferred way of spending time. Always put off anything until tomorrow that can wait until then is my firm belief.'

'I'll drink to that, sir.' I chuckled.

At first, I was more than a little intrigued as to the nature of the business Sir Richard was referring to, but I soon put it to the back of my mind. My thoughts for the rest of the evening were of Eleanor, right up to when I kissed her goodnight and made my way to my bedroom at the end of the evening a delighted and contented man.

When I awoke the following day, I felt awful. Faint. I had the most terrible taste in my mouth. My head was splitting, and I was trembling. I was sweating profusely but felt as cold as ice simultaneously. My neck was so stiff that I could scarcely move my head, either side to side or up and down.

I got up slowly, struggled to dress and staggered downstairs.

'Good grief!' exclaimed the cook as I almost fell into the kitchen.

'Sorry to trouble you,' I croaked, my voice hoarse and obscure. 'I have a sore throat and a terrible thirst. May I have a drink of water?'

The cook rushed over to me, took my arm, guided me to the kitchen table and pulled back a chair.

'Sit yourself down, sir, while I get you a glass and some water,' she invited.

I slumped down on the chair and rested my head on the table, breathing heavily. Finally, the cook returned and placed the water I had requested on the table.

'Thank you,' I whispered, barely lifting my head to look at her.

'I'll go and call my master,' said the cook before leaving the kitchen.

After she had gone, I struggled to lift my head off the table and sit upright. I picked up the glass of water and tried to take a drink, but I couldn't swallow more than the smallest of mouthfuls. I put the glass back down on the table and slumped forward. Ten minutes later, the cook reappeared, followed by Sir Richard and his manservant, Jenkins.

'Come on, my boy,' said Sir Richard kindly. 'Let's get you back to your bed, and then I'll send for the doctor.'

He and Jenkins helped me off the kitchen chair and then back up to my bedroom, where Jenkins undressed me and put on my nightshirt. With a listlessness that portrayed great physical effort, I leant against him, swaying unsteadily towards the edge of the bed and sat down. He placed his arm around my shoulder and helped me ease into bed. My breathing was rapid and shallow, and I was gasping for breath.

'Thank you,' I croaked, my voice foggy and distant.

At that moment, I was seized with a violent urge to vomit, but I managed to control it. Jenkins helped me to sit up, which seemed to help, and positioned a pillow behind my back to support me. He then bent down, picked up the chamber pot from the floor by my bed and placed it on the bed – within my reach. I lay there still, bathed in perspiration.

Sir Richard turned to Jenkins and instructed him to ride with all speed into Winchester to summon the family doctor to come to the hall before returning to my bedside.

'Try and rest,' he told me reassuringly. 'I will go downstairs and wait for the doctor. In the meantime, I will get the cook to bring you some honey in hot water. I often find that it helps soothe a sore throat.'

'Thank you, Sir Richard.'

Having tried and failed to drink a cup of the honey in hot water brought up to me, I fell into a fitful sleep until I was awakened when Sir Richard and the doctor came into my room.

The doctor was a tall, grey-haired man with a long, pitted, weather-beaten face, perhaps fifty years of age. A slightly hooked nose fell over his full mouth.

'Who have we here, Sir Richard?' he asked.

'This is Lieutenant Dunbar,' replied Sir Richard. 'Someone who has become a very dear and welcome friend to my daughter and me both.'

The doctor moved to the side of my bed and stood there, looking at me for what seemed an eternity.

'Hello, Lieutenant Dunbar,' he finally said. 'I'm Thomas Collins. Sir Richard has told me a little about your predicament, so I'll get on with a full examination of you.'

He reached down and drew the bedclothes back. He pulled me forward, lifted me slightly and removed my nightshirt before examining my body, tut-tutting from time to time as he did.

'Now, please open your mouth so that I can look at your throat,' he instructed after he had finished his external examination. He leant down over me but jerked his head away as I exhaled. 'Forgive me,' he said. 'I was caught unawares by your breath – it carries a most offensive putrid odour.'

'I'm sorry, Doctor,' I croaked, somewhat embarrassed.

'No problem, Lieutenant. It's me who should apologise. I shouldn't have reacted as I did – very unprofessional of me. So now please open your mouth wide.'

He then asked me to move my tongue – up, down and side to side. Finally, he took out a spatula to hold my tongue down and inspected my throat. Having done so, he replaced my nightshirt and drew the bedclothes back over me. He then took my hand and looked at me with a serious look on his face.

'Lieutenant Dunbar, I'm not sure what to make of your condition,' he said, perplexed. 'But I believe that you have contracted a disease that we do not have a name for in this country, although it is known elsewhere by a variety of names, including *morbus strangulatorius*,' he continued academically, 'but in plain English, I'll call it *putrid throat*. You show all the symptoms as I understand these to be. Your uvula, tonsils, pharynx, and the whole of the arched opening at the back of your mouth that leads to the pharynx, are remarkably red. There is also a white slough that has formed by your tonsils. Your face, neck and hands are also intensely red. Further, your face and body are covered with small pimples and eruptions like flea bites.'

Much of what Dr Collins had said passed over me, but I connected with the term *putrid throat* – my throat felt like it was on fire.

'Thank you, Doctor,' I whispered, struggling to speak. 'Is there anything you can do for me?'

'I would be less than honest if I said that I can prescribe a guaranteed cure for your condition,' Collins replied frankly, 'but I hope I can prescribe something that will alleviate it.' He turned towards Sir Richard. 'Do you have any barley water or syrup of roses in the house?' he asked.

'I'll check with the cook,' Sir Richard replied. 'If we do not, I will send for some. In the meantime, Lieutenant Dunbar has been provided with honey dissolved in hot water.'

'Have you been hiding your medical talents under a bushel?' Collins chuckled. 'In my experience, that offers benefits similar to vinegar in barley water or syrup of roses. You might also give Lieutenant Dunbar small draughts of mint tea mixed with red port wine in a ratio of one part port to five parts of mint tea.'

'The port wine I do have,' replied Sir Richard, 'but I suspect we may not have any mint tea.'

Collins turned back to me, his brow furrowing.

'One thing I will not prescribe, though, is leeching. Unlike many of my fellow doctors, I do not believe that bleeding a patient is helpful to him – and certainly not when a patient is already weakened by his illness. Perhaps, you may regard me as too much of a modernist. Still, I'm afraid I also have to disagree with the practice of purging by using the like of bezoar stones to induce vomiting and sweating, especially where a patient is likely to vomit unaided and who is already sweating profusely. What you need, Lieutenant Dunbar, is rest – and plenty of it. Apart from that and taking in the liquids I have prescribed, there is little else I can suggest. I will take my leave of you for now, then, but I will return daily to check on you.'

With that, Collins and Sir Richard left me.

I soon dozed off after they had gone but vomited several times and became increasingly confused as the day wore on. Gradually, I fell into a deep sleep until I woke with a start; someone was wiping my forehead with a cool cloth. I grasped the hand holding the fabric and pulled it to my chest. Clearing my mind of confusion that appeared to have wholly fogged it, I remembered where I was – and why. I assumed the hand must be one of the servants caring for me. I looked up, trying to make out who was wiping my face. No matter how hard I tried, I could make out nothing more than a pair of eyes looking intently at me, surrounded by pale mist. Gradually, my sight grew turbid again, and I drifted back into a blankness fractured by visions of war – of Dettingen and Culloden.

Sometimes, whilst in a semi-comatose state, I grasped words spoken by various people close to my bedside, which seemed to come almost from another world.

I think that we are losing him...

Wipe the vomit from the lieutenant's face and chest.

He's become delirious – almost maniacal on occasion...

Somehow, I doubted that the words could be directed towards me. It could not possibly be me that was near to death or who had vomited. Inwardly, I felt so well. It could not be me who behaved maniacally in any way. Inwardly, I was entirely sound of mind.

Sometimes, I would awake from a nightmare for long enough to find myself sitting in bed, my arms pinned down by other arms, which endeavoured to hold me. Then I would sink back into that world of horrors I had emerged from, yo-yo-ing between that world and a progressively less troubled consciousness.

Although I came close to succumbing to my illness more than once, I somehow clung on. Then, very slowly, my condition started to improve. The soreness in my throat abated, and my headache faded away.

'Hello there, William,' a familiar voice greeted me as I awoke from the first untroubled sleep I had enjoyed since being taken ill. As I looked up to see Eleanor, a smile spread over her face. 'I'm delighted to see you seem on the mend at last,' she continued gleefully. 'You did frighten us. So many times, you opened your eyes and did not recognise anyone, and you raved like a madman occasionally! But it's all over now. Hopefully, we have given you the best of care then and will continue to do so now.'

As I listened to the words, *we have given you the best of care*, I felt myself trembling. My head was spinning; I could hardly think straight.

'Do you mean to say you have been caring for me?' I gasped.

'Of course, dearest William,' she replied, laying her hand on my shoulder. 'I insisted that I alone should do so.'

I took her hand, drew it to my lips and kissed it gently. 'But you have risked catching the same disease by helping me. How could I ever thank you,' I whispered, touched by her kindness.

'Seeing you well again is thanks enough,' Eleanor replied tenderly.

A couple of days later, and feeling well enough at long last, I woke, washed and dressed and made my way downstairs for breakfast. It was a sunny day, and I fully intended to invite Eleanor to accompany me on a ride into Winchester.

As I entered the dining room, I found Sir Richard on his own, his head hanging low and looking sadder and more forlorn than I had ever seen him before.

'Is something wrong?' I blurted out.

Sir Richard looked up. There were tears in his eyes. 'It's Eleanor.' He sighed. 'She's been taken ill. I fear that she has contracted the same illness that you had. She has a terribly sore throat and has been vomiting intermittently through the night.'

I shuddered. A sense of guilt surged through me. *I've given the disease to Eleanor!*

'Dear God, please let it not be so!' I gasped.

'Amen to that,' whispered Sir Richard. 'Dr Collins has been sent for. He should be here soon. But, in the meantime, at least we have syrup of roses and mint tea to help her.'

I crossed the room to where Sir Richard was sitting and laid my hand on his trembling shoulder. 'Is there anything I can do to help, sir?' I asked.

Sir Richard placed his hand on mine and looked up at me.

'I fear that the only thing either of us can do is pray that Eleanor, like you, is spared.'

We sat together in the dining room in silence. I, for one, could find nothing to say. Then, after an agonising wait, Dr Collins arrived at the hall and was taken to Eleanor's room by Sir Richard.

A while later, Sir Richard reappeared, ashen-faced and visibly shaken.

'Our worst fears are realised,' he mumbled, almost incoherently. A spasm of fear swept over his face. 'Eleanor has putrid throat.'

During that day, Eleanor's health fell into an ever-steepening decline. Then, just when I thought things could not get any worse, they did. Sir Richard was also taken ill. He, too, was stricken by putrid throat – the disease that so nearly took me – the disease already strengthening its grip on Eleanor, threatening to take her from him and me.

I took it upon myself to ensure everything was done to care for Sir Richard. However, as things rapidly began to turn out, that was very little. Maybe it was his age or not, but he suffered a far more aggressive attack of putrid throat than Eleanor or me.

His attack had begun as mine had: shivering, headache and urges to vomit. I sent Jenkins for Dr Collins, but by the time he arrived at Chilcombe Hall, the shivering, headache and urges to vomit had abated. At first, I thought I had overreacted, but regrettably, I had not. I waited in the dining room while Collins examined Sir Richard, hoping everything would turn out well. My heart sank when Collins entered the room with a doleful expression. I looked at him pleadingly. He shook his head.

'It's not looking good, I'm afraid. Sir Richard's uvula, tonsils and contiguous parts are deep red and so swollen that they have virtually closed the entrance to his pharynx. I fear that there is little I can do – or suggest that can be done for him – other than to make and keep him as comfortable as possible while the disease takes its course.'

'Thank you, Dr Collins,' I replied. 'I'll sit with him. It's the least I can do.'

'That's very good of you. In the meantime, I'll check on Eleanor.'

I left the dining room, climbed the stairs and headed to Sir Richard's room. Dr Collins followed me up the stairs before crossing to Eleanor's room. Once inside Sir Richard's room, I closed the door and crossed to a chair beside the bed. Sir Richard was asleep. I went over to the washstand in the corner of the room, poured some water from a jug placed on the floor into the washstand basin, picked up a facecloth from the stand and put it in the basin, ready in case I needed to wipe Sir Richard's face.

I returned to the bed and sat on the chair, wondering what the day might bring.

As the day wore on, Sir Richard's condition seemed to improve. He began to breathe more easily and could take some syrup of roses without difficulty, although he occasionally spat up large quantities of phlegm.

By early evening, my hopes for Sir Richard had begun to rise when, without warning, he took a turn very much for the worse. First, he experienced severe breathing difficulties – almost like he was being strangled. Then his lips had turned blue. I rushed across the room, opened the door, shouted for Jenkins and returned to Sir Richard. I put my arms around him and lifted him forward. Jenkins appeared.

'Quickly, man,' I called to him. 'I think that Sir Richard is having a fit. Place pillows behind him as support, then fetch the facecloth from the washstand basin, wring it out and bring it back to me. After that, make all haste and summon Dr Collins.'

No sooner had Jenkins gone when Sir Richard seemed to recover. His breathing became less laboured, and the colour of his lips returned to a more normal hue. I felt a real sense of relief flood through me. I went over to the washbasin to dampen the facecloth again, but no sooner had I reached the washbasin when Sir Richard let out a mighty groan and exhaled sharply as he passed from this world to the next – barely a day had elapsed since the onset of his attack of putrid throat.

I crossed the room and looked down at Sir Richard before closing his eyes. 'May you sleep peacefully in your eternal sleep,' I whispered in despair.

I've known people who've died before, but I had never before felt the same sense of loss as I felt for Sir Richard at that moment in time. Then my mind was flooded with thoughts of Eleanor.

I rushed from Sir Richard's room and crossed to Eleanor's room. She was asleep but looked deathly pale. I stood over her, trembling, before leaning down and feeling her forehead. It seemed slightly warmer than usual, but not unduly so. Then I noticed a fetid watery discharge flowing from her nostrils. I found a facecloth, wetted it and then gently wiped away the discharge. As I did, Eleanor regained consciousness, drew a long breath and slowly passed her hand across her eyes, lips and mouth. She looked at me and seemed about to speak, but no sound came from her lips at first. Then she smiled weakly.

I, too, was speechless at first. I knew that I couldn't break the news of her father's death for the present. That terrible news had to wait until she was well enough to receive it.

'You look pale, Eleanor,' I finally said, choking up. 'How are you feeling?'

'Not so good, I'm afraid.'

'You have to get better.'

'Why, dearest William?'

'You make me want to be a better person. No, it's more than that. You alone make me want to be a better person.'

Eleanor looked up at me. There were tears in her eyes. 'God bless you, William,' she replied, her voice tailing off as she did.

Moments later, Eleanor drifted back into unconsciousness. I leant down and kissed her on the cheek before leaving the room. There was much I had to do. Dr Collins was expected to arrive soon. But, more importantly, the news of Sir Richard's death had to be broken to his eldest son and the remainder of his family.

Dr Collins came and went, and I took all steps necessary to inform Sir Richard's family of his death and Eleanor's condition. After that, the day seemed to drag by. There was nothing else to take my mind off Eleanor and how she might be faring, but I rushed back to her room as soon as possible.

Much to my relief – and my delight – I found her still in bed but feeling better than she had since taking to her bed. Her face and hands were still very red, and her throat remained sore, but her nausea was gone, and she was breathing without difficulty. She felt well enough to have some mint tea and bread and butter.

'Promise me that you will stay with me,' she whispered.

'Of course, I will,' I replied.

'Promise you will stay for as long as necessary.'

'For as long as necessary – I promise.'

She looked up at me. 'Thanks, William,' she said, her voice trailing, her eyes becoming dim.

I drew a chair to Eleanor's bedside, sat down, took her hand and kissed it gently. 'Try and sleep, dearest Eleanor,' I said softly. 'I'll watch over you while you do.'

Eleanor smiled weakly and closed her eyes. At that moment, though, she began to experience breathing difficulties. One minute she suffered breathlessness; the next, she was breathing very quickly. To my horror, things were becoming dire. Whilst the redness of her skin disappeared, her hands grew cold. Then, utterly distraught, I witnessed her body gradually shut down. I sat by the side of her bed, holding her hands in mine as she slowly lost consciousness.

I briefly closed my eyes in silent prayer. As I did, I suddenly became aware of an air of tension in the room and knew something was seriously amiss. I shot up from the chair on which I was sitting. There was an eery stillness. I looked at Eleanor's face, translucent white on the pillowcase, and knew what it was. Death had come to her. At that moment, I felt numb.

'This can't have happened.' I sobbed. 'The world has just stopped making sense.'

Numbness turned to anger and guilt for having survived when she had not. Then, finally, anger and guilt gave way to deep, heartfelt grief. In less than a week, I had lost the woman I had come to love like no other and the man who had become like a father to me.

TWELVE

It had already been a busy day for me as I made my way along Cornhill before turning towards the Jamaica Coffee House, set within a labyrinth of medieval courts and alleys, where I was to meet my cousin, Robert Campbell, whom I hadn't seen since he transferred from the Marines back to the Royal North British Fusiliers not long after Ann had begun proceedings against me. As I reached my destination, I looked up to see a magnificent glass lantern that hung above the door on which was painted a Turk's head.

I opened the door and entered, peering through a fog of thick pipe smoke that filled a room which seemed to be a constant hive of activity. A man I took to be the owner stood behind a counter that took up much of one side of the room. Armed with a pot of coffee each, several maids worked their way through the room, offering refills to anyone wishing their dish to be replenished.

'William,' a voice called out to me. 'Over here, cousin.'

I could vaguely make Robert out, sitting up at a rectangular table. I crossed the room and sat opposite him, beside a somewhat corpulent person smoking his pipe while a bright-eyed, neat-handed maid refilled the empty dish at his elbow.

'Coffee for us, please,' Robert called to the maid.

'Certainly, sir,' she replied. 'I'll be with you as soon as I can.'

Robert looked across at me.

'So, how are you, cousin?' I asked as he did. 'It's been a long time since we last met.'

'Too long, William,' Robert replied affably. 'I'm very well, thank you – and you? Although judging by how prosperous you look, I guess my question is answered already.'

'I mustn't grumble, that's for sure.' I chuckled. 'But thank you for the compliment. Have you been waiting for long?'

'Not really, but I have learned something while I have,' he declared. 'This was the first coffee house in London. It was frequented by no lesser a person than Samuel Pepys.'

'And now it's been frequented by us,' I replied light-heartedly. 'Let's hope the coffee is at least as good now as it was in his time.'

'Well, here come our dishes, so we'll find out soon,' Robert guffawed as the maid arrived.

She placed a dish of coffee in front of each of us and left. I picked up my dish and took a sip. Robert did the same before giving me a puzzled look.

'Now, tell me what you want to discuss with me,' he said.

'To the point, as usual,' I quipped, putting my dish down. 'It's simple. I have a business proposition to put to you.'

A quizzical brow arched above Robert's left eye.

'A business proposition. How intriguing. So, tell me more.'

I looked straight at Robert. A sense of pride was rising inside me. 'Thanks to a very fortunate change in my circumstances, I have become a shipowner—'

'A shipowner?' Robert interrupted, looking slightly aghast. 'But how – why?'

'Steady on, cousin, give me a chance, and I'll explain all,' I chided. 'Life has been very kind to me in recent months. First of all, I met several businessmen and landowners in Winchester and Southampton after your return to the Royal North British Fusiliers. I developed a lucrative sideline operating as a financial intermediary through them and my contacts here in London. One of the landowners, an architect by profession, became almost a second father to me. Then, to my greatest sadness, he died suddenly in the most unfortunate circumstances and bequeathed me a small fortune in his will. Following this, I sold my commission and repaid Uncle Mark the money he had loaned to me to buy it in the first place, and there was even a small profit for me upon the sale.'

'And they say that the devil takes care of his own,' Robert joked.

'I don't know about that,' I replied, looking first at Robert and then up above me before continuing, 'but someone, something, up there must like me.'

Robert threw his head back, pressing the fingers of his left hand against his forehead. 'And how did that... *someone, something, up there...* steer a financial intermediary and beneficiary into becoming a shipowner?'

'Well, through my Southampton contacts, I was introduced to an agent in Bristol who acts for several investors in transporting goods between Bristol and Africa and from Africa to the Americas. He told me of a vessel that had been taken by a French privateer on its way to Africa but was later retaken and sent into Plymouth before returning to Bristol, where it was sold and refitted. So, to cut a long story short, I saw the ship as an interesting business opportunity and bought it.'

'So, that's the "how" and the "where", I guess, but what is the "why"?'

I picked up my dish of coffee, drank the remaining contents, wiped my lips with my forefinger and looked back at Robert with a smile. 'I propose to turn my investment into a fortune,' I replied gleefully.

Robert looked at me, this time tapping his forehead with his fingers, at the same time raising his eyebrows in interest. 'That leads to a further question,' he said. 'In what way?'

'I am putting the ship to the same purpose that it was put to originally.'

Robert sucked in his cheeks as if deep in thought. He looked down at his dish of coffee, saying nothing at first. 'Where do you see me fitting in?' he finally asked, breaking the silence that developed between us.

'I would like you to invest in my venture,' I replied.

Robert shot me a troubled look before picking up his dish of coffee, emptying it and calling the serving maid over. 'Another dish, cousin?' he asked.

'Not for me, thanks,' I replied.

'Then just a refill for me, please,' Robert told the maid. After she had left, he looked back at me. 'But why do you want or need me to invest in the venture, cousin?'

'The cost of the refitted ship was £2,146. The further cost of the initial cargo that will be shipped on the outward leg of the voyage to Africa is £1,734. My intention has been to find four or five other interested parties who would purchase a half share in the vessel from me, repay me half of the fitting out costs and cover half of the cost of the cargo, with me covering the other half. So far, four individuals have committed to joining the venture. They each want to take a one-eighth stake in the venture but are happy to accommodate one further partner. Therefore, the total cost of the venture has already been underwritten, but I would like you to become a partner as well. Would you be interested in doing so?'

'Possibly, but first, a few questions.'

'Of course, what are they?'

'How will the profits be shared?'

'Each partner, including me, would share the profits of the

venture pro rata with their investment. Thus, my share of the profits would be fifty per cent.'

Robert gave a little whisk of a smile. 'And what profit are you hoping to achieve?'

'I have been advised that ten per cent is to be expected as the return on one's total investment in the African trade, but I'll go so far as to say I would not risk my capital on a venture to Africa for less, and I expect to receive a significantly higher return in the present instance.'

'Ten per cent seems reasonable – albeit a little less than I would expect,' Robert observed.

'Well, as I said, I expect to receive a significantly higher return. On our projections, the venture will return something closer to twenty-three per cent.'

'A return of that magnitude sounds nice, but it also sounds too good to be true, and I've always held the view that something that sounds too good to be true inevitably is.' Robert looked around the room for a while, clearly in deep thought. 'What insurance arrangements are, or will be, put in place?' he finally asked, looking back at me.

'The individual partners will need to purchase their own cover. In my case, I will insure my half of the vessel and cargo solely against the perils of the sea. I do not wish to incur any expense beyond such a policy. However, it goes without saying that if any other partner wishes to extend cover beyond that level, it will be a matter for him. Partners are also free to take the risk themselves – to self-insure – and, thereby, incur no insurance costs. For my part, the cost for me to insure my total investment is £140.'

Robert leant on one elbow; his expression slid into a frown. 'One final question, William. You have not said so in so many words, but am I correct in thinking that your intended cargo between Africa and the Americas will be slaves?'

'Oh, yes, isn't it obvious from what I've been saying? Does that bother you then?'

'If I'm honest, it does a little,' came Robert's slow reply. 'It does not seem to me to be right to profit directly from the suffering and misery of other human beings.'

'But people have been the victims of slavery for centuries – even we English were taken from this country as slaves by the Romans. Have you forgotten the story of Pope Gregory the Great, who saw some fair-skinned children in a Rome slave market and asked who they were? *Angles* came the answer, to which Gregory responded, *non Angli, sed angeli* – "not Angles, but angels".'

'But do two wrongs make a right?'

'A good question, perhaps, cousin. However, it seems that there have been slavers for as long as there have been prostitutes – each of them pursuing a morally reprehensible means to earn a living.'

'Well, I would find it difficult to argue with you on that point.'

'In any event, don't forget what I told you once before.'

'You will have to remind me, William.'

'I fully intend to possess the fullest of purses and do so as soon as possible. But, as I have told you before, I am not... *too full o' th' milk of human kindness to catch the nearest way...* and my proposed venture now represents the nearest way for me.'

Robert nodded, a half-smile crossing his face. 'Ah, yes, I recall you saying something along those lines.'

'Then will you join me as a partner in my venture?'

Robert's face changed to a rather serious expression. 'I am tempted,' he replied, 'but I'm not sure that I can afford to take the risk of a direct investment in the venture; I do have a suggestion though: what if I lend you £485 – at a rate of interest of five per cent per annum against your note of hand? You could then use that money to increase your investment in the venture, thereby increasing your profit share – even after repaying the loan from me, plus interest. As for me, I would earn a greater return than if I kept my money either in the form of government consols or deposited with my bank, and I wouldn't be taking on the inherent risks of your venture.'

I threw my hands in the air.

'If you'll excuse the pun, that sounds like a capital idea.' I chuckled. 'I'm all for making more money rather than less. I'd be delighted to take up your suggestion.'

'In that case, William, time for lunch, I think. We can thrash out the details over a decent meal and a few tankards of porter.'

'Never a truer word, Robert,' I replied enthusiastically. 'Let's go to the inn across the way – the one in Castle Court – and it will be my treat.'

*

It was December. Winter had well and truly set in. The year was almost at an end, but my new venture had just begun. Until now, the weather had been unusually mild, but, of late, a bitterly cold, numbing, north-westerly wind had sprung up. From where I stood on the shore to the horizon, there was nothing but angry, churning grey tipped by whitecaps that looked keen-edged enough to slice through the hull of a twin-masted ship, now named *The Archer*, as it inched its way forward. It had started the first leg of its journey from Bristol to Calabar, towed by rowing boats. Its hold was packed with iron bars, copper rods, manillas, neptunes and cowrie shells, all to be used as currency in the purchase of slaves for transportation to the Americas to be sold there. It carried the hopes of me and my co-investors.

As I watched, my heart was pounding, fuelled by excitement and trepidation. What lay in store for *The Archer*? Would I see a return on my investment? There was a lot at stake. My investment in the venture was nearly £2,600, including the money I had borrowed from Robert – almost as much as I had received as one of Sir Richard's beneficiaries.

But you have to speculate to accumulate, I told myself as I made my way from the docks to meet one of the major Bristol agents to prepare for the next voyage of *The Archer* when she returned to England in about seventeen months' time. By then, I hoped to have earned sufficient profit to recover my initial investment, repay Robert, acquire an additional ship and finance a second financial venture to Africa and the Americas for both it and *The Archer*.

A second venture – and further ventures after that – will undoubtedly ensure that I fulfil my ambition always to have sufficient wealth for my purposes.

MERCY GRUNDY

THIRTEEN

I sat opposite Mama in the front parlour. I was anxious. Dejected. It had been almost a year since William had returned to Southampton after the revelations about Ann Macclesfield. I had heard nothing from him since then; heard nothing of him. He had not replied to the numerous letters I had written to him. I was at a complete loss. Distraught.

'I just don't understand it, Mama,' I murmured. 'Why haven't I received any news of William since he returned to his regiment? Has Ann Macclesfield's claim against him succeeded? Has he returned to Scotland to be with her? Has something happened to him? Has he been transferred back to Flanders? Has he been wounded – or worse?'

Mama looked across at me, a concerned frown joining her eyebrows together.

'Hush, hush, dearest daughter,' she said sympathetically. She came over to me and put her arms around my neck. 'I am certain there will be a very good reason why you have heard nothing from him,' she continued gently, 'and also why he hasn't replied to your letters. Don't fret yourself so, dearest Mercy, I'm sure he's safe and—'

Mama didn't finish what she was saying. At that moment, Papa came through the door. 'You're sure who is safe?' he said, looking at Mama enquiringly.

'William,' Mama replied.

'William – William who?'

'Why, William Dunbar, of course, Papa,' I said, taking Mama's arms from around my neck.

A look of repugnance crossed Papa's face. 'Oh, him – the married man. The man who betrayed my trust. The man who wanted to destroy your honour,' Grundy hissed, revealing an abusive nature I had scarcely witnessed before. 'He is someone you must never see again!'

I felt my jaw drop. Something inside me snapped. A wedge of anger mixed with tears filled my throat. I shot up from my chair.

'Papa, I have every intention of seeing William again!' I fumed, exasperation etched into my voice.

'You dare to defy me?' Papa barked, clearly livid at my outburst.

I was feeling rebellious but found it almost impossible to put my feelings immediately into words. I knew what I wanted to say, but at first, I didn't seem able to. Then I exploded, determined to stand my ground.

'I love you, Papa, but yes, I dare defy you. William is the only one in the world for me. There is nobody else who could take his place. To me, he has become the very essence of living.'

'If that man has become the "very essence of living",' Papa sneered, 'God help us all.'

By then, I was at a complete loss for words. I stood staring at Papa. Motionless. Papa returned my stare. Silent. He was breathing heavily. All the colour had drained from his face. Mama, a spectator until then, went over to Papa and took his hand. He turned and faced her.

'Why has that man got such a hold over Mercy?' Papa pleaded.

Mama smiled kindly. 'Dearest husband, why can't you see she loves him?'

'Loves him? How? Why? She hasn't seen him for months.'

With that, I immediately found my voice again. 'That may be the case, Papa, but yes, I love William – and know, with every moment that has passed, that love for him has become far deeper than I ever thought possible – but you don't care at all, do you?' I hissed.

'Care? About him?' Papa sneered. 'Absolutely not!'

I sat down. I felt aggrieved by Papa's lack of empathy, my face downcast. My head was spinning, but I was determined not to remain silent.

'Why would you?' I sputtered. 'You can't ever see beyond a man's wealth or social standing. I am happiest when I am with William. My only hope is to make him half as happy as he makes me.'

'I don't know why,' Papa replied, aghast.

'How could you, Papa? You're not me.'

'Where Dunbar's concerned, I'm grateful I am not.' Those were Papa's parting words as he stormed out of the room.

*

The following morning, my eyes flickered open. The first bright rays of the sun were piercing through the curtains and falling slanted across my bed. I had scarcely slept. No sooner had I dozed off when I woke with a start, alternately reliving my argument with Papa the previous evening and wondering why I had had no contact with William for so long. With solemnness, seemingly my only friend, a feeling of guilt and shame constantly haunted me: *have I permanently damaged my relationship with Papa when, in truth, I have no idea whether William cares for me at all?*

That question remained with me as I made my way down to breakfast. As I approached the dining room, I heard Papa cough. My heart skipped a beat. I had been hoping Papa might have already set off for his office. I opened the door with trepidation and, head down, came to a halt half in and half out of the room.

'Forgive me, Papa,' I mumbled, my eyes suddenly moist with tears.

'Forgive you for what, daughter?' Papa replied.

I looked up.

'For my behaviour yesterday evening.'

Papa stood up, turned towards me and walked slowly to where I stood. He reached towards me, framed my face with his hands and looked deeply into my eyes.

'Many words best not spoken passed between us yesterday,' Papa said softly, 'words now best forgotten. I still believe you should have nothing more to do with Dunbar, but it's not for me to tell you how to live your life. In any event, the Scottish court may yet determine that he is free to marry you. In the meantime, I will accept his word that there was no marriage between him and Ann Macclesfield. Accordingly, if he returns to Henley, I will welcome him into my home as I would anyone else lucky enough to be the future husband of the daughter I hold dearest above everything in this world.'

I could scarcely believe my ears.

'Papa!' I cried in delighted astonishment as I reached up, took Papa's hands from my face and clasped them firmly between my own.

Papa looked at me and smiled.

'That's settled then.' He chuckled. 'Now let me finish my breakfast and get off to the office… I have important business to deal with this morning.'

'And I will join you for breakfast,' I replied. 'After that, I will ask Mama if I can go with her when she visits Uncle Henry this afternoon, especially since I can't remember the last time that I saw him.

*

The coachman held open the door of Papa's carriage, and Mama and I climbed in and settled down for the short ride to Culham Court, Uncle Henry's magnificent country house. Once there, we were escorted into the parlour.

As I habitually did when I first entered the room, I gazed around enviously. I never ceased to be amazed by its splendour. A large crystal chandelier hung from the ceiling. There was an *étagère* to house numerous figurines. A small chinoiserie collector's cabinet stood on a walnut lowboy. A pair of bronze sphinxes stood on its twin. Marble portrait busts stood on various pedestals placed around the room.

A portrait of Uncle Henry's father, Richard, hung over the exquisite Palladian fireplace mantel that framed a roaring fire. Mama and I each sat on one of the rose damask upholstered wing chairs on either side of the fireplace, our hands folded in our laps, me staring at the flames of the fire, almost spellbound.

We were soon joined by Uncle Henry, looking as prosperous as ever, a stoutly, powerfully built man bordering on being portly. He walked to Mama, kissing her on the cheek, before crossing over to me and doing likewise. He then moved to the settee facing the fireplace and sank onto it.

'Dearest sister, dearest niece, it's so nice to see you again,' Uncle Henry greeted us cordially.

'It's been too long, Henry,' scolded Mama. 'I'm sure Mercy had almost forgotten what her uncle looked like.'

'I know – I know.' Uncle Henry chuckled. 'But you have to appreciate that I have been unbelievably busy of late.'

'That's as may be, Henry, but remember this, no one on their deathbed ever wished they'd spent more time at work.'

The afternoon passed uneventfully until Mama changed the subject to William – without warning.

'Henry,' she said. 'Do you recall my mentioning a certain Lieutenant William Dunbar to you last year?'

Uncle Henry's eyes narrowed thoughtfully.

'Lieutenant William Dunbar? That name does ring a bell…' he muttered. 'Dunbar – ah, yes – the fellow against whom a declarator of marriage action had been raised before the Commissary Court in Edinburgh.'

'Yes, that's him,' Mama confirmed. 'Did he ever contact you? Seek your counsel?'

'No, he didn't. Why do you ask?'

Mama looked at me, her eyes darting. 'It's because of something that happened yesterday evening,' she murmured. 'I'll spare you the details, but Mercy and her father had a most frightful argument about him.'

I felt a knot of nerves in my stomach as Uncle Henry looked at me disapprovingly.

'I'm disappointed to hear that, Mercy,' he said sternly. 'It's never right for a daughter to argue with her papa, is it?' I felt my face go warm with shame but had no answer for Uncle Henry. 'Your mama told me last year that you and Lieutenant Dunbar were betrothed, so I assume that the action brought against him has not yet been resolved,' Uncle Henry continued. 'That being the case, it's only natural for your papa to be concerned about your relationship, isn't it?'

My head dropped, and I stared at the floor.

'Yes, uncle,' I whispered.

'So why would you want to challenge your papa's concern if that was at the heart of the argument?'

'I know I was wrong in speaking to Papa as I did and have

apologised to him. He told me this morning that he accepts William's word that there was no marriage between him and Ann Macclesfield and that he will welcome him into our home if he returns to Henley. The problem is that I have heard nothing from William since he returned to Southampton after Mama and Papa learned of the court proceedings.'

'And that's why I raised the issue with you just now,' Mama added. 'Is there anything you can or could do to help us, Henry – either regarding the court action or William? We hoped William's great uncle, Lord Mark Campbell, could help us. He had taken a house in Henley but has since left the town. Unfortunately, before then, he and Francis crossed swords over the lease on the house and became estranged.'

Uncle Henry looked at me and smiled kindly. 'I'm afraid there is little I can do about the court action. That must run its course – as determined by the judges hearing the case. I will, though, do whatever I can to try and make contact with Lieutenant Dunbar. I will also see what I can learn from Lord Campbell. I know him, having advised him in the past. He may be willing to talk to me even if he wouldn't talk to Francis.'

I felt as if a great weight had been lifted from me. Whilst nothing for me had changed, I nursed a real hope that it would – and a change for the better. All I had to do now was to wait and hope.

*

A few weeks later, Uncle Henry invited Mama and me to meet him at Culham Court. He had some news for us.

I sat beside Mama on a sofa, fidgeting nervously, my heart beating fast with anxiety and apprehension. She squeezed my hand gently as Uncle Henry entered the room. He drew up a chair close to us and sat down.

'I've some news to share with you at last about William Dunbar,' he announced without further ado. 'Mixed news, I have to say. Firstly, by chance, I met a long-standing client who told me that he was a business associate of a certain Sir Richard Archer. This client had been invited to a ball at the home of Sir Richard as a pretext for an introduction to a lieutenant in the Marines based in Southampton who might act as a financial intermediary between the client and his London business associates—'

'A lieutenant in the Marines based in Southampton,' I gasped. 'William?'

'Let Uncle Henry finish,' Mama scolded.

'Quite.' Uncle Henry chuckled. 'Funnily enough, Mercy, I asked a similar question. And, yes, the client was talking about William Dunbar.'

By then, I could scarcely contain myself. 'Do you mean to say that your client and William are in business together?' I gushed.

'I'm afraid not, Mercy,' Uncle Henry replied. 'My client saw Dunbar at the ball – but only very briefly. He did not get to meet him. Dunbar left the ballroom almost as soon as my client spotted him and had not returned before my client had to leave. In the event, he never got to meet Dunbar at all. My client learned that Dunbar was taken seriously ill the day after the ball. He also learned that Sir Richard and his daughter were taken ill within days of Dunbar and that, sadly, both Sir Richard and his daughter had died within a day of one another. My client did not know whether Dunbar had also died.'

I only heard the words "Dunbar" and "died". Shocked, I broke into tears, buried my face in my hands and sat there bewildered. 'My William is dead.' I sobbed, nearly distraught with sorrow, believing all my hopes and dreams had been shattered.

Mama came over to me, sat beside me and embraced me. Then, she pulled me gently towards her. 'Mercy,' she said softly but sternly. 'Uncle Henry did not say William was dead – only that his client didn't know whether he was alive or dead. I am sure Uncle Henry has more to tell us if you let him finish what he has to say.'

'I'm sorry, uncle,' I apologised.

'Calm yourself, niece, please,' replied Uncle Henry. He looked at me, his eyes narrowing as he did. I quickly looked away. 'There is more,' he continued. 'I followed up on what I had been told and discovered that Dunbar survived his illness and prospered. According to his great-uncle, Lord Mark Campbell, he no longer serves with the Tenth Regiment of Marines in Southampton. He has sold his commission and repaid Lord Campbell the money advanced to purchase it in the first instance—'

'That might explain why William hasn't replied to your letters, Mercy,' Mama chipped in.

'Quite,' replied Uncle Henry, showing just a little frustration at being interrupted once more. 'Anyhow, as I was about to say, whilst no one seems to know the full details of how he has, it is the case that Dunbar has prospered to the extent that he has acquired a half share in a ship that is at present en route to Africa and from thence to the Americas. In short, he has become a slave trader. This turn of events so appalled Lord Campbell that he severed all links with Dunbar and now wants to have nothing more to do with him. I have also discovered that Dunbar has developed a lucrative sideline operating as a financial intermediary. That sideline sees him not only in London from time to time but also in Windsor, where he has taken a house, and from where he occasionally drives to London in his curricle – drawn by a carefully matched pair of horses.'

As Uncle Henry continued, my heart began to beat so fast that I felt myself becoming breathless. Eventually, I couldn't contain myself and interrupted Uncle Henry yet again. 'I just don't understand it,' I cried. 'Windsor is so close to Henley. Why hasn't he come to see me?'

Uncle Henry looked at me, then up to the ceiling, and sighed loudly. 'I think there may be a simple but regrettable answer to that question,' he replied. 'It could just be the case that Dunbar was only ever interested in marriage to you because of the prospect of receiving the dowry promised by your papa. Now that Dunbar is wealthy, perhaps any such interest has vanished.'

'What a cruel thing to say,' I gasped. 'William would not – could not – behave in such a way.'

'I would agree with Mercy on that score,' Mama added. 'When I last saw William, he left me in no doubt that he loved Mercy for her sake alone – he had no interest in receiving any dowry from Francis, of that I am certain.'

'Perhaps the case in the Scottish court against Dunbar has succeeded. Perhaps it is a fact that Dunbar is a married man and that he recognises that any liaison with Mercy would be improper.'

'But William is not married,' I protested tearfully. 'He has a letter from Ann Macclesfield that proves there was no marriage between them.'

'There may be a letter, dear niece, but my understanding is that its bona fides is questionable. Still, my understanding may, of course, be incorrect. But, doubtless, all will be revealed in due course.'

*

I was deep in thought, mentally pulling myself this way and that. Speaking to Papa as I had, I felt ashamed. I rejoiced the fact that William was safe and well and prospering. I feared the possibility that Ann Macclesfield's action had succeeded – that the Scottish court had decided that William was, in fact, a married man. Above all, though, I felt anger and disappointment because William had sometimes been so close to Henley, but he had made no contact with me. Then, I came to with a start as I realised Mama was talking to me.

'What's troubling you, daughter?' asked Mama.

'I just don't know what to make of it all, Mama.' I sighed, perplexed. 'It's all so confusing. One minute I'm the happiest woman in the world, looking forward to sharing my life with William. But then, Papa and I have just had the most dreadful quarrel about him. Next, I learn that there is some doubt over the outcome of the court case against him. Worst of all, though, I find out that William is sometimes in Windsor, not twenty miles from here, but he doesn't think to call and see me.'

Mama laid her hand on my shoulder. 'Everything will turn out well; you'll see,' she said affectionately.

'But I can't help worrying about Papa – about William – about the court case – about everything.'

Mama lifted her hand and stroked a finger against my cheek. 'Hush there, Mercy. No good can ever come of worrying about things you have no control over,' she said in a soothing voice.

I lifted my eyes to meet Mama's eyes and smiled weakly. 'I know you're right, Mama, but I just can't help it.'

'Well, let's just look at the concerns you have expressed to me. Firstly, you and Papa have settled the differences between you and him. Secondly, I firmly believe the Scottish court will exonerate William – as do you, I am certain. Finally, as your papa has made clear to you, he will welcome William into our home any time he is in Henley, and I will make sure that he does visit us soon.'

I could barely believe what I was hearing. 'How?' I gushed, my delight ringing warm.

'I will send William an invitation to visit us via Uncle Henry. I know William will soon return to Henley once he receives it.'

FOURTEEN

Almost for the first time in my adult life, I suffered from an attack of real girlish excitement. I had barely slept the previous night and had been on tenterhooks for most of the day. I was sitting by the parlour window, my head leaning against the frame. Then, suddenly, I started to my feet, trying to suppress a cry of delight. At long last, William Dunbar was driving his curricle up the street.

I watched with mounting anticipation as he slowed the curricle to a halt. A diminutive, liveried groom, sporting a top hat almost as tall as himself, leapt down from the carriage and ran to the horses' heads. He seemed little more than twelve years of age and had been perched behind William, occupying the tiger's seat between the carriage's springs. William climbed down from the curricle and started walking towards the house.

I gasped. He looked so smart – so resplendent – in an exquisite silver-grey suit that matched a waistcoat made of luxurious brocaded *gros de Tours* taffeta embellished with threads of silver and gold woven into a stylised shell pattern. Roses with two leaves were brocaded in red-, yellow-, purple- and green-coloured silk threads on the front. His breeches were fastened below the knee. His shirt was frilled at the cuff. A knotted lace cravat was tied around his neck. His sandy-coloured hair fluttered, seemingly being blown by a gust of breeze.

'Mama,' I gushed. 'William is here – William has arrived.'

Try as hard as I could, I was unable to control myself. Casting any vestige of decorum aside, I rushed out of the parlour and through the hall. I threw open the door and hurried down towards William. Looking astonished, he caught hold of me and lifted me clean off my feet and up to his chest as we met. He kissed my forehead and gently lowered me down. I looked up at him, tears of joy streaming down my face. There had been so much I had wanted to say to William, but for now, I was struck dumb.

'Well, you surely are a sight for sore eyes, William,' Mama purred as she slowly made her way towards William and me, her face a picture of delight. 'You don't know how pleased I am to see you again,' she continued, her sincerity audible. She held her hand to William, who took it and raised it to his lips.

'The pleasure is mine,' he replied warmly. 'It's been such a long time since we last met. After I left Henley, I feared I might never see you again. So I can't tell you how delighted I was to receive your invitation to visit you for a few days extended to me through your brother, Henry Stephenson.'

'And I can't tell you how delighted Mercy and I were when you accepted.' Mama turned to me. 'Come, daughter, let's get back to the house,' she said. 'We'll send Jarman to fetch William's luggage and tell the coachman to show William's groom to the stables and then to his quarters.'

Mama and I moved on either side of William and escorted him back to the house and into the front parlour. Mama sat down on her favourite armchair by the fireplace.

'Sit down, please, William,' she invited. 'May I offer you some refreshment – tea or a glass of port, perhaps?'

'Not for me, thank you, Mrs Grundy.' William sat down on the armchair opposite Mama.

I hovered, standing close to the seat near the window I had occupied before William's arrival.

'Mercy,' Mama called across to me, 'please ring for Jarman and then sit down and relax, for Heaven's sake. I'm sure we'd all appreciate it.'

I did as I was asked, and shortly afterwards, Jarman appeared.

'Please go to Mr Dunbar's carriage to collect his luggage and take it to the guest bedroom. After that, please tell the coachman that he is to show Mr Dunbar's groom to the stables and, as soon as the carriage and horses have been stabled, take him to the servants' quarters, where he is to stay during Mr Dunbar's visit.'

'Yes, madam.'

'Yes, thank you, Jarman,' added William, 'and please ask the coachman to tell my groom that, once he has attended to my horses, I shall have no further need of his services until tomorrow morning.'

Jarman left the room. Shortly afterwards, I could make out Papa talking to him before I heard the front door closing. Moments later, Papa breezed into the room.

'Welcome, dear boy,' he cheerfully greeted William, holding out his hand. William stood up from his chair and grasped Papa's hand. A wide smile spread across his face.

'Thank you, sir,' he replied. 'I hope you're keeping as well as you look.'

Papa pursed his lips together in a faint smile and nodded.

'And you're looking as if you have prospered since I last saw you,' he replied softly, albeit somewhat coolly. 'Now, sit down, and tell us what you've been getting up to since your last visit.'

At first, it pleased me to witness how well Papa and William seemed to be getting on as the afternoon and evening progressed – even when the conversation turned briefly to Ann Macclesfield's claim and the fact that the Scottish court had yet reached no decision. However, it soon became clear that the bonhomie that Papa was showing had more to do with William's new-found wealth than anything else when I overheard him whisper to Mama: 'I am delighted to learn that Dunbar is now not only a man of noble birth but also has become a man of wealth. Breeding and money is a far better combination, that's for sure.'

Still, some progress towards a more cordial relationship between Papa and William was preferable to none.

*

The sun rose bright and clear and shone warmly through the window of my room. Outside, I heard birds carolling their morning hymn of praise. It was one of those mornings which promised a day to be celebrated. And yet, at that moment, I was filled with sorrow, for William's visit to our home was ending all too soon. He would be travelling back to Bristol the following morning. At least, though, Papa had agreed for William and I to spend the afternoon together on our own. To go for a drive in his curricle. Finally, I would have the chance to be alone with him for the first time since he arrived in Henley.

I was on tenterhooks from the moment I got out of bed until the time arrived for William and me to begin our afternoon's drive. He was waiting for me as I swept into the front parlour, wearing my finest day dress – a present from Mama for the occasion. William stood up as I entered. As I caught sight of him, I gasped. He had looked magnificent upon his arrival a few days earlier, but today he looked even more so. Today he was wearing a coat of rich shot green and black silk, a waistcoat of yellow silk brocaded with coloured silk and silver threads and featuring large flowers and leaves, breeches of black velvet, silk stockings with silver trees and buckle shoes.

'This old outfit?' He laughed after I told him what exquisite dress sense he had. 'Why I've had it for over a year – albeit it's been quite a while since I last wore it. Besides, it seems so very ordinary compared to the dress you are wearing.'

At that moment, I caught sight of myself in one of the wall mirrors in the room. My face had gone bright red.

Heavens above, I'm blushing.

William came over to me, took both of my hands, lifted them to his lips and kissed them. As he did, Jarman entered the room.

'Your carriage is outside waiting for you, sir,' he announced.

'Thank you, Jarman,' William replied. He turned to me. 'Time to go,' he said.

William took my hand, led me out of the house to his carriage and gently helped me up to my seat before climbing up to sit next to me. The groom, who had been holding the head of one of the horses, came over to William, handed up a whip to him and then went to the rear of the curricle and climbed up to sit on the tiger's seat. William placed the whip beside him before lifting the reins and urging the horses into motion.

Once we had crossed Henley Bridge, he flicked the reins, urging the horses into a brisk trot, and we headed towards Remenham. It was a glorious afternoon, one of those which seemed more perfect than any I could have ever imagined: the air was pure, the sky bluer than any sapphire, the grass greener than any emerald, the hawthorns that lined either side of the road were bedecked with clusters of small, cup-shaped white and pink-red flowers, while cherry blossom snowed gently on the ground.

Our path was not alongside a crowded pavement. Here, there was neither the hum of any village nor the hustle and bustle of a town. A solemn and beautiful wood stood on our left. Its glad and beautiful language, the music of thousands of birds unseen in the leafy shades and green arches, rose heavenwards.

We continued until we reached Remenham, where we headed towards Aston, following the curve of the Thames as we did. I lay my hand on William's arm.

'It's such a beautiful day,' I said. 'There's an inn just up ahead. Why don't we stop there, leave the carriage with your groom and walk to the river?'

After leaving the curricle with the groom at the inn at Aston, William and I headed hand in hand slowly towards the river. At first, we walked across some meadowland where the richest moss grew on the low turf at our feet. Then I let go of William's hand, skipped ahead, stopped and looked back.

'I cannot remember the last time I felt as happy as this,' I cried, throwing my arms open.

William said nothing but ran towards me. I gave a cry and, lifting my arms, caught him about his neck as he reached me. He clasped me to his breast, still saying nothing.

'I love you, William – above everything on earth. I always have, and I always will,' I whispered. 'And you, William, tell me that you love me. You have never done so before.'

'You know I love you, Mercy,' he answered after a while, 'and if you didn't love me as you do, I should not want to live. I love you above everything, and you are in my thoughts day and night.' He took my face in his hands, drew me to him and kissed me.

'I am always thinking of you, too, dearest William. Now I can't tell you how happy I am to hear you say you love me. I was sure you had forgotten me. I am more in love with you than ever,' I cried. At that moment, no words could describe the flood of joy and unutterable wonder that had rushed over me. I stood there in the afternoon sunshine with William, feeling like someone who had just been surrounded by a radiant cloud and who half exulted in the brightness but half dreaded its excess of splendour.

'Mercy,' I heard William whisper. 'Mercy – are you with me?'

The sound of his voice made me start, bringing me gently back to the life around me.

'Sorry, William. I was miles away. Oh, William, I had almost forgotten what we came for in the happiness of being with you – we've got a little way to go yet. Quick, come with me,' I cried, grasping his hand and drawing him on again.

We reached a small wood.

'How much further?' William gasped.

'Nearly there now.' I giggled, pulling him into the wood, where bluebells, some still in full bloom, while others now fading, stretched like a patchwork quilt between each tree.

Before long, we were standing on a shady bank with myriad buttercups and daisies all around. We walked on a little further until we found a spot of sweet and rare beauty. It was dark with verdure. The boughs of a lordly oak were laced above it, and only patches of the bright blue sky shone down through its twinkling leaves. Even the lustre of the hot afternoon seemed like a clear twilight as it found its way through the masses of waving green above us.

I moved over to the oak and sat down with my back to it. Looking up at William, I patted the ground next to me. William came over towards me, but to my surprise – and if I'm honest, my slight disappointment – he didn't sit down. Instead, and chuckling as he did, William lifted his head upwards. Once. Twice. He then held his hands out to me. I took them, and William helped me to my feet. I stood and faced him. He stared at me. A gentle breeze swept softly over our faces as he bent his head towards me. I smiled faintly. As I did, he gently kissed my forehead. A shiver of excitement passed through my whole body. My heart beat faster and faster, half in trepidation, half in anticipation. Then his lips met mine. Even though only briefly, my brain started to fizzle. He gently guided me towards him, gathered me in his arms and kissed me.

I lay my head on his shoulder and turned my face towards his. I felt his breath on my cheek. I sighed, a sigh of joy and contentment. I had always understood that life takes unexpected twists and turns, sometimes the result of making a deliberate choice, sometimes through happenstance. But, until that moment, I hadn't realised what it felt like to be with someone and know without a doubt that the whole part of my life until then – every twist of fate along the way – was just a journey to get to that person. Now, I knew that William was mine, and I was his. Now, I realised how much I loved him and how much I looked forward to the day I would become his wife.

'Life for me is now so wonderful,' I whispered. I paused before repeating the word "wonderful" joyously.

William kissed me again. A quiver passed through my entire body. I caught my breath for moments of pure joy. The kiss was long, twenty seconds or more, but it ended all too soon for me. I rested there in his clasp, my eyes gazing up into his. A fierce passion swept through me to be held by him like that, warm, close and secure. I trembled at the thought. My eyes closed, and then I kissed him, yielding utterly to the swirl of mad impulse. We clung together. Time seemed to stand still.

This is happiness. True happiness.

I eased my head back and looked at William. He stared at me with eyes wide open for a few seconds; then, a smile broke over his face, lighting it up with a sudden radiance which entirely changed his expression. He put his hand into his coat pocket and took something out that I could not quite see. He lifted his right hand, and as he did, I could see what looked like a small, dark-blue box between his right thumb and index finger. Then, steadying himself, William opened the box with his left hand.

'Something for you as a token of my friendship and love for you,' he said softly, handing the box to me.

I gasped. My mouth gaped open. I was looking at the most beautiful ring I had ever seen. I stood there spellbound.

'Well, aren't you going to try it on?' William asked with a broad grin spreading across his face.

I could only nod in answer; my tongue failed me. My heart pounded as I eased the ring from the purple velvet cushion. I looked at it in awe. It was a gold ring embellished with scrollwork and decorated with a large, rose-cut diamond set in a silver, heart-shaped mount, on either side of which was a smaller diamond. All three diamonds dazzled and sparkled even in the shadowy light permeating the oak tree leaves.

'Here, let me,' said William, gently taking the ring and easing it on the little finger of my left hand. 'There,' he said, 'it fits perfectly. You were destined to wear it!'

'Oh, William. It's so beautiful,' I whispered.

He leant into me and kissed me again. Blissfully happy, I drew in close to him, rested my head on his shoulder and started to shed tears of pure joy. At that moment, I knew that there was nothing I wouldn't do for William – nothing I wouldn't do to be with him forever. We stood there silently for what seemed like an eternity, but it was only five minutes in reality. Then William raised his hands to my face and gently brushed away my tears with his thumbs.

'Why don't we continue to the river as we planned? After that, we must start back towards Aston, and then back to Henley.'

My heart sank at the thought of returning home again, but in my heart, I knew that we had to. I knew that William had to make an early start the following day. He had a long drive back to Bristol ahead of him. Hopefully, though, he would conclude his business there before too long, and he would return once more, and we could be together again.

FIFTEEN

In the weeks that followed William's return to Bristol, he became a frequent visitor to Henley, either en route back to his house in Windsor or by making the trip from there to see us. Very occasionally, Papa invited William to stay with us for a day or two – almost invariably at Mama's insistence.

I'm not sure whether it was Mama or me who was happier of the two of us when William stayed with us in Henley; she seemed to regard him almost as if he were her own son and treated him as such. Papa, though, treated William somewhat distantly, notwithstanding his assurances that William was always welcome in our home.

Mama and I also saw William occasionally in London – whenever we visited Mama's very old and dear friend Abigail Poole at her home in St James's Square – and he was in town on business.

Everything seemed to be going so well for Mama, William and me until Mama was suddenly struck down one afternoon with a mysterious ailment whilst she and I were staying with Mrs Poole. One minute Mama was laughing and joking as we sat in Mrs Poole's parlour, and the next, she leapt up from her chair, clutching at her stomach and screaming in pain. Moments later, she collapsed to the floor.

Horrified, I rushed across to Mama and knelt over her. She was still holding her stomach but was now speechless. There was a terrified look in her eyes. Her face was strangely discoloured and distorted.

'Oh, Mrs Poole,' I gasped as I looked back across the room filled with anxiety. 'What's happening?'

'I just don't know – I cannot say, Mercy,' Mrs Poole replied. 'We'd better send for my doctor immediately.'

'But is Mama dying?' I whispered in terror and distress.

Mrs Poole came over to me and knelt beside me, placing a hand gently on my shoulder.

'Wait for the doctor,' she replied quietly and reassuringly. 'He'll know better than me. Hopefully, whilst things may look serious for now, this attack will soon pass. So you stay here and comfort your mama while I go and instruct the footman to fetch the doctor and get my maid to bring us some pillows for your mama to rest her head on and a blanket to cover her with and keep her warm.'

Mama lay there silent and speechless while I waited for Mrs Poole to return, with nothing to show that she was conscious of my presence except a piteous expression of fear and dumb entreaty in her eyes. I felt helpless. All I could think of to do was to smooth Mama's hair away from her brow, speak to her again and again, begging her to answer me, and when I found that all my efforts to rouse her were unsuccessful, I began to panic.

At that moment, Mrs Poole returned with a pillow and a blanket. I took the pillow from her, lifted Mama's head gently, ever so gently, and placed the pillow behind it. Mrs Poole covered Mama with the blanket and then went back out of the room to fetch a glass of water, which she handed to me. I held the glass to Mama's lips, lowering myself stiffly to the floor where I sat with my skirts puffed up around me. When Mama showed no interest in the glass of water, I placed it on the floor next to me and sat there holding Mama's hand, stroking it until the doctor arrived and swept into the room.

'Good afternoon, Doctor,' greeted Mrs Poole. 'Thank you for coming so promptly. Mrs Grundy, who is lying over there, is my friend and guest. She was suddenly taken ill, clutching her stomach and screaming in pain before collapsing to the floor. The young lady with her is her daughter, Mercy.'

The doctor looked at Mama and then me, nodding towards me as he did. He was a stout, ruddy-faced man with dark hair, perhaps forty years of age. He moved across to Mama and knelt beside her. I stood up as he did and moved away slightly.

'I will need to examine Mrs Grundy,' said the doctor, 'but I cannot do so here. We need to get her to a bed.'

Mrs Poole immediately called for two servants to help carry Mama to her room. This was a most difficult and distressing process, with Mama constantly crying out in pain as she was moved. Eventually, though, she was lying on her bed. Finally, the servants left the room, and Mrs Poole and I managed to undress Mama and put on her nightgown.

Once we had done this, the doctor sat on the bed next to Mama. He then placed a hand behind her shoulder and tried to pull her forward and lift her slightly. As he did, she screamed out in pain once again. He stopped immediately, settling Mama back onto the bed.

'I fear that I will not be able to examine your mother at all for the present,' he said, turning towards me. 'I must calm her first by giving her something to soothe her pain.' He then looked at Mrs Poole. 'Do you have a posset or a sweet syrup handy?' he asked her.

'I'm sure we will have,' Mrs Poole replied. 'I'll go back down to the kitchen immediately and look.'

She left the bedroom for a short while, returning with a bottle of syrup of roses and a glass, which she handed to the doctor.

The doctor reached for his bag and rummaged around briefly before pulling out a packet containing a brown-coloured powder. He poured the powder into the glass and added some of the syrup of roses, shaking the glass slightly as he did.

'Mercy, would you please help me give this to your mother?' I moved over to Mama and knelt down. 'Now hold her head up so I can get her to drink this,' the doctor continued.

Mama seemed to regain her senses somewhat as I started to lift her. This time, she winced but did not cry out in pain.

'You must drink this,' said the doctor softly. 'It will help soothe the pain in your stomach.'

To my relief, Mama managed to drink the potion in the glass as the doctor held the glass to her lips.

'Thank you,' she whispered when she had finished, struggling to speak.

'Is there anything that can be done now?' I asked the doctor.

'Not at present,' he replied. 'I suggest that you and Mrs Poole leave me with your mother. I will wait here whilst the potion takes effect.'

'What kind of potion is it?' I asked.

'The powder I mixed with the syrup of roses is a compound of opium and ipecacuanha. It is known as "Dover's powder". The reason for using the syrup is that the powder is very bitter tasting if taken by itself.'

'And how will it help Mama?'

'Hopefully, it will help your mother greatly, inducing a feeling of well-being and warmth that will flood through her veins,' the doctor replied. 'I should then be able to examine her without her feeling further distress, which I will do as soon as is possible.'

I heaved a huge sigh. Tears were streaming down my face. I felt empty. I wanted to stay with Mama but realised I could not do anything if I remained in the room. I looked at Mama, then the doctor, then Mrs Poole. I could find nothing to say.

'Come, Mercy,' Mrs Poole said softly. 'Let's leave the doctor with your mama. I'm sure he will let us know what might be wrong with her as soon as possible. But, in the meantime, there seems to be very little you and I can do for her.'

I felt a sense of panic well up inside me.

'No, Mrs Poole,' I murmured. 'I must stay here with Mama. I'll draw a chair up to her bed and sit by her. I won't get in the doctor's way. You can both be sure of that.'

Mrs Poole looked at me kindly and smiled.

'Very well, dear Mercy,' she said. 'I'll leave you and the doctor together with your mama. Then, if you need me, I'll be in the front parlour.'

With that, Mrs Poole left the room. The doctor also drew up a chair beside Mama's bed, and we sat there silently for what seemed an eternity. I took Mama's hand, stroking it gently as I gazed at her lying on the bed. Gradually, I noticed that she appeared to calm down. Her breathing rate slowed noticeably. She seemed at peace.

'I think the potion has taken effect,' said the doctor, breaking the silence. 'Let's see if I can examine her now.'

With that, he sat on the bed next to Mama. Then, he pulled the bedclothes away, placed a hand behind her shoulder, pulled her forward and lifted her slightly.

'How does that feel?' he asked Mama.

'Rather better than before,' Mama replied dreamily. 'But there is still some pain.'

'Just where is the pain?'

'It starts just under the ribs on my right-hand side and spreads to my side and up to my shoulder,' Mama whispered.

The doctor lay Mama back on the bed. 'I need to feel around your ribcage and the right side of your abdomen. May I do so?' he asked.

Mama nodded weakly before closing her eyes. The doctor stood over Mama and began to examine her. I saw him place his hands on either side of Mama's waist. He ran one hand slowly across her abdomen, squeezing her gently occasionally. He then felt under her ribcage. First, to the right of it, then the left.

'Does that hurt?' he asked Mama. She shook her head. 'I'm now going to turn you onto your left side while I check the right,' he continued.

Once he had finished this, the doctor turned to me, looking a little perplexed.

'I would be less than honest if I said I knew what the matter is with your mother. The fact is that, at present, I cannot. It could simply be that she has eaten something that disagrees with her. If so, the condition should pass quickly. If not, please call me again – immediately. In any event, I will return in two days to check up on your mother. In the meantime, I will leave some Dover's powder with you. If your mother continues to experience pain, mix a teaspoon with some syrup of roses or stir it into a posset and serve it to her – but not more than twice daily and not less than six hours between each dose.'

'Thank you, Doctor,' I replied, albeit with a slight sense of foreboding as I did. 'I—'

The doctor didn't allow me to finish what I was about to say. 'I also suggest that I leech Mrs Grundy before I leave and repeat the leeching when I return to check up on her,' he interrupted. 'Apart from that and the use of Dover's powder as I have prescribed, there is little else I can suggest. I will take my leave of you for now.'

*

Mama remained confined to her bed for longer than I hoped she would. She seemed to be making plodding and intermittent progress. The doctor became a regular visitor to the house. Worryingly, Mama became increasingly reluctant to take any medication offered to her. I became increasingly fearful for her.

Then, when no one expected it, she received a surprise visitor – indeed, a visitor who was as much a surprise to me as to Mama. William. There I was, sitting with Mama, trying to persuade her to take her evening medication, when the bedroom door opened, and Mrs Poole appeared in the doorway. I looked up at her as she did.

'You have a visitor,' she announced with a beaming smile before stepping into the room with William following close behind her.

With a scream of surprise and delight, I shot up from my seat, almost spilling Mama's medication as I did. I looked at William. I closed my mouth, but my jaw went slack when I saw him.

'William – oh, William,' I burbled. I whipped my head around to look at Mama. 'Oh, Mama,' I gushed. 'Looks who's here – who's come to visit – it's William!'

Barely able to take in what was happening, I watched in amazement as Mama threw aside her bedclothes, climbed out of bed, rushed over to William, took him about the neck and kissed him affectionately.

'Dearest William.' She sighed. 'I am so glad you have come; I shall get well again soon, you'll see.'

The corners of William's mouth curled upwards into a wide grin.

'I'm delighted to be here, Mrs Grundy. I'm only too sorry not to have got here sooner, but I only learned this morning when I called in at your house that you were unwell.'

I anchored my attention on William and raised my eyebrows.

'You spoke to Papa, did you?' I asked.

'Yes. He told me that your mama had been taken ill. So I came here as soon as he had. He also said he would come here tomorrow or the day after.'

I lifted my hand, my index finger making tight circles in the air while I considered my words.

Why hadn't Papa come to London with William?

'Papa couldn't come with you then?' I eventually questioned.

'No, he had clients to see still, but he beseeched me to drive up to London immediately,' William replied. He pulled his head back and looked at Mama. 'Come, Mrs Grundy,' he said softly. 'Back to bed now.'

'Yes, Mama,' I added, 'and you still have to take your medication.'

Mama looked at me, her expression sliding into a frown. 'Only if William will administer it to me,' she replied, almost childlike.

William looked at me, winked and then turned towards Mama, a broad smile on his face. 'It would be an honour to do so.' He chuckled.

Mama settled back into bed. I swear she almost purred as William spooned a posset laced with Dover's powder into her mouth. Not long afterwards, she had nodded off to sleep.

As soon as she did, I looked at William. 'Let's go downstairs,' I mouthed.

William nodded, and we both crept out of the room and went downstairs to join Mrs Poole in her parlour, where she was reading a book. She looked up as we entered the room.

'How's your mama?' she enquired.

'Thankfully, she's asleep now,' I replied.

Mrs Poole turned to William. 'You're very welcome to stay here tonight,' she said.

'That's very kind of you,' William replied. 'I would be delighted to, but I will have to leave early tomorrow morning – no later than nine o'clock – I have a business meeting in Throgmorton Street that I cannot miss.'

My heart sank. 'Oh, William, must you go?' I sighed.

William looked at me with a sad expression on his face. 'I'm afraid so,' he replied softly.

'But you will return as soon as the meeting is finished, won't you?' I pleaded.

'Yes, you must. I insist,' Mrs Poole interposed. 'You must stay here for a few days more at the very least.'

William looked at me, then at Mrs Poole. His lips parted in a grin. 'How could I refuse?' he replied.

I gave a little shriek of joy that prompted Mrs Poole to laugh out loud.

'In that case,' she said. 'I will have a room prepared for you and some supper for us all. Then, William, you must tell me about this business you are engaged in.'

*

I came to suddenly. I had fallen asleep sitting on a chair beside Mama's bed. Almost doubled over, my head was resting on the bed covers. For a moment, everything about me seemed to swim before my eyes like a confused evanescent dream. I lifted my head slowly and a little stiffly. As I did, I became conscious that the sun was streaming through a gap in the curtains and was warming my face.

'Mercy, dearest,' I heard Mama call out. 'What are you doing here – why aren't you in bed?'

Still somewhat bleary-eyed, I looked at Mama and grinned.

'Hello, Mama,' I greeted. 'After supper yesterday evening, I returned to your room and must have dozed off. But never mind me. How are you feeling?'

Although she seemed a little pale still, Mama's eyes brimmed warmly, and a broad smile spread across her face.

'So much better, darling daughter,' she gushed, 'and I owe it all to you and my dear William. His arrival has given me new health and fresh spirits. I was fearful that I would not survive what has been ailing me and, worse, that he was not here to comfort and protect you, but he is now here with us. To care for us. Both of us.'

'Whatever else, William's arrival has certainly made a world of difference for you,' I replied. 'If I hadn't seen it for myself, I would never have believed it – never have thought that just the presence of one man could have such a healing effect.'

'Yes… it's a miracle. I can't wait to see him again – where is he now?' asked Mama.

'I will go and check,' I replied. 'But he did say that he had to go into the city early today to attend a business meeting.' As I stood up, I looked at the clock on the mantlepiece over the fireplace in the room. 'Goodness,' I gasped. 'It's gone nine o'clock. I'm sure he will have left already.' Mama's face dropped. I could see tears welling in her eyes.

'Oh, no!' she exclaimed. 'No! He couldn't have gone without seeing me first. Without saying goodbye.'

I quickly took Mama's hand and kissed it.

'Hush, Mama,' I whispered. 'If William has gone, it won't be for long. He will be returning here after his meeting – that is certain. Mrs Poole invited him to stay for a few days, and he accepted the invitation.'

I left Mama and rushed downstairs, but William had already left, so I returned to break the news to Mama. Fortunately, she had dozed off again, so I left her sleeping peacefully and went back downstairs to try and busy myself. At the same time, I waited impatiently for William's return later that afternoon.

*

Papa eventually arrived at Mrs Poole's house as William had said he would, but it was several days later than expected. However, if truth be told, I don't think that Mama noticed the delay – she was so taken by William's presence, especially when he accepted Mrs Poole's offer to stay for as long as he wanted. For his part, William was only too happy to stay and to spend hours talking to Mama and attending to her needs.

Papa seemed happy that William was there with Mama and me. Indeed, when he arrived, he took William up in his arms, saying, 'I am glad to see you here.' He then turned towards me. 'How's your mama?'

'Oh, Papa,' I replied. 'She's so much better – albeit still not one hundred per cent.'

'I suppose both you and she are happier now William has come,' Papa said, smiling.

'And she'll be so much happier now that you are here, sir,' William chipped in.

I moved over to Papa, kissed him on the cheek and took him by the hand.

'Come on, Papa,' I said. 'William is right. Come up and see Mama, now.'

Papa seemed to be in good humour for the whole of the first day he was at Mrs Poole's house. Then, however, his mood changed dramatically after meeting the doctor the following morning to discuss Mama's prognosis.

Sitting in the parlour with William and Mrs Poole, I heard Mama and Papa arguing fiercely in Mama's chamber. I rushed upstairs to see what was amiss. As I entered the room, I saw Papa standing over Mama, red-faced and animated.

'There's no alternative,' he grunted, staring at Mama. 'You'll have to return to Henley immediately to continue your recuperation.'

With that, Papa turned, pushed past me and stormed out of the room, leaving Mama in tears. I rushed over to Mama, sat on the bed and cradled her.

'What on earth has been going on?' I gasped, horrified.

Mama looked up at me, struggling to speak. Then she burst into tears. 'Why is your papa treating me as he is?' She sobbed.

At that moment, William came into the room. 'What is the problem?' he asked, outwardly concerned.

'It's all about money,' Mama whimpered. 'The doctor has told my husband of the cost to date of his attendances and that of the apothecary. My husband says that these are prohibitive – that any further costs must be mitigated – that I must return to Henley to do that. If I do not, I, and I alone, must assume full responsibility for the costs of my treatment – past, present and future. He will not pay a penny towards those costs.'

William looked aghast. Shocked.

'But, as I understand it,' he replied calmly but annoyed, 'you are still not well enough to travel, Mrs Grundy.' He reached towards me and took me by the hand. 'Come with me,' he said. 'We need to have this out with your father.'

Still holding my hand, he strode purposefully out of the bedroom and down the stairs to look for Papa, whom we eventually found sitting in the parlour drinking a dish of coffee.

'Sir, we need to have words about Mrs Grundy,' William uttered as he let go of my hand and approached Papa.

'What about?' snapped Papa, looking up at William. 'My wife is no concern or business of yours.'

There was a brief, awkward pause. William's face reddened at first, then went white.

'With respect, sir,' he hissed, 'I'm making it my business. I understand that you insist on Mrs Grundy returning to Henley, even though she is too weak to be removed there at present.'

Papa's lip curled up into a sneer as he continued to look

straight at William. 'Oh, really, and you are an expert on these matters, are you?'

'No, sir, I'm no expert, but anyone who cares about Mrs Grundy can see how sick she still is – that she needs to stay where she is for a while longer.'

'It will not harm Mrs Grundy if she makes the… the short journey back to Henley in the comfort of my carriage,' Papa snapped. 'Once there, she will receive equally good care from my doctor and apothecary… and at half the cost being incurred here in London.'

As I watched William, I saw his jaw drop and a look of complete incredulity cross his face.

'So that's what it's all about, is it?' he replied, raising his voice sharply as he did. 'Money – not your wife's health and well-being. I cannot believe that a man would wish to treat his wife in the way you appear to want to. The cost of Mrs Grundy's treatment here in London cannot be so much greater than in Henley to merit uprooting her from here at this time.'

Papa shot to his feet. The chair he had been sitting on shot backwards before clattering to the floor. His face was scarlet, his eyes bulging – almost to the point of exiting their sockets. 'I'll take no lectures from a man who abandons his wife and child about the health and well-being of my wife,' he screamed.

'I have no wife,' came William's almost instantaneous reply.

'That, Mr Dunbar, remains to be determined by the Scottish court.'

'Aye and, as you will discover in due course, determined in my favour.'

An uneasy hush followed, with neither William nor Papa saying anything. Instead, they just stood and stared at one another.

Papa was the first to break the silence. 'If you're so concerned about my wife, why don't you cover the cost of her treatment to date, and the cost of her accommodation and her keep here at Mrs Poole's home, and all further costs to be incurred?'

William placed his hands on his hips and leant forward towards Papa. 'And just what are the costs incurred to date?' he hissed.

'The doctor's and apothecary's costs are £40. You'll have to check with Mrs Poole as to the cost incurred by her during my wife and daughter's stay.'

William did not reply. He just spun around and walked quickly out of the room.

'Just as I would have predicted,' Papa sneered. 'Dunbar has run away at the thought of backing up his words with money.'

Moments later, William returned. He walked up to Papa and thrust out his hand in which he held a leather purse.

'Here's £60,' he said in a clear but calm voice. 'That should more than cover the medical fees incurred to date and those likely to be incurred in the near future. I will settle any costs incurred by Mrs Poole during the stay of your wife and daughter directly with her.'

Papa said nothing at first. He just snatched the purse from William, turned and headed towards the door. When he reached it, he looked back at William. 'So be it,' he called out angrily. 'Mrs Grundy stays here with Mrs Poole, but I am returning to Henley immediately. If our paths never cross again, Mr Dunbar, it will be too soon.'

As Papa left, I rushed over to William. I took him by the hand and led him into the parlour. I was in the throes of thanking him for his goodness to my mother when he prevented me from so doing by kissing me.

'That is all the thanks I need,' he said softly before kissing me again, following which he led me back upstairs to Mama's room.

As I went with William, a thought crossed my mind: *I fear we may not have heard the last of all this from Papa.*

*

In the two weeks following Papa's departure back to Henley, Mama made a steady recovery, which seemed to be accelerated whenever William visited her. Finally, at the end of that period, Mama was well enough to return to Henley.

Whilst I was delighted that Mama and I were on our way home, I began to experience an increasing feeling that something was amiss. It was a feeling I couldn't put my finger on; it seemed illogical until our carriage pulled up outside our house, and we got out. Then I saw Papa standing outside the front door, looking smugger than I had ever seen before. He held a document in his hand, which he waved towards Mama and me as we walked towards him.

'I knew it! I always knew it!' he called out gleefully. 'Here is the unequivocal confirmation of what I have always known.'

Mama reached Papa first. He handed the document to Mama, who read it slowly.

'Oh, dear heavens,' she gasped, letting go of the document. 'No... it can't be true.' She burst into tears.

I rushed to where the document had fallen. I bent down and picked it up. My heartbeat quickened with every word I read. It was a letter from an attorney in Edinburgh.

Dear Mr Grundy,

Further to your letter of the 15ᵗʰ ultimo, I write to advise that the Commissary Court has found that Ann Macclesfield, eldest lawful daughter of the deceased David Macclesfield of Leith, merchant, the lawful son to the deceased Sir David Macclesfield of Stanhope, is the lawful spouse of William Henry Dunbar, merchant, and formerly a lieutenant of the Regiment of Marines.

The court found that the said William Henry Dunbar and the said Ann Macclesfield were married on the 22ⁿᵈ of May 1744.

The court further found that Margaret Dunbar, born on the 19ᵗʰ
of February 1745, is their lawful daughter.

My hands were shaking. I looked up at Papa, inwardly horrified
at the smirk almost covering his face, before looking again at the
letter and reading on.

The court has ordered that William Henry Dunbar shall pay Ann
Macclesfield an annuity of £125 together with an additional £25
per annum by way of support for Margaret Dunbar. William
Henry Dunbar was further ordered to pay Ann Macclesfield's
legal costs, assessed at £100.

I dropped the letter, staring down as it fluttered to the ground. I
felt empty. Hollow. Drained. Papa brushed past me, bent down,
picked up the letter and raised it triumphantly above his head.

'Now, perhaps, you'll have nothing more to do with Dunbar,'
he yelled before returning inside the house. Mama followed. I
brought up the rear, my mind whirring. I didn't know what to
think. What to believe.

Matters worsened a few days later when William unexpectedly
visited Henley to see Mama and me. Unfortunately, he arrived
when Papa, Mama and I returned home after visiting Uncle
Henry at Culham Court.

Papa must have spotted William's curricle before either
Mama or me, for he gave out a loud cry. At that moment, I saw
an instant and horrible change come over Papa's face. It faded
to dead paper white. His eyes became fixed like lenses. His jaw
dropped, a strangled gurgle came from the open mouth and then
a hoarse cry of anger.

'Halt!' he screamed at our coachman. He didn't wait for the
carriage to come to a halt. I watched in horror as he threw open

the door and flew towards where William was waiting. 'What the hell are you doing here!' he roared.

A shaken William seemed transfixed by Papa's outburst. He made no reply. In the meantime, Papa rushed past William's groom, who was holding the head of one of the carriage horses, and stopped to the side of the curricle. He looked up at William.

'You are a debased profligate, sir, absolutely unfit for any respectable people to know,' Papa blazed out. 'You, you...' he spluttered a little, 'you are a positive danger to society. Of itself, just the thought of a vile creature like you visiting my home is a repugnance to me.' He was snorting in earnest now. 'But worse than that, you dare contemplate a bigamous marriage to my daughter! You, a man who has abandoned his own wife and child!'

William's eyes flashed. 'I allow no one to call me a vile creature... and especially not you... and once and for all, I have no wife.' He spoke defiantly, looking Papa full in the face.

For a moment, Papa was speechless, and then he attempted to take refuge in scorn. 'Are you so foolish as to believe you are not married when—' he began.

But William cut him short sternly. 'You have said more than enough already. Good morning.' He turned to his groom. 'Get back on the carriage. We are leaving.'

As soon as the groom sat down on the tiger's seat, William flicked the reins and drove off along Hart Street. Then something appeared to strike him before he had gone more than ten yards. He stopped his curricle, and he faced round again.

'May I venture one suggestion? The next time you preach at me, you might take the Gospel according to St John, chapter eight, verse seven, as your text, *He that is without sin among you, let him first cast a stone.* Have you forgotten that you rushed off from your wife when she was ill as soon as you learned the cost of her care and her and Mercy's keep in London?'

With that, William started off along Hart Street again. Papa, pale already, went, if possible, a shade paler, with anger.

'What…' he screamed out after William. 'Do we now have the devil quoting scripture?'

But, by now, William was well out of earshot.

I looked anxiously along Hart Street after William had disappeared from sight, hoping to see his returning carriage. However, any hope that I would gradually disappeared with each passing moment.

I felt sadness coupled with anger at Papa for his treatment of William as I eventually made my way into the house when I realised he would not be coming back – at least not that day. That sadness and anger increased as I walked through the front entrance to witness Mama and Papa engaged in a fearful argument. They were standing face to face, only a pace or two apart.

'Mercy has set her heart upon William!' Mama screamed out. 'I'll not have you… or anyone else for that matter… say anything to spoil that state of affairs. Just accept her wishes, for Heaven's sake!'

'Can't you see… will it never get through to you?' Papa thundered back. 'That man is not a suitable match for Mercy! She deserves far better!'

'That's for Mercy to decide… not me… and certainly not you!'

With that, Mama spun round and flew out of the room. Moments later, she returned. She looked at me, her face white.

'Mercy,' she called over to me. 'I want you to stay with me tonight. Your papa can use the guest room.'

I turned open-mouthed to look at Papa. Mama had gone again by the time I looked back.

'You'd better go and see to your mama,' Papa growled at me. 'Hopefully, I'll find her in better humour in the morning.'

With that, Papa stormed off in the direction of the kitchen.

*

Mama scarcely left her room in the two days that followed. She took her meals there and refused to have any dealings with Papa. Then, on the third day, Mama came downstairs after lunch and found me in the front parlour, where I was sitting by the window reading a book.

'Ah, there you are,' she greeted me cheerfully. 'Will you join me on a walk by the river? It looks like it's nice outside today. Afterwards, perhaps we could go to the Red Lion Inn and see Mrs Dawes. I haven't seen her for ages.'

I looked up at Mama, closing my book as I did. 'I couldn't think of anything better to do,' I replied elatedly. I got up from my chair, moved to Mama and kissed her on the cheek. I stood back and looked at her. She looked better than she had for a long while. The colour had returned to her cheeks, and there was a renewed sheen to her hair. She was dressed in her best ivory silk dress over which she wore a cloak of tightly fulled scarlet wool with a collar above an attached shaped mantelet. The cloak was fastened at the neck with a large steel eye and a brass hook. A hood, lined with white silk, was sewn to the cloak's neckline above the collar and mantelet. The cloak's edges were left unhemmed, while the hood's front edge was lined with red corded piping. The front edges of the cloak were faced with narrow strips of white silk.

'It's so good to see you up and about again, Mama… especially looking so stunning.'

Mama blushed. 'Shush, daughter,' she replied. 'I have to look my best when I go out, don't I… especially if I am to be accompanied by my daughter?'

'Then I must change into something more glamourous than what I'm wearing.'

'Nonsense, daughter,' Mama said, taking hold of my arm. 'You don't need to. You look just wonderful as you are. Just put on a cloak.'

'Oh, all right.' I chuckled. 'I'll just go up and get one… the dark blue one you gave me on my last birthday.'

Moments later, Mama and I left the house into the fresh air. We headed past St Mary's Church before crossing over Henley Bridge, stopping frequently as we met little groups of friends and neighbours who were congregated here and there, swapping greetings and snippets of news. Once across the bridge, we rambled by the riverside and along several meadow paths, heading nowhere in particular.

It was only during this time that Mama recounted for the first time what she and William had discussed when she visited him while he had first stayed at the Red Lion Inn.

'When I saw William just before he left,' she told me, 'I did not doubt that you and he were meant to be together. He also left me in no doubt about his love for you. Nor was there any doubt in my mind that Ann Macclesfield's claim was anything but a false one… or that he would marry you as soon as possible after it was dismissed. I still hope such marriage will shortly come about, whatever the view of William your papa expressed just a few days ago.'

As Mama spoke, I could feel tears well in my eyes. It suddenly hit home that I had heard nothing from William since the altercation between him and Papa.

'Why does Papa resent William so much? Why is it that one minute he says that he will welcome William as he would anyone else lucky enough to be the intended husband of the daughter he holds dearest above everything in this world… and the next that he is a "debased profligate"… someone who is "absolutely unfit for any respectable people to know"… "a positive danger to society"… "a vile creature"?'

Mama stopped and turned to face me. She reached up, cupped my face with her hands and looked into my eyes.

'It may not seem it… but it's because Papa loves you more than anything else. He does not want to see you hurt… lose your virtue… lose your friends… become a social outcast… as you surely would if you give yourself to William, only to find that, despite what you and I believe, what Papa's attorney in Edinburgh said in his letter is true – that William's marriage to Ann Macclesfield really is valid.'

I lowered my head and began to sob uncontrollably.

'That's as may be,' I blubbered, 'but he's driven William away… it's been days since William left… and I've heard nothing from him… nothing of him.'

Mama lifted my head again, brushed away my tears with her thumbs and kissed me gently on my forehead.

'There, there, daughter,' she whispered. 'Don't fret yourself so. There will be a good reason why you haven't heard from him, you'll see.'

'Maybe.' I sniffed. 'Maybe not.'

Mama reached inside her cloak. She brought out a handkerchief and gently dried my eyes.

'He'll be back soon. I know it. He'll probably stay at the Red Lion Inn as he did before. When he does, Mrs Dawes will surely send news of his arrival the minute he gets there.'

In the days that followed, I grew ever more despondent. William did not return. He did not write or make any other contact with me. Throughout, Mama did her best to comfort me. She remained steadfast in her belief that William would return – that there was a straightforward explanation for his continued absence. She made a point of getting me out of the house daily to ensure I didn't just sit around moping. Invariably, she took me for a walk by the riverside or a drive to Culham Court to see Uncle Henry.

Then, out of the blue, things took a dramatic turn for the worst. All thoughts of William vanished from my mind.

SIXTEEN

There was a loud banging on my bedroom door. As I roused to consciousness, or rather to semi-consciousness, my mind played tricks on me as I imagined myself reposing among billowy white clouds in an atmosphere of crimson light. Gradually, however, the white clouds resolved themselves into the white linen and coverlets of my bed, whilst the crimson light proved to be the breaking dawn, lighting up the ruby-coloured hangings of my bed and the windows draped to match.

'Miss Mercy. Miss Mercy,' Mama's maid called out. 'Come quickly. The mistress has been taken ill.'

Those chilling words jerked me into full consciousness. I shot out of bed, rushed to the door and opened it. The maid stood outside, holding a silver candlestick with a flickering lighted candle, a horrified look on her face.

'Have you roused the master?' I demanded.

'No, Miss Mercy,' the maid replied. 'The mistress told me not to bother him. I was only to call you.'

'Here, let me have the candlestick,' I said, taking it from her before she could hand it to me even though the light was sufficient by then to no longer need a candle.

I hurried across the landing and into Mama's bedroom. Mama stirred and murmured my name. I rushed over to her and put the candlestick on her bedside table before bending towards her. Mama's hand found its way around my neck and nestled there. I took the hand from my neck, softly caressed, and tenderly kissed it.

'Mama, what is wrong... what can I do for you?'

'My dear Mercy, don't take on so. The stomach pains I suffered from when we were in London returned, waking me from my sleep... but now you're here with me, they will soon go, and I shall be well again before we know it.'

My mind was racing. At first, I couldn't think of what I could do. Then I remembered I still had some Dover's powder in my room. So I picked up the candlestick, blew out the candle and turned to Mama's maid.

'Here, take this,' I said, 'and go to the kitchen and fetch me a glass of syrup of roses mixed equally with water. Bring a spoon also... quickly... quickly, no time to waste.'

'Yes, Miss Mercy,' the maid replied before disappearing downstairs, taking the candlestick with her.

As soon as she had gone, I returned to my room to collect the few packets of Dover's powder I had brought back from Mrs Poole's house. I returned just as the maid appeared with a glass of diluted syrup of roses and the spoon I had asked for.

I took the glass and poured the contents of one of the packets into it before taking the spoon and stirring the powder and liquid together. Once I had done that, I returned to Mama's bed and placed the glass on the table.

'Over here,' I called to the maid. 'Prop the mistress's pillows behind her as I lift her upright.' I placed my arm behind Mama's shoulder and gently eased her forward while the maid manoeuvred pillows behind her.

'Here, Mama,' I said, handing her the glass once she was comfortable. 'Drink this.'

Mama laughed. 'As you command, madam.'

She slowly emptied the glass's contents and settled back, shuffling her shoulders as she did. I pulled a chair up to the side of the bed and sat down, taking Mama's hand in mine and stroking it. I leant forward to kiss her face. The texture of her cheek felt strangely soft with the give of an overripe plum. I gasped.

'What's troubling you, daughter?' Mama whispered.

I didn't get a chance to answer. Mama had fallen into a deep sleep before I could. The Dover's powder had taken an almost immediate effect. I drew the bedclothes over her before sitting by her side again.

Mama slept peacefully through the remainder of the morning and seemed well on the way to recovery by mid-afternoon.

'Why don't you go and get some fresh air?' she suggested shortly after she awoke.

'But I must stay with you for the time being,' I replied.

'I'm feeling much better now, Mercy. Tell my maid to bring me some light refreshments – perhaps some cold pork, bread and cheese. She can then remain with me while you're gone.'

'But I must stay,' I protested.

'No, daughter,' Mama insisted. 'I'll be fine... and you need a break. Why don't you go for a walk along the riverbank... perhaps you might like to pick me a posy of flowers from the meadow... oh, and some roses from the garden.'

Mama was right. I did need a break. Some fresh air. As she had suggested, I walked by the riverside, over the meadows, up towards Remenham and then back home again. In the process, I assembled the posy of flowers Mama had requested. I carried this carefully as I walked along Hart Street from St Mary's Church, picking my way through the townsfolk heading in the opposite direction to attend the evening service. I had forgotten that it was Sunday. Before rejoining Mama, I went into the garden and cut a mix-coloured bunch of roses.

Back in her bedroom, I sat by Mama's bedside while the evening sun shone outside; the birds sang gaily; and the church bells filled the air with solemnly joyful music.

The shadows crept round and lengthened; the soft breeze, laden with the scent of late summer, came in through the open window. Now the clang and the clash of the bells ringing for evensong had ceased, and in the silent chamber, I caught the faint rise and fall of the hymns sung to the dear familiar tunes. It soothed my anxious sorrow listening thus, and presently I hummed softly in accompaniment to the distant music. Mama joined in, the words falling like balm on my heart.

*

Mama's maid woke me in a near-blind panic in the early hours of the following morning.

'Miss Mercy,' she cried. 'It's my mistress. She has been taken ill again. She has terrible pains in her stomach and has been vomiting. I fear that if you want to see her alive, you must go to her immediately.'

Tendrils of terror curled in my stomach. I leapt out of bed, put on my shoes and a single petticoat and ran across the corridor to Mama's bedchamber. I threw open the door and rushed over to Mama. She put her hand out as I did and took hold of my petticoat, pulling me towards her. I gasped as I caught sight of her in the flickering candlelight. Her face was distorted. Colourless. Her eyes were screwed shut. I fell to my knees by her bedside and put my arms on either side of her shoulders, fighting back my tears.

'Mama... Mama! What can I do for you?' I blubbered.

Before she could answer, Mama screamed with pain. Then, her expression drawn in agony, she pulled the sheet from her and reached down to her stomach, seemingly trying to massage away knots of painful tension ravaging her insides.

I don't think I've felt more helpless in my whole life – not knowing what to say... or do. Then the pain that Mama was suffering eased its grip on her. She sighed as her body relaxed, propped herself on her elbow and turned to face me.

'I fear I soon must meet my Maker,' she whispered. 'I am almost ready to submit without question to what God has ordained for me, but I still have one ambition to fulfil before I do... I need to be certain that your future is secured – by which I mean your future with William.'

Mama's words sent me into a state of utter panic and confusion. Then I stood up, turned about, ran to Papa's room and hammered on the door.

'For God's sake, Papa, come to Mama's room now. I fear that she may be dying.'

When I heard Papa stirring, I ran into the kitchen, where I found the coachman. I ordered him to drive to Reading and bring Dr Hetherington to Henley. Having done so, I hurried upstairs to find Papa sitting by Mama's bedside in deep discussion with her. So it seemed they had been talking about me during my absence.

'You and Mercy have had your differences of late,' I heard Mama say as I entered the room, 'but she is everything you could ever wish for... and has been the best of daughters to me. Trust her. She will never abuse that trust. But you must also accept that she has set her heart on marrying William Dunbar; when I am gone, let no one set you against a match between them.'

'Rest assured, dearest wife,' Papa replied immediately, 'it will be through no fault on my part if such a match does not occur. However, you must know and accept that there can be no marriage between Mercy and Dunbar until the question of his marriage to Ann Macclesfield in Scotland is finally resolved in his favour... and at present, it has not been.'

'God bless you, husband, for saying that,' replied Mama, 'and for all your kindnesses you have shown to Mercy and me.'

I crossed the room and sat next to Papa as he reached over and kissed Mama on her forehead. There were tears in his eyes. Mama took his hand and placed it in mine.

'Be both a father and a mother to Mercy,' she told him. 'Never forget that you mean everything to your papa,' she told me.

Papa began to cry. Something I could not remember happening before. He pulled his hand from mine and stood up.

'Forgive me.' He wept. 'Forgive me... I can't help myself... please excuse me while I go downstairs and regain my composure. Once I have, I will send for Dr Hetherington.'

With that, he turned and headed out of the room. I rushed after Papa, catching up with him as he reached the top of the stairs. I took him by the arm.

'Papa, I've already sent the coachman to fetch Dr Hetherington. Hopefully, he'll be here before too long.'

'Thank you, Mercy,' he mouthed. 'I should have known you would... now, please go back to your Mama and care for her while I go into my study to await the doctor's arrival.'

With that, Papa continued on his way downstairs while I returned to Mama, spending a little time tidying up her bed before sitting beside her.

'Sorry for rushing off as I did, Mama,' I said. 'I just needed to tell Papa I had already sent for Dr Hetherington.'

'Thank you,' Mama whispered. She then took my hand, drew me to her and kissed me. 'Mercy,' she whispered. 'I have so many things to say to you. Firstly, when I am gone—'

'But, Mama,' I interrupted, 'let's not forget what is said in the Bible – *there is hope for whoever is joined to all the living.* The doctor should be here soon. He will surely be able to restore you to full health again.'

Mama looked up at me, her eyebrows lifting as she did. She

smiled. 'Maybe, Mercy, dear... maybe. But I fear that that will only happen if, somehow, he can replace my insides. Now – as I was about to say – when I am gone, take special care of your papa. If you think he has been hard on you sometimes, it is only because of his deep love for you... don't be angry with him. You must also take care of William. I know how much he loves and cares for you. I only wish that you and he would have married by now.'

I couldn't contain the sense of sorrow welling inside me. I began sobbing uncontrollably, almost drowning in tears. Mama caught me in her arms.

'How could I survive you and face all the challenges I might face if you die now?' I whimpered. 'You have been the best of mothers to me. But, not only that, you have been the best of friends to me. How will I ever be able to face all the challenges life will surely throw at me throughout the coming years without you to advise and guide me?'

'My dearest daughter,' Mama replied, 'your papa will be here for you. Now dry your eyes, fetch me my favourite book – *The Pilgrim's Progress* – and read to me.'

*

As soon as he arrived, Dr Hetherington was shown up to Mama's room by her maid just as Christian had met Faithful outside the Valley of the Shadow of Death. I put down *The Pilgrim's Progress* as he entered Mama's bedroom and stood up.

'Good evening, Miss Grundy,' Dr Hetherington greeted me. He turned to face Mama. 'Good evening, Mrs Grundy. I'm sorry to learn that you have been taken unwell.'

Mama looked at the doctor, smiling weakly. 'It's nothing, really,' she replied. 'I'm so sorry to be such a nuisance... bringing you all this way so late in the day.' At that moment, I started to move away from the bed and head towards the door. 'Oh, Mercy,' Mama called to me. 'Please don't leave me. I'm sure Dr Hetherington will not mind if you stay.'

'Of course not, Mrs Grundy... but perhaps Miss Grundy would move away from the bed so I can chat with you before I examine you fully.'

I said nothing as I crossed to the chair by the bedroom window and sat down.

'Thank you, Miss Grundy, that's very good of you.' Dr Hetherington then moved to the side of the bed and sat down. 'So, Mrs Grundy, tell me about your illness.'

He listened intensely as Mama rehearsed what had happened, firstly in London and, more recently, in Henley. Then, when she had finished, he stood up.

'Right, Mrs Grundy, let's have a look at you.' With that, he reached down, drew the bedclothes back and, pulling Mama forward and lifting her slightly, started to examine her. 'Now,' he said. 'So the pain you have been experiencing starts just under the ribs on your right-hand side and spreads to your shoulder?'

'Yes, Doctor,' Mama whispered.

Dr Hetherington lay Mama back on the bed. 'As was the case when the doctor examined you in London, I need to feel around your ribcage and the right side of your abdomen. Are you happy for me to do so?' he asked.

'Yes, of course, Doctor,' Mama replied, nodding.

Dr Hetherington stood over Mama and began his examination, which followed an identical pattern to the examination carried out by the doctor at Mrs Poole's house. Once he had finished, he sat down again at Mama's bedside.

'I have a few questions for you now, Mrs Grundy. Firstly, have you had regular bowel movements?'

'No,' Mama replied, looking somewhat embarrassed. 'I have not had one for several days now.'

'I see… and have you been sick at all?'

'Yes, Doctor. I was very sick last night.'

'That's right, Doctor,' I added. 'The maid told me that Mama had vomited.'

'Thank you, Miss Grundy,' Dr Hetherington replied. He turned to face Mama. 'Have you eaten anything today?'

'No, Doctor,' Mama replied. 'I haven't felt like it as yet.'

'When did you last eat?'

'I had some bread, cheese and cold pork yesterday afternoon. Oh, and a glass of milk late yesterday evening.'

Dr Hetherington paused for a moment or two before looking at me quizzically. 'Tell me, Miss Grundy,' he said, 'have you noticed a slight yellowing of your mother's skin? If so, when did you notice it?'

I leant forward to look closely at Mama. Dr Hetherington was right. There was a change in her complexion.

'I hadn't until now, Doctor,' I replied, 'although I did notice how different her cheek had felt when I kissed her yesterday.'

Dr Hetherington's face slid into a frown. His eyes narrowed as his eyebrows pulled together. He looked at me, then down at Mama.

'I'll be honest with you, Mrs Grundy. I am not yet certain what your problem is. My first thought was that you had eaten something that disagreed with you… causing the stomach pain and vomiting, but your constipation and the yellowing of your skin are a little concerning to me – albeit these may also have been caused simply by something you may have eaten. So, what I propose for the moment is that I bleed you immediately, after which I will leave some medication for you with Miss Grundy. I also suggest a change of diet for the next few days, which I will explain to her before I leave.'

Mama looked up at Dr Hetherington.

'Thank you, Doctor,' she said, almost in a whisper, 'but if you don't mind, I would prefer if you left any bleeding until your next visit. For the moment, I would just like to sleep for a while.'

'As you wish. Then I will take my leave of you for now. I will return tomorrow afternoon. In the meantime, perhaps Miss Mercy would come down with me, and I will give her the medication I want you to take and explain the change in diet I propose for you.'

Dr Hetherington took his leave of Mama, and I led him to Papa's study.

*

Things seemed to quieten down after Dr Hetherington's visit. However, Mama was not overly concerned by having nothing to eat other than a thrice daily serving of broth made by boiling mutton and a chicken in water with added raisins, prunes and the roots and leaves of ditch fern. Her only consolation was that she was additionally served a small portion of blackberries mixed with raspberries after she had finished the broth. She was also allowed an apple or a pear once a day. However, whatever Mama may have felt about her diet, it and the medication Dr Hetherington had prescribed seemed to do the trick as, over a period of five days, she gradually began to recover from whatever it was that had ailed her. This recovery, though, proved to be the lull before the terrible storm that followed.

It was mid-afternoon, and I had not long since returned from a walk along the riverside. As had become my habit, I was sat at Mama's bedside reading *The Pilgrim's Progress*. Christian's wife, Christiana, together with their sons, had begun her pilgrimage, together with my namesake.

As I read, Mama suddenly screamed out and jerked forward into a sitting position before falling back again. Blood was pouring from her mouth. She lay there shuddering. I dropped the book I was reading. My heart began to race. A feeling of dread began to envelop me. I was in danger of heading into a state of blind panic.

Pull yourself together! Think!

I rushed to Mama's washbasin and poured water into it from the jug next to it. I grabbed a facecloth, wetted it, wrung it out and returned to Mama. I had just started to wash the blood from her face when she screamed again, thrusting her pelvis forward. Seconds later, she gave out a loud, lingering gasp. Her body went limp. At that moment, Mama died. I stood in a momentary state of shock before running to the bedroom door.

'Papa… Papa!' I screamed. 'Come up here… now!' I ran back to Mama, sat on the bed and cradled her, tears flooding my face. 'Wake up, Mama. Wake up… please,' I pleaded, even though I knew she never would again.

Papa burst into the room, looked at Mama and stood there transfixed, his jaw open and a horrified look on his face. I got up from the bed, went over to Papa and wrapped my arms around his neck. Tears were streaming down my face.

'Mama's gone, Papa.' I wept.

Papa tore away from me. 'Dear God!' he exclaimed before falling to his knees at the bedside. He looked again at Mama and buried his face in her midriff, sobbing. 'No… no… no,' he kept repeating.

I left Papa with Mama and hurried out of the room to fetch Mama's maid so that she and I could attend to Mama's body – a task that was to bring home to me the horror of her death and the manner of it.

We carried a jug of hot water from the kitchen, together with soap and some towels. I had sent Papa out of the room, telling him to go and send for an undertaker, and begun to wipe the blood away from Mama's face when I noticed that she had bitten through her tongue in her death throes: the cause of the bleeding. We then pulled the sheet covering Mama away from her and were met with a horrific sight that caused me to recoil, gagging as I did. Mama's night dress was soaked in blood that ran from her lower body towards her knees. It was as if her bowel had exploded.

Trying to hold myself together, I worked as carefully as possible to wash Mama's body clear of all visible signs of the cause of her death. We then stripped the bed and replaced the bedding. Once these duties were completed, we dressed Mama in her best clothes, and I summoned Jarman, to carry Mama's body down to the front parlour to await the arrival of the undertaker.

Mama was buried in the churchyard at St Mary's Church three days after she died. The funeral was well attended. In addition to family members, many of the great and good of Henley and its surrounding towns and villages were there. Despite my having sent the coachman to William's house in Windsor to deliver a letter there to inform him of Mama's death, and sending a similar letter to Bristol by messenger, the one notable absentee was William.

I was distraught at this. If there was ever a time when I needed him, it was then. In contrast, Papa seemed completely nonplussed that William was not there when I raised the absence with him.

'I might have guessed that he would not show his face,' was his only comment.

*

In the days that followed, I wrote almost daily to William – to both his address in Windsor and that in Bristol – but received no reply to any of my letters. Then, several weeks later, Uncle Henry visited me as I sat on a bench in the garden enjoying a rather pleasant autumn afternoon. As he approached, I noticed that he was carrying a packet. He was also looking very serious. I stood up and moved towards him.

'Uncle Henry, what a pleasant surprise. It's so nice to see you,' I greeted, embracing him as I did. 'To what do I owe this pleasure? I thought you were in London… with Papa.'

Uncle Henry seemed strangely distant.

'May I sit down?' he replied.

'Of course, Uncle,' I mumbled. 'Is something wrong?'

Uncle Henry led me back to the garden bench and bade me sit down. He then sat next to me.

'I've something I need to give you,' he said. With that, he handed me the packet he had been carrying. 'This arrived at my office yesterday morning. A similar packet arrived at the same time and was addressed to your papa. He has shown me the contents of the packet sent to him… and I do not doubt that the contents of both packets are identical.'

I took the packet and opened it with my hands shaking. There was a letter and several official-looking documents. I started to read the letter.

Dear Madam,

I am sending this letter via Mr Henry Stephenson, whose address was given to me by my attorney in Edinburgh.

To my horror, surprise and consternation, I recently discovered that you had received a marriage proposal from the Honourable William Henry Dunbar. Having since instructed my attorney to investigate further, I now learn you have accepted that proposal.

I write to advise you that no marriage between you and Mr Dunbar would be lawful as Mr Dunbar is already married – to me.

In this regard, I refer you to the enclosed documents.

One is a copy of the decree of the Commissary Court of Scotland, which you will note unequivocally declares that Mr

Dunbar and I are legally married. The other is a copy of the Order of the Court requiring Mr Dunbar to pay me an annuity of £125, plus an annuity of £25 as support for Margaret Dunbar, the lawful daughter of Mr Dunbar and me.

I am sure this letter will shock you, but you should learn the truth now rather than later.

I remain, madam,

Your most humble and obedient servant

Ann Dunbar

As I finished reading, I felt an increasing inquietude within me. The letter and documents sent by Ann confirmed everything that the attorney in Edinburgh had reported in the letter I had seen a few days before William left Henley.

Is this why I haven't heard from William… why he didn't come back to Henley to see me… to be with me after Mama died? Have I lost not only my mama but also the man I love so dearly?

WILLIAM DUNBAR

SEVENTEEN

My mind was filled with hot and bitter thoughts as I drove my curricle along Hart Street, heading back to my house in Windsor.

Do I need all this? I asked myself. *Does Mercy mean that much to me?*

These were questions I found answers to long before I reached my destination. It was true to say that I had developed strong feelings for Mercy over the weeks that followed our reunion when I visited Henley after Eleanor died. It was also true to say that I still had a financial advantage if Mercy and I married. However, the motive for my actively seeking marriage to Mercy in the first instance no longer existed; any tocher I might receive from Mr Grundy were I to do so was no longer necessary. I was now a wealthy man who was about to become an exceedingly rich one as soon as *The Archer* returned from the Americas with the profits of her present venture and the future profits to be earned from new ventures. The fact was that Mercy was dispensable – or so I concluded then. However, the fates had other plans for me, as I was soon to discover, but first, I took time to travel to Edinburgh and Newbattle to visit my brother, James, and my mother.

It was while I was staying at my mother's home that I received a letter from Walter Lougher, the agent appointed to manage the venture of *The Archer*. He needed to meet with me urgently, but no reasons were given for the meeting or its urgency.

'It all seems rather odd, Mama,' I explained to my mother as I took my leave of her. 'I hope that the meeting is a beneficial one, but I can't help fearing the worst.'

'You were always such a pessimist,' my mother chided. 'I'm sure that everything is well – that you have nothing to concern yourself about.'

'I hope you are right, Mama,' I replied before embracing her, kissing her on her forehead and going out to the coach that James had arranged to take me all the way to Bristol – a long, tedious and, at the time, altogether unwelcome journey. It had been a long time since I had last seen my mother, and I had been looking forward to an extended stay with her.

As soon as possible after I arrived in Bristol, I visited Lougher and was shown into his office. As I entered the room, I saw him standing with a man with heavy jowls and longish hair starting to grey at the temples. He appeared to be in the throes of explaining something. His brown eyes were animated, his face flushed, and he was gesticulating to Lougher, whose expression was thoughtful, his head tilted to one side and his arms crossed. My entrance immediately brought the conversation to a halt.

'Good afternoon, gentlemen,' I greeted.

'Good afternoon, Mr Dunbar,' said Lougher as he moved towards me. I took his outstretched hand and shook it. 'Do you know Captain David Wiltshire, master of *The Archer*?' he continued, turning towards Wiltshire.

'I have heard of him,' I replied, 'but we've never met before now.'

I offered my hand to Captain Wiltshire. As he took it, I realised the thumb and two adjacent fingers on his hand were missing.

'Good afternoon, Mr Dunbar,' he said, coming to attention and nodding towards me.

I could feel my heartbeat quicken: a sudden spike in anxiety.

Something's not right... what on earth is Wiltshire doing here with Lougher? He can't have completed the venture already... it's far too soon for that.

'Shall we be seated?' asked Lougher before moving behind a desk and sitting on the chair behind it. Two chairs sat in front of the desk. I sat on one, Wiltshire on the other.

Lougher leant forward, his fingers laced before him on the top of the desk.

'I'll cut to the chase, Mr Dunbar,' he said. 'We've some bad news for you. *The Archer* is lost.'

I gasped. At that moment, I felt as if I had been punched in the stomach. Completely winded.

'What... what do you mean *The Archer* is lost?' I eventually sputtered.

'Let me explain,' said Wiltshire.

'Please... do.' I gulped.

'Everything started so well,' Wiltshire began. 'We enjoyed fair winds and clement weather throughout most of the early part of the journey, arriving at the Sierra Leone River four days earlier than we had planned. We subsequently set sail from the Guinea coast with a cargo of 124 slaves, comprising eighty-seven men, twenty-two women and fifteen children. These were held in chains on the lower deck of the ship. Whilst we could have carried more, I had deliberately limited the number of slaves to be transported. I wanted to mitigate the number of losses that would inevitably arise during the voyage to the Americas. I aimed to land and sell at least 105 slaves on our arrival – to limit cargo loss to less than fifteen per cent. I knew that the more crowded the cargo deck, the greater the risk of significant loss.

'Four days after we set sail, a number of male slaves freed themselves from their shackles. They released others and broke through the ship's bulkhead with them. This was at around four-thirty in the morning. They gained the deck, where, as I later learned, they killed two of the crew and seized weapons. Five men, a boy and I took refuge in the cabin below and barricaded the door, not knowing what to expect. We had my pistol, two muskets, a small number of musket balls and powder with us. We could hear slaves talking and moving outside the cabin, but no immediate attempt was made to break in.' Lougher paused and took a deep breath before continuing. 'I felt I needed to do something. We couldn't just sit there doing nothing—'

'So, what did you do?' I interrupted, showing my impatience.

'I looked around me and spotted a bottle of rum,' Wiltshire continued. 'I emptied the contents onto the cabin floor, took some powder, fashioned a fuse and packed it and the powder into the bottle to make a grenade. Once this was done, I moved to the barricaded door and turned to one of the men. "When I give the signal – a nod in your direction –" I told him, "remove the barricade and open the door. In the meantime, I will light the fuse and throw the grenade to clear the area around the cabin. We will then attack and attempt to retake the ship." I took several deep breaths—'

'Yes... and did you?' I muttered, feeling ever more anxious.

Wiltshire looked at me, then up to the ceiling, and then, showing just frustration at being interrupted once more, gave a loud sigh. 'As I was about to say,' he recontinued, 'I took several deep breaths, picked up a lighted candle, gave the necessary signal and started to light the fuse. There was an instantaneous flash and an explosion as the grenade detonated prematurely. The explosion blew open the cabin door, raised the deck... took half my hand off and seriously wounded the sailor to my right. There was no possibility of making our planned attack, so we used various items of furniture in the room to construct a barricade and took cover behind it—'

'So, what happened then?' I interrupted yet again.

'All we could do then was to wait and see what the slaves would do next.'

'And did they do anything?'

'Nothing except to subject us from time to time to intermittent musket fire—'

'But surely that's not all they did?'

'No. The slaves controlled the ship for several days while we remained below,' Wiltshire went on, his face showing increasing frustration at my continuing interruptions. 'Unbeknown to me then, the slaves had captured the remainder of the crew, forcing them to return the ship to the Guinea coast. To achieve this, the slaves threw two of the men overboard when they refused to help bring *The Archer* about. Soon after we entered the Sierra Leone River, the ship ran aground on a bar. At that moment, we heard screams coming from the deck, which we soon realised were the screams of the crew members pressed into sailing the ship back. The slaves were slaughtering them.' Wiltshire paused again, almost anticipating my further interruption, before continuing. 'The sole focus of the slaves at the time seemed to be the murder of the crew. This allowed us to lower a boat and escape – an opportunity we took. As we rowed away, we could see the ship on fire. We spent the next nine days at sea before, barely alive, we were rescued by a Royal Navy frigate and brought back to Portsmouth.'

I sat motionless and silent for what seemed like an eternity, mentally stunned by the blow dealt to me by Wiltshire's account of the demise of *The Archer*.

Mr Lougher finally broke the silence. 'There you have it, I'm afraid, Mr Dunbar,' he said, setting my mind racing.

Insurance. We took out insurance.

'Have the other owners started claims against the insurance they took out before *The Archer* set out on the venture?'

'Some have, others—'

'And?'

'One claim has been paid. But, unfortunately, several have not,' replied Lougher.

'And… do you think my claim will be paid?'

'I fear not, Mr Dunbar. The critical restriction under the insurance policy taken out by you – and all but one of your fellow owners – was that any losses to be claimed for under its terms had to arise from a "peril of the sea". Accordingly, had *The Archer* simply been lost due to it sinking in a storm, an insurance claim for the loss arising would have been paid. But, unfortunately, *The Archer* was lost because it was set on fire and destroyed during an insurrection by slaves; its loss was not a consequence of a "peril of the sea". Such loss, therefore, is not covered, and any insurance claim you may wish to make in its regard will fail. Similarly, had the cargo of slaves perished because *The Archer* sank in a storm, an insurance claim for the loss would have been paid. However, in your case, any claim you may wish to make now for the loss of the slaves will fail; the loss was not a consequence of a "peril of the sea" but the result of their escaping from the ship following an insurrection.'

I heaved a mighty sigh and dropped my head into my hands as the enormity of what I had just been told began to sink in. In less than a quarter of an hour, I had learned that every penny I had invested in *The Archer* and her voyage was gone. Lost.

*

I urgently reviewed my finances in the days following my meeting with Lougher and Wiltshire. On the negative side, I had lost some

£2,100 with the loss of *The Archer* and its cargo. Additionally, after investing in *The Archer*, I needed to repay several hundred pounds borrowed against further notes to finance my lifestyle. Hopefully, they would not press me for this money.

More worryingly, though, I owed my cousin Robert Campbell more than £500, including accrued interest, for the money he had advanced me against my note, which I had invested in the failed venture to Africa. Unfortunately, and sadly, he had recently been killed in a tragic accident whilst out hunting, and inevitably, my note would form part of his estate, placing me in the hands of his executors in its regards. Inevitably, they *would* press for early repayment.

On the positive side, even though the annuity arising under my father's will was reduced to zero following the order made in favour of Ann and Margaret by the Commissary Court in Edinburgh, I still enjoyed an acceptable income by continuing to act as a financial intermediary between clients in London and Southampton. There also remained a small balance of Sir Richard's bequest to me.

The overriding problem for me, though, was a realisation that I had become all too used to the lifestyle I had enjoyed since I had been named Sir Richard's beneficiary. The realisation sank in that, at that point in time, I could no longer ensure that I fulfil my ambition always to have sufficient wealth for my purposes. That being said, I quickly realised that there was a step that I could take to mitigate my new circumstances; killing two birds with a single stone, so to speak. That step would repair the damage caused to me by the finding of the Commissary Court, removing the need for me to pay maintenance for Ann and Margaret. But, more importantly, it would open the way for me to marry Mercy: the way for me to get my hands on the £20,000 tocher promised by Grundy.

Using some of my remaining capital, I tracked down and purchased a number of registers of the Entries of Marriages in the Fleet Prison maintained by Edward Ashwell, who had officiated at a great many weddings in and around the vicinity of Fleet Prison and was once described as one of the most notorious of parsons. After he had died, the registers of the marriages he had performed were sold. The ones I bought covered the period that bracketed my marriage to Ann.

I eventually found a page in one register that lent itself to the insertion of a record of a fictitious marriage between Mercy and me and then hired a skilled forger to add the words: *9 The Honourable Lieutenant William Henry Dunbar, Royal North British Fusiliers, and Mercy Grundy of Henley, S.* The same forger also prepared a parchment certificate confirming the marriage. Once this was done, I headed up to Scotland to attend a meeting with my attorney, John Balfour.

Armed with the register in question and the certificate, I instructed Balfour to commence an appeal in the Court of Session against the finding of the Commissary Court that Ann and I were lawfully married.

In support of my appeal, I prepared a sworn written statement of evidence as part of that process.

I, William Henry Dunbar, of Crailing, Roxburgh, Scotland, Gentleman, make oath and say:

I aver that I am not now, nor have I ever been, married to Ann Macclesfield. I could not lawfully marry her as alleged because I was already married at the time of the alleged marriage between Ann Macclesfield and me. Such marriage was purported to have occurred on the 22nd of May 1744. However, on that day, I was already married to Miss Mercy Grundy of Henley in the County of Oxfordshire, England.

The marriage between the said Mercy Grundy and me occurred in the Hand and Pen Inn in Fleet Street on the 9th of April 1744. It was conducted by Dr Edward Ashwell, whom the court may be familiar with.

I paid Edward Ashwell the sum of 2gns to conduct the marriage and ½gn to produce two parchment certificates recording the marriage. I additionally paid him ½gn to enter the names of Mercy Grundy and me in the register.

I did not have access to the register when I filed my defence to the defender's claim and did not produce the certificate at the time as I knew it was insufficient by itself since I would also need to simultaneously produce the register. Accordingly, I relied solely on the letter sent to me by the said Ann Macclesfield in which she stated that whilst she and I lived under the same roof and became lovers, our relationship never progressed beyond that state of affairs.

My previous difficulty regarding the register has now been resolved.

About eight months ago, I purchased a series of registers containing the Entries of Marriages in the Fleet Prison from the year 1743 to the year 1746. They were bought from someone who had acquired them from a beneficiary under the will of the said Edward Ashwell, who died in January 1746.

I produce one of these books, which covers the period from the 29th of January to the 17th of April 1744.

As the court will note, this book contains the entry for my marriage to the said Mercy Grundy dated the 9th of April 1744. It is recorded as the sole marriage set out on the eighth to last page – opposite the marriage on the same day of Henry Hulbird, Butcher, and Martha Shirley, Spinster, and that of Joseph Parkhouse and Ann Purdy, Widow.

I also produce a certificate signed by Edward Ashwell to confirm the marriage.

I left Balfour with high hopes that the Court of Session would allow my appeal. In the meantime, I could turn my mind towards Mercy and a reunion with her.

*

I returned to England with my brother, James, and his wife, accompanying them to his house in Portman Square – not far from the home of Abigail Poole.

A few days after arriving in London, I took the opportunity to visit Mrs Poole, where I learned the shocking news of the death of Mrs Grundy and that Mercy had been trying to contact me.

I immediately sent my footman to Henley with a letter for Mercy in which I expressed my deep sorrow at learning the news of Mrs Grundy's passing and begged her forgiveness for not contacting her sooner. I told her I was staying with my brother and hoped with all my heart that she would see me again as soon as possible.

I must confess that I didn't know what to expect from Mercy as my footman set off for Henley with the letter. But, in the event, I need not have entertained any doubt or worry. My footman returned the following day with a letter of reply from Mercy to tell me how overjoyed and relieved she was to receive my letter. She planned to make an immediate visit to London, hoping to stay with Mrs Poole. Her greatest wish was that we could meet there.

Mercy also told me that her father had said that he would welcome me as a guest in his home if I was ever in Henley. Notwithstanding this, I was sceptical that Mr Grundy would actually welcome me anywhere – let alone at his house. He might tolerate my presence there, but I was sure that that was about as far as it would go.

My scepticism soon proved to be well founded.

A week or so after I received Mercy's letter, I was invited by Mrs Poole to join her and Mercy for dinner at her home. To my surprise, she and Mrs Poole arrived at my brother's house on the day in question in a coach Mrs Poole had hired to collect and take me to her house.

Just as we approached our destination, a voice suddenly rang out. 'Halt!'

To my consternation, the coach was brought to a sudden halt. I could hear the sound of horses snorting and leant out of the window of our coach to find out what was going on. Another coach was standing immediately to the side of us and facing in the opposite direction. Its door was open. Someone began to approach us.

'Mrs Poole!' the same voice rang out clearly through the evening air. It was unmistakable. It was the voice of Grundy.

'What in Heaven's name...' Mercy gasped.

I pushed open our carriage door and started to get out.

'Don't trouble yourself,' Grundy shouted at me. 'Stay where you are, man! I am only here to give my daughter a piece of my mind, and then I shall be on my way again.' Then, he stopped a couple of paces away from our coach. 'For God's sake, daughter,' Grundy snarled. 'What are you doing with rubbish like Dunbar?'

'Rubbish, do you call him?' Mercy called out defiantly. 'Rubbish? He's the man I love... the man who may one day be your son-in-law.'

'Yes, he's rubbish,' Grundy snapped back at Mercy. 'You are far too good for the likes of him. How could you ever entertain the thought that a man who is married... who has a wife and child in Scotland... could ever become a son-in-law of mine.'

I stepped from the coach and took a step towards Grundy.

'How many times must I tell you? I am not... nor have I ever been, married,' I called out as calmly as I could manage.

'That's not what the Commissary Court in Scotland found, is it?' Grundy sneered.

'The Commissary Court was wrong... as you will surely discover before too long,' I replied, trying to suppress my rising anger. 'I have appealed the decision and provided unequivocal evidence that will result in it being overturned by the Court of Session... as will become clear.'

Grundy looked at me, his face now drained of all colour.

'And pigs will fly before that ever happens,' he retorted. He started to turn away from me, then stopped. 'I've said what I came to say. I've better things to do than stand idling any longer, wasting time talking to the likes of you.'

I watched as Grundy stormed back into his coach, shut the door and ordered his coachman to drive on. Moments later, his coach had disappeared.

Mercy came to my side and took my hand. 'I'm so sorry, William,' she whispered.

I lifted her hand to my lips and kissed it. 'You've nothing to be sorry for,' I replied with a smile. 'What your father says and does is outside your control... and it's for me to try and find the way to rebuild the bridge between him and me, which I will try and do.'

*

Several months after the altercation with Grundy outside Mrs Poole's house, I received a wholly unexpected invitation from him via Mercy. He wished to meet me at Nando's Coffee House the following week. Apparently, he had urgent business to discuss with me. Mercy was almost as surprised as me by this turn of events when I raised it with her the day after I received the letter.

'Perhaps he has had a change of heart about you,' she commented optimistically.

'Stranger things have happened, but I highly doubt it in this case,' I had replied pessimistically.

That pessimism was well founded, as it became all too clear from the moment I entered Nando's and caught sight of the sneer on Grundy's face as I approached him. He was sitting at a table in a corner of the room with a pile of papers spread out in front of him.

'I'll not get up,' he said charmlessly.

Not replying, I sat on the chair opposite him and looked around me. I caught sight of a serving maid and called her over.

'Can I offer you a dish of coffee?' I asked.

'You can... it's perfectly possible, I'm sure... but no, thank you. I want nothing from you.'

I smiled, determined not to rise to Grundy's deliberate rudeness, and turned towards the serving maid. 'Just one dish of coffee, please.'

We sat in silence as Grundy started to move the papers in front of him before picking up one and holding it up.

'Your great-uncle, Lord Campbell, has informed me that your cousin, and his great nephew, Robert Campbell, Master of Lothian, was killed in a hunting accident recently. He has also informed me that he is appointed as the sole executor of the will of Robert Campbell.' I gulped, a feeling of anxiety swelling up inside me. 'I gather that Lord Campbell does not think at all highly of you,' Grundy continued.

My hand was shaking slightly as I lifted my dish of coffee, took a sip and put it back on the table. 'And just where are you going with all this?' I asked.

Grundy didn't answer at first. Instead, he looked over me to catch the attention of a serving maid and beckoned to her.

'A dish of coffee for me, please,' he ordered. Still saying nothing to me, he took a sip of coffee as soon as a dish was placed in front of him. He then looked straight at me. 'Lord Campbell told me that one of the assets in your cousin's estate was your note in your cousin's favour in the sum of £485 with interest accruing at five per cent per annum – by then amounting to a total of £512/4/9½d. He wondered if I might be interested in purchasing the note.' Grundy paused, looking at me with a supercilious grin on his face. 'Naturally, I was… and eventually paid £491/15 for it,' he continued. 'The note continues to attract interest at a daily rate of about 1s4d… so as of now, you owe me £515/3/3, give or take.'

I sank back in my chair and looked up at the ceiling, my mind racing, not knowing what to say.

'But… as you know only too well, there are more of your notes in circulation other than the one you gave to your cousin.' Grundy put down the note in favour of Robert and picked up the other documents, which he held out towards me. 'There are thirteen to be exact – see. If it helps you, these total £320 – plus accrued interest, of course. I have identified and bought them in their entirety. So, all in all, you owe me £850 in round numbers.'

By now, what Grundy had told me had completely knocked the wind out of my sails.

'What do you want of me… repayment?' I gasped. 'If so, when?'

Grundy laughed, placing the notes he was holding on top of the one in favour of Robert. 'I know you can't pay what you owe. Lord Campbell also told me about your investment in your venture to Africa and the loss of your ship… *The Archer*, I think it was called… but I have a little proposal for you – one that would work to our mutual benefit.'

I felt a twinge of relief at Grundy's sudden mention of a proposal. But what sort of proposal might suit us both? 'A proposal?'

'Yes… and one you might want to consider very carefully, I suggest,' Grundy replied. He emptied his dish of coffee, placed it on the table and looked at me. 'If you unequivocally agree never to see Mercy again and undertake to have nothing more to do with her,' he continued, 'I'll sell these notes back to you for just 1gn. Your agreement and undertaking would be reduced to writing with the proviso that if you ever acted in breach of the agreement and undertaking, you would forthwith pay to me on demand the sum of £850 together with interest accruing at the rate of ten per cent from the date of the agreement until the date payment is made to me in full. So, if you agree to this proposal, you'll be left with no debt after payment to me of the guinea. However, if you do not agree to it, I will require your immediate and full repayment of the value of the notes, plus accrued interest, and if you do not repay in full, I will start proceedings against you forthwith. So, there you have it – give up Mercy once and for all or face the debtors' prison… since we both know you cannot pay your debts.'

With that, he swept up all the notes, stood up and headed out of Nando's. As he reached the door, he suddenly stopped and returned. 'Oh, I should have said… you have one week to make up your mind about my proposal.'

Moments later, he had disappeared from sight. As he did, I put my head in my hands and sat motionless, mentally stunned by the blow which had been dealt me.

What am I to do? The most sensible option is to accept the proposal. If nothing else, there is absolutely no prospect that Grundy would ever pay a penny as a tocher if I married Mercy, but how could I live with myself if I just let him ride roughshod over me?

*

I had always believed that bad news arrives in clusters, seldom as single, spaced-out instances, and the contents of a letter I had just received from John Balfour reinforced that view.

Dear Mr Dunbar,

Below is a transcript of the lead judgment of the court hearing your appeal against the decision of the Commissary Court in the case of Ann Macclesfield against you:

[His Lordship] *believed that registers such as that submitted by* [you] *are not evidence to authenticate any marriage recorded in them. Firstly, it is a fact that they have been used on occasion as vehicles of fraud and abuse. Secondly, they are never made with the same degree of care that other documents are. Whilst it may be significant that the register before* [his Lordship] *was not previously relied upon by* [you], [he] *did not necessarily suggest that the register submitted to* [him] *is a vehicle of fraud and abuse, nor that the content of it is flawed. However,* [he was] *of the view that the register was not receivable in evidence, to say nothing of the question of whether it should be submitted to the court for consideration to determine its validity or not.* [His Lordship] *also believed that the same could be said of certificates purporting to confirm a marriage. Accordingly, and in the absence of any admissible evidence to substantiate* [your] *claim that* [you were] *lawfully married prior to the marriage to Ann Macclesfield,* [he] *concluded that* [you] *were not so married and, therefore, free to enter into a marriage with her.*

His Lordship then went on to address the finding of the Commissary Court:

That then led to the question of whether the Commissary Court fell into error when it determined that the marriage to Ann Macclesfield on the 22ⁿᵈ of May 1744 was lawful. In that regard, [I am] *of the opinion that* [I have] *heard nothing to suggest that it did. In* [my] *judgment, therefore, the appeal fails.*

The other judge hearing the appeal concurred with this

judgment. Accordingly, your appeal was dismissed, with costs assessed at £100 awarded against you.

It is, of course, open to you to appeal further to the House of Lords. My advice to you, though, is not to pursue that option, but I will await your further instructions once you have had the opportunity to consider your next steps.

I remain, sir,

Your most humble and obedient servant

John Balfour

Moonlight streamed in through the window, firelight through the open door. The beam and glow kindled the old-fashioned furniture in the room into something that seemed almost lifelike. I lay in bed contemplating what to do next.

I had read and reread the letter several times, perhaps subconsciously hoping the contents would change, but they never did. So now, I remained married to Ann. I continued to be liable to pay £150 per annum as support to her and Margaret, and I was a further £100 poorer due to having to pay her legal costs. If that was not bad enough, the notes held by Grundy hung over me like the sword of Damocles, for there was no way I could ever hope to redeem them.

One thing that was certain, though, was that there was no way I could ever risk being sent to the debtors' prison. I was fond of Mercy but not sufficiently fond of her, per se, to turn my back on Grundy's offer. However, she remained the only immediate way for me to recover my wealth – the wealth I craved.

Can I have my cake and eat it? Possibly, but I will need to consider a way to achieve this.

As I lay there, thoughts of murder began to fill my head. I

began to see a possibility – albeit a very risky one – where the fact that Mercy was almost certainly Grundy's sole heir came into play. If she was, and if he were to die, she alone would surely inherit his estate – an estate that, in contrived circumstances, I could benefit from.

EIGHTEEN

I had just five days left to accept or reject Grundy's proposal but had still not thought of a way of avoiding having to accept it as I headed towards St James's Square. I had arranged with Mrs Poole that I might visit Mercy in private at her house. I approached the front door and pulled the bell handle.

'Good afternoon, Mr Dunbar, sir,' said Mrs Poole's footman as he opened the door. 'Come into the hall. Mrs Poole is out, but she told me to expect you. If you wait here, I'll let Miss Grundy know you have arrived.'

Several minutes later, Mercy appeared. A beaming smile lit up her face. She was dressed in a silk gown that moulded itself to her figure and fell into graceful curves.

'William!' she exclaimed excitedly. 'I can't tell you how pleased I am to see you again. Come into the parlour. I'll order some tea.'

I followed Mercy into the parlour. A window looked out onto the street, on either side of which hung long, blue velvet curtains drawn open. I sat on a leather upholstered, throne-like gentleman's chair. Mercy rang the bell and sat on a chair opposite me with her hands folded in her lap.

'A pot of tea, please,' she said as a maid appeared.

'Yes, Miss Grundy,' replied the maid, curtseying.

As the maid left, I looked around the room with its panelled walls, all painted pea green. Behind me stood a burl bureau cabinet with its broken architectural pediment. In front of me, an ornately framed mirror hung over a magnificent fireplace designed in the style of a Roman temple with its feature columns and projecting cornices. A decorative vase stood on its mantel. A column plinth showcasing a classical bust stood to the left of the fireplace; a walnut longcase clock ticked metronomically on the other side. There was an *étagère* to house numerous Meissen figures. Plants in elegant pots were displayed on pedestals discretely placed around the room.

'This is such a comfortable and comforting room,' I said, breaking the silence that had descended.

Mercy glanced around the room before looking at me, her eyes twinkling, a broad smile on her lips.

'Yes, it is. I prefer it to any other room in the house,' she returned. 'Especially in the winter when the fire burns brightly in the grate.'

Tea appeared, and we began to chat away merrily as we drank. For the present, I did not dwell on my recent meeting with Grundy – any mention of that needed to be confined somewhere away from the house. Mercy, though, continued to try to return to it.

'Oh, William.' She sighed. 'There must be so much more about your meeting with Papa than you have told me already.'

'You're right, dearest Mercy,' I replied, 'but not here. Why don't we take a walk in the park? I can tell you everything as we do.'

Mercy and I left the house and strolled towards the park. At first, nothing was said by either of us. In my case, I was waiting until we were well on our way, and I was sure that no one might overhear what I had to say. But Mercy had other ideas.

'So, tell me about your meeting with Papa,' she said after we had gone about thirty yards.

I turned my head to look at her as we continued our walk.

'Your father has contrived a situation where he has a very real hold on me at present, and he wanted to ensure that I knew it.'

'But how? Why?'

'For a while, I enjoyed some extraordinarily good fortune. To cut a long story short, I helped a man and his daughter when a highwayman was robbing him. He died a little while afterwards from a very unpleasant disease known as *putrid throat*, and to my great surprise, he named me as a beneficiary in his will. This enabled me to leave the Marines and set up my own business. Almost before I knew it, I owned a half share in a ship – *The Archer* – and the cargo it was to carry on a venture, firstly to Africa, then to the Americas, before returning to Bristol. When we last met in Henley, I learned that *The Archer* was about to leave for Africa. That was what prompted me to leave so suddenly—'

'But why didn't you say something before you went?' Mercy interrupted, stopping as she did.

'I didn't know the full details… but in any event, I wanted to wait until after *The Archer* had returned, by which time I would have been set for life… and able to properly provide for a life together with you.'

'And wasn't the venture a success?'

'Sadly, no… as I have only recently discovered. *The Archer* was lost in tragic circumstances… and my entire investment was wiped out – and more besides.'

'What do you mean "and more besides"?'

'I borrowed money from my cousin, Robert, against my note of hand. You may recall him. He was with me when you and I first met. I used that money as part of my investment in the venture. I also borrowed money from others against notes pending the return of *The Archer*. I was hoping to redeem some of those notes with what little capital I still have and the remainder over time as my business as a financial intermediary permitted. But, unfortunately, your father has found out about all these notes and has purchased them... making him my sole creditor.'

'How much are we talking about, William?'

'Let's continue walking; I'll explain as we go.'

We set off again.

'So, tell me, William. How much are we talking about?' Mercy asked, sounding somewhat impatient.

'Roughly £850... and he is now threatening me with debtors' prison if I cannot redeem the notes from him within the next five days.'

'Oh, William, dearest William... if only I had the money myself to give you to buy the notes. I would gladly do so.'

'I know you would... but I could not let you do that – it wouldn't be right. I got myself into this mess; I alone must get myself out of it.'

'Is there any way out of this for you?'

'Yes... but—'

'But what?'

'Your father... your father will sell the notes back to me for just one guinea... if... if I undertake never to see you again... never have anything more to do with you...'

Mercy came to an abrupt halt and turned to face me open-mouthed. The colour had drained from her face. 'How could he... do that to you... do that to me? He knows just how much I love you and need you.'

'Don't be too hard on your father. He is concerned for you. He will still not accept that I am not lawfully married to Ann Macclesfield. He knows that any relationship between you and a married man would surely sully your reputation, result in the loss of your honour and see your friends desert you in droves.'

'And just what is the position with Ann now?'

'As you know, the Commissary Court found for her. I appealed against that decision, but the appeal was dismissed... wrongly dismissed, I am convinced... and I will be appealing to the House of Lords.'

Mercy stopped, turning to look at me. Tears were welling in her eyes. 'Oh, William – it doesn't matter. I will stand by you, whatever. I have never loved anyone as I love you. I don't care what others may think of me. You are all I want.'

I placed my hand gently on Mercy's shoulder.

'But I can't let you sacrifice everything for me... and to make matters worse for you, your father will cut you off without a penny.'

'That is a risk I'm prepared to take, so long as I can be with you.'

'Mercy... I still have time before I have to do something. I'm sure I can think of a way forward for both of us that will ensure our future happiness... and, more importantly, your financial security.'

'But how, William?'

'Don't worry, Mercy. I will think of a way. In the meantime, let's enjoy today and put your papa from our minds while we do – let's not allow him to spoil things for us now. After today, let's meet again in a couple of days – by which time I will have a plan, I am sure.'

'Where shall we meet? I have to return to Henley tomorrow.'

'I will go to my house in Windsor, drive to the Red Lion Inn and meet you there the day after tomorrow – in the afternoon. It's a bit close to your home, but hopefully, that will not create too much of a problem for you.'

'No, it won't – Papa and Mrs Dawes do not see eye to eye in any way. He won't go near her or the Red Lion Inn.'

*

Mercy and I met at the Red Lion Inn as we had arranged and decided to go for a walk. We eventually passed through a little wicket gate and, hand in hand, followed a trodden path that led across the springy turf towards the river. At first, the ground sloped gently downhill, a sunny expanse of grass broken by great trees, oak, ash and beech, but it soon became much steeper.

The little path dropped down among bramble bushes. Then, after a few moments, the ground flattened out again, and we found ourselves on a broad, sheltered, natural terrace with a glimpse of the river curving away through the valley below. I stopped, turned to face Mercy and kissed her gently.

'Let's stay here a while, William,' she said before kissing me, our mouths opening slightly as she did. My heart began to race.

'Let's try and find a place to sit and enjoy our surroundings,' I whispered, gently guiding Mercy towards a spot where reeds and wildflowers fringed the riverbank.

We sat down on the grass, supported by our arms. Mercy slowly moved her arms backwards as she lay down and looked up at the sky. I turned my head towards her, looked down and lay down slowly. My left hand touched her right hand briefly, and I took it gently when Mercy left her hand where it was.

Slowly, I lifted myself to lean over her. I gently lowered my head and kissed her. I could feel her trembling and her heartbeat quicken as I did. I lifted my head again and looked at Mercy. Her eyes were closed but quickly opened.

'Don't stop.' She sighed.

I kissed her again. A lingering, sensual kiss. I could feel the passion rise inside me. I wanted to caress her. Feel her. Make love to her. I was sure that Mercy felt the same way, but I needed to talk to her now about what I was planning to do about the situation I found myself facing concerning her father. There was a time and a place for everything.

'What's wrong, William?' Mercy asked as I eased myself back to lie next to her again. 'Don't you want me? Have I done something wrong?'

'There's nothing wrong, sweet Mercy – I do so want you – and you have done nothing wrong,' I whispered. 'It's me.' I put my arm under her head and pulled her gently towards me. 'It's the position your father has placed us in – there's so much to do and so little time left to do it.'

'You have a plan?'

'Yes. But it will involve you placing a great deal of trust in me.'

'But… you know I will. Just tell me what I must do.'

I looked at Mercy, smiled and began to weave my web. 'I will arrange with your father to meet him at his office… where I will tell him that I accept his offer—'

'You'll do what—' Mercy pulled away from me, a look of horror on her face.

I kissed her on the top of her head. 'I said that you would need to trust me, Mercy… I will enter into the agreement your father wants me to. I will agree to give you up – to have nothing more to do with you. I will buy my notes from him and then leave to go to Scotland and prepare to put the next part of the plan into action.'

'What will that be?'

I stood up. 'I still have things I need to sort out and people to see, but as I said, trust me. I will find a way to convince your father he does not need to harbour any concerns about me. So, let's walk on further and enjoy the rest of today.' I helped Mercy to her feet and took her arm as we set off again. 'I will write to you while I am in Scotland – via Mrs Poole. I will use code whenever necessary – a code I'll explain as we walk on. I will travel down to see you as often as I can, hopefully at Mrs Poole's house if she'll permit it.'

NINETEEN

Returning to Scotland was a blessing in at least a couple of ways. Firstly, it allowed me to be with my mother, whose health had taken a turn for the worse of late. Secondly, it offered time for me to develop a plan to settle my score with Grundy or, more specifically, a plan to kill him – for that is what I intended to do.

That plan had been triggered as I walked to have lunch with my brother at his club when I was confronted by a man who handed me a leaflet intriguingly entitled "The Famous Love-Drops".

My usual reaction would generally have been to either hand it straight back to the man or jettison it in the street, but on this occasion, I stopped and read it.

Any man in love with a woman, and she won't return it, let him come to me, and I'll make her glad of him. Only giving her a few drops of this love philtre will make her feel she can't rest without him. So likewise, if a woman is in love with a young man, and he won't comply, let her give him a little of this liquor of love, and he will not be able to rest without her.

The words "love philtre" brought to mind my study of the book *Metamorphoses* by Apuleius and the story of a woman with a reputation for being able to do whatever she liked with the help of charms and drugs. She was hired to reanimate a baker's love for his unfaithful wife and did so, I assumed, by using love potions.

I also remembered that old women who dealt in abortifacients sold love philtres in imperial Rome – and that people used such potions so frequently that the authorities eventually promulgated a decree declaring them poisonous. The first piece of a jigsaw puzzle fell into place.

As I sat in my mother's house with the advertisement spread out on a desk in front of me, I began to devise a plan.

Love… hate… there is very little to choose between them after all. Using a deadly "love philtre" to eliminate Grundy has a somewhat ironic appeal.

I decided, therefore, that, as a first step, I would manufacture my own philtre – one comprising of some form of deadly poison; in truth, a "hate philtre".

But what poison should I use?

It soon became evident to me that my only choice was arsenic. It had many attractions: it was readily available; it was tasteless, making it easy to add to food without arousing suspicion. Further, arsenic poisoning was very difficult to detect when administered in small doses over a long period. Its symptoms – gastrointestinal pain, diarrhoea, vomiting and dehydration – mimic many common ailments, often leading a casual observer to believe that an elderly victim was growing sicker for no other reason than age.

I have the method, but someone else must administer the philtre.

It would always be the case that I would not be able to dispense any poison to Grundy personally. Not that I would want to. I had no wish to place myself as the focal point of suspicion – let alone get caught doing or having done so.

Mercy was the obvious means to feed the arsenic to her father on my behalf. If he died, no one would ever suspect such a loving daughter as her of playing any part in his death, let alone think she could commit parricide. Further, Grundy had such absolute faith and trust in her that he would never question what she was feeding him.

How is Mercy going to administer the arsenic?

I was aware that, whilst arsenic was easily ground into a powder, it was not soluble. It would, therefore, need to be disguised somehow. It certainly needed to be administered to Grundy gradually and in a way that would not arouse any suspicion on Mercy's part that I was using her to kill her father.

At that moment, my mother invited me to join her in her parlour for a dish of tea. As I entered the room and passed the tea table, I noticed a small, cone-shaped sugar loaf on a salver and a pair of silver sugar nips beside it. As I did, the final piece of my plan fell into place.

All that remained for me to do to put my plan into action was to think of a scheme to dupe Mercy into drip-feeding arsenic to her father. After that, a trip to London to meet up with Mercy would be in the offing.

*

It was a humid day. Heavy, dark clouds dominated the sky, but at least it was dry as Mercy and I set off from my brother's London house on a walk around Portman Square. I explained my plan as we walked.

'My dearest Mercy,' I said. 'I think I may have discovered the way and the means to change your papa's feelings towards me – to allay his mistrust of me – to see that I am not as black as he paints me.'

Mercy looked at me, her bright face looking brighter still. 'Have you?' she ejaculated. 'But how?'

Mercy was excited and showed it in the flush of her cheek, the twinkle in her eyes and the energy of her tone. I chuckled inwardly at her reaction.

'Well,' I began. 'I promise that what I am about to say is no lie... but I must warn you that you will find it incredible.' Then, without further delay, I began to explain my revelation to Mercy. 'You will recall that in Shakespeare's *A Midsummer Night's Dream*, Oberon asks Puck to find a magical flower which expels a juice that can be placed on a person's eyelids while they sleep so that when they wake, they will fall deeply in love with the first living creature they see.'

'Yes... but what has this to do with us?' Mercy asked.

'It is often the case that fictional accounts have a factual basis,' I returned. 'As with Shakespeare, so here. While in Edinburgh, I was told the whereabouts of a particularly skilled, cunning woman—'

'By "*cunning woman*", do you mean a witch?' Mercy interrupted, unable to hide a shade of scepticism in her voice.

If I am honest, hers was not an altogether unexpected reaction. I turned towards her and took her hand. 'Yes, but not in the way you might think.'

Mercy looked at me quizzically, seemingly at a loss for words. 'So, what happened next, William?' she eventually asked, barely above a whisper.

I smiled at Mercy before spinning a yarn so convincingly that *I* almost believed it. If nothing else, I am a skilled and accomplished liar, especially when my audience is as naïve and gullible as Mercy.

'Picture this... I entered a rather gloomy, small cottage with white painted walls and a low, beamed ceiling. The only light in the room came from a heavily smeared, almost opaque window, a fire burning low in the grate and a flickering candle on a much-used kitchen table. The cunning woman sat in front of the table. It wasn't easy to ascertain her age. She could have been forty; she could have been seventy. She wore a grey shawl over her shoulders and arms, covering a dark grey dress and a white lace stomacher. Long, straggly strands of grey hair hung loosely on either side of her face, emerging from under a white cap, on top of which she wore a floppy, black hat.'

'Oh, William,' Mercy gasped. 'She sounds terrifying. Weren't you afraid?'

'No, Mercy,' I replied, smiling at her. 'Not at all.'

'I'm sorry, William. Forgive my interruption. Please continue.'

'I could make out a line of four large tarot cards that ran from near the top to the middle of the table. To the side of this line were a tattered, red, heart-shaped cushion and a crystal ball. A dark dresser stood along the wall to the right of the table. A variety of bottles were sitting on each of its shelves, some green, some blue, others clear, some full, some partly full, some empty. A pestle and mortar rested on the dresser itself. "Good morning," I said to her. "I am told that you can help me." I then told her about you and how your father had favoured our relationship initially but had now turned his face against it. I said that I needed to find a way to restore his original feelings towards a union between us—'

'And was she able to?' Mercy interrupted once more.

At that moment, I realised I had Mercy in my grip – I had taken her in, hook, line and sinker. 'Oh, yes,' I replied, looking straight at Mercy before continuing. '"Sir," the cunning woman said, "you have arrived just in time to receive my help. But unfortunately, in cases like yours, time and tide wait for no man. But have no fear... I can help you... even at so late a stage." She turned to the dresser and removed a green glass jar from the shelf. She opened it and took out what looked like a small lump of chalk. She then ground the chunk in her mortar with her pestle until she had rendered it into a fine, whitish powder. Having done so, she poured the powder onto a sheet of paper before folding the sheet carefully so that none of the powder could spill out, forming a packet. She then handed the packet to me.'

I paused for greater effect, looked at Mercy and then continued. '"This is a love philtre," she said. "If it is administered to the father without his knowledge, you will soon find that his attitude towards you will change for the better – he will start to welcome you at all times with open arms."

'"But how should I administer it?" I asked.

'"Sprinkle it on the father's food," she replied. "It has no taste or smell, so he will be none the wiser. I recommend that the powder is administered secretly, as the father might otherwise suspect *mala fides* and refuse it."

'"What if it doesn't work?" I asked.

'"It may not, of course," she replied. "But have no fear, sir; I am confident it will. I do not usually give any guarantee with my remedies, but, in your case, I am so confident that it will work that I will return your money if you come back and tell me that it has not."'

'What happened next?' asked Mercy before I could say anything else.

'I paid the 3s4d she asked for the powder, bade her farewell and left.'

'William!' Mercy exclaimed. 'That's all too fanciful for words.'

'I can understand your scepticism, sweet Mercy,' I replied, 'but I have tried the powder already. It does work, I can assure you. After a disagreement, I secretly administered some to a friend I had fallen out with. Within days of doing so, all animosity between us after the disagreement disappeared. In the light of this, I have had no cause to claim back my money from the cunning woman.'

'It all seems so very far-fetched to me,' replied Mercy.

'Oh, ye of little faith,' I said, smiling. 'I'll leave the thought with you. I am sure that the powder works – as sure as God made little green apples. But, in the meantime, let us change the subject and continue to enjoy our walk.'

MERCY GRUNDY

TWENTY

It was late afternoon on an unusually windy day before William finally called for me at Mrs Poole's house. I had waited all day for his arrival, growing ever more despondent with each passing moment. Finally, to my great sadness and disappointment, the time had come for William to leave London. He would be returning to Scotland the following morning. I had wanted to spend as much time with him as I possibly could before he left, but what time remained was dwindling at an alarming rate.

Decorum should have dictated otherwise, but I leapt to my feet like an excited child and rushed across the room as Mrs Poole's footman finally ushered William into the parlour. I threw my arms around his neck.

'Where have you been?' I whispered. 'I was beginning to think you were never coming.'

William took my arms and stepped back half a pace before lowering his head slightly and kissing me on my forehead.

'I'm sorry, Mercy, I had planned to be here much earlier, but I had to attend a meeting with my brother that went on much longer than expected.'

We crossed the room, hand in hand, and sat down together. William put an arm around my shoulder; I sighed and rested my head on his chest. We sat there in near silence for the next ten minutes before William suddenly leant forward and turned to look down at me.

'Will you come out and walk with me, Mercy?' he asked softly.

I went out willingly, and William drew my hand through his arm, and we walked for a long while in silence. I knew he had something to say and waited, not knowing what that might be. Then he stopped and turned to look at me.

'Do you still love me?' he asked, his forehead creased, seemingly with worry, and yet his eyes were filled with tenderness.

Slightly flummoxed, I stood there. Mouth slightly open. I was still trying to figure out how to respond. 'Why do you ask?' I replied, drawing up a shallow breath.

'Do you still love me?' William repeated.

'What a question!' I exclaimed, standing there, saying nothing at first. 'Of course, I do… you know I do… I will always love you,' I eventually spluttered, a sense of foreboding passing through me. 'And you… is it still your wish for me to become your wife?'

'Dearest, sweet, Mercy,' William replied, 'you know that nothing could give me greater happiness than to take you for my wife… that I would gladly give everything I possess and hold dear for that to be so. My one regret is that your father has turned against me in the way that he has… forcing us apart.'

'Amen to that,' I whispered, 'but haven't you discovered a way to change Papa's feelings towards you?'

'You mean the love philtre?'

'Yes, William. You seemed so sure that its use offered a way to allay his mistrust of you – to make him realise that you are not the villain he thinks you are.'

William looked at me questioningly. 'Perhaps we could give it a try?' he said.

'If you are sure it will not harm Papa,' I replied softly, trying to mask the uncertainty in my voice.

William looked straight into my eyes. 'Of course, I am sure… I would never dream of hurting him,' William replied. With that, he reached inside his coat and pulled out three small paper packets. 'Try these in the first instance,' he said, handing them to me. 'Mix the contents of one pack into a cup of tea once every other day. As you will see, they will not harm him in any way – on the contrary, you should see a change for the better in his general demeanour insofar as I am concerned. However, if you do not… and you may not, because your father's feelings towards me are so deep-rooted, you may need to administer the love philtre over a more extended period. In such a case, write to me and let me know, and I will send you some more.'

*

I rose from my bed, crossed the room and drew the curtains to witness a glorious sunrise stealing softly into the pure, peaceful sky. I stood there in wonderment for several minutes before going to my washstand, completing my ablutions and then dressing for the day ahead. It had been a fortnight since I had returned to Henley, and William had returned to Scotland. Finally, the time had come to start putting his plan into operation.

I headed downstairs and entered the dining room just as the maid, Susannah Gosswell, brought in the tea set on its silver tray and placed it on the demi-lune tea table.

'Good morning, Miss Mercy,' she said. 'The master is in his study. I'll go and call him.'

'Thank you, and while you do so, I'll pour the master a cup of tea ready for him when he comes for breakfast.'

'Yes, Miss Mercy,' the maid replied. She curtseyed before turning and leaving the room.

As soon as the maid left, I rushed to the tea table. There wasn't much time. I knew Papa would come for breakfast as soon as he was called. I opened one of the packets William had given to me and poured the contents into Papa's favourite dish. I hesitated. I was having second thoughts.

I can't do it… it feels wrong… surely no good can come of it?

But before I could do anything more, Papa entered the room. Left with no choice, I picked up the teapot and filled his dish.

'Ah… a dish of tea,' he said, crossing over to me. 'That's just what I need, Mercy. Thank you.'

He took the dish from me, added some sugar he nipped from the sugar loaf on the adjacent glass scrutore, crossed to the dining table and sat on his chair. He took a large sip of his tea and swallowed before looking at me with a quizzical look on his face.

'This tea tastes different… rather sweeter than usual. Is it our usual blend?'

'Yes, Papa, I'm sure it is. Shall I send for a fresh pot?'

'No, daughter… I wasn't complaining… in fact, I liked it.'

Papa finished his tea and asked me to refill the dish. So, I got up, collected it, went to the tea table and filled it before handing it to Papa. As before he added a nip of sugar.

Papa tasted his tea and looked at me, somewhat astonished. 'Very odd,' he said. 'I can't understand how the last dish of tea I drank could taste so different from this. Had you already added sugar before you poured my tea, perhaps?'

I felt a cold tingle pass down my spine. I felt my insides tighten. I sensed every nerve, cell, muscle, drop of blood and hair individually.

'No, Papa,' I mumbled. Then, to hide my confusion, I hurried from the dining room into the parlour. 'I'm not hungry myself, Papa. I'll leave you to enjoy your breakfast in peace,' I said as I passed Papa. He gave no more than a grunt as I did.

Moments later, I settled myself for a morning's reading in the comfortable window seat of the parlour, which looked out over the garden. I hoped nothing could disturb my enjoyment of the book of poetry Mrs Poole had given me a few days before I left London.

That evening at dinner, it seemed that Papa's previous ill humour had melted away. Once again, he was his old self, at ease, ready to joke with me and, unusually, to talk to me about William, or so I thought.

'I'm sorry, Mercy, I fear I have not made your life as pleasant as I could recently, but I couldn't bear the thought of you wasting your life on someone like Dunbar.'

Momentarily silenced, I looked across at Papa, my mouth open.

'Oh, Papa!' I eventually gasped out. 'Yes... we have become such strangers,' I continued, my voice trailing as I did. 'But that's because you've made me feel that you know so little of me... of what I need... of what I want... and that I wanted a life with William.'

Papa hesitated before he replied, almost as if he was unsure what tone to take, but at last, he reached across the table and placed his hand on mine.

'Not such strangers as you think; rather, such strangeness is more common than you can imagine. But I have not been so blind in this matter as you might believe, Mercy. I promised your mama two things where you are concerned: firstly, that no marriage should be forced upon you and, secondly, no reasonable choice of a husband by you be thwarted. I took to Dunbar the first time I met him, even though he had little or no wealth. I felt that he and you were made for one another, but then came the revelation that he was already married. After that, I tried to let you judge Dunbar for yourself, and I gave him his chance to show he was free to marry you. Alas, to no avail. Ultimately, I was left with no choice. I had to step in to spare you from him. Now, thankfully, Dunbar is gone; the matter is done with… and well done with.' Then, as if Papa was afraid of saying too much, he added hastily, 'Now let us both forget this business as soon as we can.'

I looked back at Papa. Tears were starting to well in my eyes.

'I wish I could, Papa, but I can't.'

Papa stood up and walked slowly round to me.

'Perhaps, my dear,' he said, touching my cheek with as gentle a caress as I had ever received from him. 'But tell me the truth, without any reserve or foolhardiness, are you seriously saying you want Dunbar to come back again?'

I stared at Papa. There was a silence between us for a moment or two.

'Yes, Papa… that is precisely what I am saying.'

Papa gasped before turning away from me and heading for the door. 'Then I fear that there is no hope left for you,' he muttered as he left the room.

I followed Papa out of the room and ran upstairs to my room. I fell on my bed and burst out crying.

I lay there thinking about what had happened during the evening and how Papa's mood had changed dramatically during dinner. One minute he'd seemed so happy; the next, all he showed was anger and resentment. Finally, I concluded that the philtre must have had some effect on Papa initially. That explained why he was so cheerful, to begin with. I also figured that the powder's impact must be accumulative – taking effect over time – which was why William had given me more than one packet.

One dose has been administered – two to go.

*

In all the time since William and I had parted, I had only had one short letter from him – which came via Mrs Poole – telling me of his arrival at his mother's home and saying that he would let me know when I might expect him to return to England. Naturally, this wasn't very pleasant. But, to be fair, he had had no letter from me – an omission I had just corrected, writing to him with good news.

I reported that, by then, I had served Papa his tea three times after adding the love philtre. He had said that the first cup tasted a little odd but made no comment on the two subsequent occasions I prepared it for him. The tea had not harmed Papa in any way, as William had promised. Further, Papa's whole demeanour towards me had changed for the better.

He had been so good-tempered, even though I was almost rude in my attempts to be nothing more than civil towards him for several days. If it wasn't for the fact that Mama was no longer with us, it seemed as if the clock had been turned back to when I was a child – a much-loved and cherished, and some might say, overindulged, child.

Deep down, though, I feared that things with Papa were almost too good to be true. I couldn't help but think that the current state of affairs would end sooner or later. Papa would revert to how he had been before William left, especially since I had told him I wanted William back when he asked me. I knew that my reply would rebound on me sooner or later. My problem was that I had now used the three packets of the philtre William had given to me in London. I would not be prepared when Papa reverted to the type he had become since he first learned of the existence of Ann Macclesfield. I desperately needed William to send me a further supply as soon as he could in case Papa did.

*

As had become my habit of late, I sat in the window seat of the parlour reading – I was now about halfway through *Clarissa: or the History of a Young Lady*. After a while, my eyes wandered from their task and rested abstractedly on the frost-covered tips of the garden shrubs, vaguely visible like pale ghosts in a white mist hovering outside, through which the sun had succeeded in forcing a few struggling beams.

There was a knock on the door, and Papa's footman, Jarman, entered the room.

'Sorry to disturb you, Miss Mercy,' he said. 'There has been a delivery for you. I've had it taken to your room.'

I looked up from my book at Jarman, my curiosity aroused. 'Thank you,' I said. Then, as Jarman turned to leave, a thought struck me. 'Is the master home?'

Jarman stopped and turned to face me. 'No, miss,' he replied. 'The master had to go to Culham Court to meet Mr Stephenson. He's not expected back until this afternoon.'

I heaved a sigh of relief. The delivery could only have come from William, and Jarman would inform Papa of its arrival sooner or later. Inevitably, Papa would go to my room to investigate, and I was afraid that I would reveal the truth in answer to some direct question from him. But, on the other hand, his being away would at least give me time to prepare an explanation for the delivery and answers to any questions I could expect.

I put my book down and hurried upstairs to my room. As I entered, I stopped still in my tracks. Standing proudly against the wall opposite me, I saw a magnificent mahogany low linen press on a cabriole leg stand.

I stood slightly open-mouthed as I admired the press: brass handles on either side, a stepped and dentil moulded cornice above a pair of shaped fielded panel doors below which were two cock-beaded drawers.

I crossed over the room, bent down and turned the key in the lock of one of the doors. Then, with mounting anticipation, I opened the door to see four shelves stacked with linen, beneath which were two drawers. Something resting on top of the first shelf caught my eye. I reached in to find a sheet of paper. I took it out and looked at it.

It's a note – a note from William!

By now, my hands were trembling, and my heart was racing. I drew deep breaths, sat on my bed and read the note.

My dearest Mercy,

Words could not convey my happiness when I received your last letter.

I can scarcely wait until you finally join me in Scotland. My mother also looks forward to seeing you when you come – so much so that she is busily preparing an apartment at her home for your use while you're here.

In the meantime, I am sending you this linen press – a belated Christmas come early birthday gift. I hope you like it.

Look in the right-hand drawer below; a small box is hidden among the contents. You will find a pair of agate earrings I commissioned for you inside this. For sure, you will be the envy of all the most fashionable noble ladies of Edinburgh when you wear them here. You will also find a packet containing powder that should be used to clean the earrings – if you know what I mean.

Affectionately yours

William

P.S. I suggest that if your father or anyone else asks where the press came from, you tell them that Mrs Poole sent it – it had been used

by your dear mama when she stayed in London, and it seemed
fitting that you should have it as a gift.

I was rereading William's note when there was a knock on the door, and Papa walked into my room.

'Jarman tells me you've…' At that moment, he caught sight of the note in my hand. 'What's that you're holding, Mercy?'

'Nothing, Papa,' I lied, secreting away the note as I stood up and glided towards him. 'Look, Papa. I've received a wonderful present – a gift from Mrs Poole. Come and see it.'

'Later, perhaps,' replied Papa, giving nothing more than a cursory glance at the linen press. 'Hmm… very thoughtful of Mrs Poole. Make sure you write immediately to thank her,' was his only comment before he turned and headed back out of the room.

I gave a silent prayer of thanks and rushed to the linen press. I found the box and its contents and hid them and the letter in my escritoire until I needed to use the powder on Papa again.

*

Just before lunch the following day, I saw Papa and Uncle Henry walking together in the garden. Neither appeared to be saying much, but my father looked angry and Uncle Henry apologetic. A turn or two more around the garden seemed to put matters right between them, for my father stopped and held out his hand, simultaneously placing the other on Uncle Henry's shoulder. Then, after facing one another a final time, they came slowly into the house together.

'Your uncle, Henry, will be joining us for lunch today, Mercy,' Papa announced when he and my uncle entered the parlour.

Nothing was said at lunch about what Papa and Uncle

Henry had been discussing in the garden, but not long after Uncle Henry had gone, when Papa and I were in the parlour together, he soon made it clear to me what it was.

'I had an interesting chat with your uncle this morning about Dunbar.'

I tensed.

'A-About William?'

'Yes… Dunbar, and nothing your uncle told me could have ever surprised me.' Papa chuckled. Then, out of the blue, he asked, 'Have you had anything to do with Dunbar recently?'

Not for the first time recently, an icy chill curled up my spine.

'N-No, Papa,' I lied, and how I hated lying to Papa. 'Why do you ask… and what did Uncle Henry tell you?'

Papa could scarcely conceal an outburst of joy as he paused and looked at me long and hard before answering me almost triumphally. 'There is one answer to both questions, Mercy, dearest – your uncle has recently been in correspondence with an attorney in Edinburgh who informed him that Dunbar has lost his appeal against the decision of the Commissary Court that he and Ann Macclesfield are man and wife… but that's just the half of it—'

'The half of it?' I interrupted.

There was a wingbeat of silence before Papa gave out a raucous laugh. 'The half of it, yes! Have you any idea of the grounds of appeal put forward by Dunbar?'

'Of course not, Papa,' I replied. 'How could I? Why would I?'

Papa sighed, and his eyes had a faraway look. 'I guess not… since I must believe you when you tell me you have not had anything to do with him recently. Dunbar claimed he had married *you* in April 1744 – a month before the marriage to Ann.'

I raised my eyebrows at Papa in disbelief.

'He did what? Did I hear you right? W-William claimed that… he and I were married?'

Papa's reply was instant and sharp. 'You heard right, and he even supported the claim by producing two documents. Firstly, he produced a register containing the Entries of Marriages in the Fleet Prison and pointed to an entry for a marriage between him and you – performed by a certain Edward Ashwell. Secondly, he produced a certificate purportedly signed by Ashwell himself to confirm the marriage.'

Initially, I was stunned into silence. I couldn't think of anything to say. My mind was a complete whirl of emotions. Astonishment. Shock. Horror. But also, a sense of joy at the lengths William seemed prepared to go to so we could be together.

'So… why… was the appeal lost?' I finally sputtered.

Papa looked at me and laughed again, a laugh that reached his eyes, spreading small lines outwards. He was sadistically enjoying every moment of his account of what had befallen William.

'In short, the Court of Session saw through him and the fraud he was attempting – saw that he was nothing but a base liar. They refused to allow either the register or the certificate into evidence. With nothing else to support the appeal, it was dismissed. Once again, costs were awarded against him, diminishing further any remaining assets Dunbar holds. Don't you see, Mercy, I have always been right about him. He's nothing but a complete fraud. He has no purpose… no money – why… he scarcely has enough to afford the glass of gruel I have for my supper each night. You deserve so much better than Dunbar – or his ilk.'

I folded my arms and clenched my fists. 'Oh, Papa,' I snapped. 'How short-sighted men are compared to women regarding their nearest and dearest. A man's perception is only skin-deep; a woman dives into the heart. In me, you see nothing more than a child… your child… one you cannot bear to share with anyone else. In William, you see the person you will have to share me with… and you despise him for that. In you, I see a man I love and respect… a man I always have and always will… you are my papa. In William, I don't see him for what money he has or doesn't have – I see him as the man I love… the man I want to spend the rest of my life with – whatever you may say or think!'

I had scarcely finished what I was saying when Papa let out an audible gasp. The transformation in his face had to be seen to be believed. His expression was now one of helplessness; the lustre of life seemed to have faded beyond recall, and the look in his eyes was despair as he looked first at, and then away from, me.

'In Dunbar, you see the *man you love… the man you want to spend the rest of your life with?*' he hissed.

'Yes, Papa.'

'Then there is no hope for you. Is there?'

Then, and not for the first time after we had discussed William, Papa stormed off and headed for his study. Sobbing, I rushed up to my room and wrote a letter to William, thanking him from the bottom of my heart for the linen press and telling him as near verbatim as possible about my argument with Papa. I stopped after each sentence, as if doubting whether to say more or less. After finishing, I read my letter twice before folding and sealing it, ready to be sent to William in the morning.

In the days that followed, I saw little or nothing of Papa. He tried to avoid me at all costs. When he couldn't, he snubbed me. His days were spent in his office, his evenings at the coffee house or the Lion or the Bell, where he would smoke and drink whisky with his friends. Invariably, he was in a foul mood when he came home – towards both the servants and me. My thoughts turned to the powder William had sent me in the linen press and of giving some to Papa.

*

Several days later, I rose early. After washing and dressing, I went to my escritoire, retrieved the box that William had sent me, opened it and stood looking at its contents.

How much powder do I need?

Thinking I should err on the side of caution, I took a farthing coin and scooped a small amount onto a sheet of paper. I folded the paper carefully to form a packet before going to the dining room, carrying it tightly in my hand. As usual, Susannah had placed the tea set on its silver tray on the tea table, and as she was not in the room, I assumed she had gone to call Papa.

I had only a little time to do what I had to. I quickly unfolded the paper and sprinkled the powder into Papa's dish before pouring tea into it. To my horror, the powder floated on the surface of the tea. I picked up a teaspoon and stirred vigorously – to no avail. At that moment, Papa walked into the room. I was in a state of near panic – there was no way I could hand the dish of tea to Papa.

What can I do? What can I say?

'Is that my tea you have there, daughter?'

'S-Sit down, Papa,' I croaked. 'I… I'll bring it over to you.'

My hand was shaking. I was in danger of dropping the dish. Perhaps it might be best if I did, but the dish was Papa's favourite. It was the only one he would use. Hoping that Papa would not see me, I quickly poured the contents of his dish into another one sitting on the tea table and refilled it. There was nothing else I could do. I took Papa's dish to him, leaving the other on the tea table.

Papa and I sat in near silence while we ate breakfast. The sole topic of conversation between us was a brief exchange about the weather. Papa thought we were facing the prospect of a cold, wet day, and I could not disagree with him. Susannah came and went on occasion as Papa and I ate, serving us and clearing the table when we had finished. What I failed to see, though, was that she had cleared away the dish of tea I had left on the tea table, and I gave it no further thought until it eventually came back to haunt me.

*

I sat down at my escritoire and picked up my white cylindrical china ink pot with its double walls, the outer wall pierced with perforations in the shape of the four different symbols of a pack of cards. Holding the ink pot firmly, I unscrewed the tapering cylindrical lid with its rounded end and took out the quill it contained. It was immediately apparent that it had seen better days.

Muttering, I opened a drawer and took out a new quill. Having done so, I reached for my quill cutter in its shagreen-covered case. I took the cutter from the case and inserted the quill in the aperture in its base until it protruded from the U-shaped aperture at the rear and then cut a nib by operating the cutter's key and screw.

I took a sheet of paper and readied myself. I picked up the quill twice and twice put it down again. I just wasn't sure what to say. I went to the window and looked out, trying to clear my head. I returned to my escritoire, sat down, picked up the quill for a third time, dipped it in the ink and took it out. Again, the quill was poised in mid-air. A further brief pause for thought; then I began to write.

Once I had, the words flowed across the page. Line by line, I recounted the violent disagreement Papa and I had had and his seeming never-ending ill humour; how all I could hope for was that Papa would have a change of heart and welcome a union between William and me. I was almost at my wit's end. I had tried to administer the powder I'd received so that it could work its magic on Papa but had to abandon my attempt when it floated on the surface and would not mix into his tea. I closed by telling William how desperately I needed his advice on what I should do next.

Before I knew it, I had filled the page. All I could do was fold the paper carefully, seal and address it, send it off to William and await his reply.

*

Several days passed, giving me plenty of time for all the pleasures and torments of expectation as I waited impatiently for William's answer, which would be sent to me via Mrs Dawes at the Red Lion Inn. She would get her maid to bring it to me once she received it.

Then, finally, Mrs Dawes' maid delivered the letter late in the afternoon. It arrived less than five minutes before Papa returned from his office. As I had done before, I secreted the letter away before sitting through an excruciatingly long dinner time with it concealed unopened until I could go up to my room and read it.

My dearest,

I cannot tell you how happy I was to receive your letter, but I was sad to read about your father's continued attitude towards us. I only wish that I could speak to you face to face about that, tell you how much I love you and discuss the other matters so dear to us both.

Sadly, I cannot do any of these for reasons we know only too well. So, I have written you a poem which, for now, must suffice.

Mercy, please understand the passions I now convey herein,
Infinite, neverendingly, genuine,

Real, undying, eternal love
Mercy, I shout out to the stars above
The hope from deep within my heart,
That when we're one, we'll never part.

Affectionately yours

William

I put the letter down and smiled. I now knew what I had to do, and clearly, my written account of my disagreement with Papa of a short while ago had resonated with him.

TWENTY-ONE

Now silent and motionless, I sat with my eyes shut tightly, experiencing a lacuna of sensation that followed a series of outbursts of sobbing and recrimination which had swept over me one after the other. I was in a state of *la mort dans l'âme* – one of total disheartenment – a wholly alien state of mind for me.

After what seemed an eternity, I opend my eyes and stared up at the ceiling, trying to process in my mind what had happened. As I did, a deep hatred for Papa consumed me, filling the lacuna. He and I had had our disagreements before, but none on the scale of the one we'd had during dinner not an hour ago and none so hurtful to me.

With heightened anger and flashing eyes, Papa had ranted about how I had gone my own way, my own headstrong, foolish way, and I had ruined myself. I had turned my back on everything my loving parents had offered me, everything my loving father continued to provide me with. My cheap attitude towards life of late had rendered me a worthless, ungrateful daughter who was in danger of making herself the laughing stock of her friends, her family and any members of respectable society who knew her. I was wasting myself on a man whose moral attributes were only less attractive than his physical imperfections. A man who possessed many characteristics of the serpent. Someone who may have gone to hell and been mistaken for the devil.

Papa saved his worst until last – his parting shot. I had caused Mama's death.

With Papa's accusation ringing in my ears, I remained sitting at my escritoire, my head now in my hands, weeping silently – consumed by a strain of suppressed anger and contempt. I might have been able to pity Papa, but I could never forgive him for what he had said.

I eventually stood up, wandered to the window and stared out. A silent drama was unfolding outside. The evening was a strange. Now and again, torn and ragged clouds swept across the setting sun. A storm was on the horizon. The wind rattled the window, and the top branches of the trees in the garden thrashed angrily. But neither wind nor storm mattered to me at that moment.

I returned to my escritoire, took out William's letter and reread it for the umpteenth time. If there was ever a time to use the powder he had sent me, this was it. I put the letter back, retrieved the box of powder, took a pinch and, as I had done previously, placed this onto a sheet of paper. I folded the paper, wrapped it in a handkerchief and put it inside the linen press. Afterwards, I readied myself for bed.

In the end, I got very little sleep that night. Occasionally, I awoke from a shallow sleep engulfed either in momentary panic, my heart thudding inside me, or in a state of near euphoric excitement. On top of all that, the wind blew in great gusts while rain pounded the window panes like an almost continuous drum roll.

In the event I overslept, waking up in mid-morning. By then, the storm that had raged through the night had passed to wherever it was eventually headed. The clouds had ceased to pour out their flood, and shafts of sunlight now streamed through the gaps that had appeared between them. The sound of the rain hammering on the window had given way to birdsong. There was a sweetness in the air but bitterness in my heart.

That day, and for the first time, I surreptitiously emptied powder into the pan of water gruel that Susannah had prepared for Papa's supper, which she had placed in the pantry, ready for him.

*

I spent the next week waiting for the right moment each day to go into the parlour and stir some of the powder William had sent me into the gruel that would be taken up to Papa for his supper that evening. On one occasion, though, I had a narrow escape from being discovered. I entered the kitchen, with its massive hearth, stone flag floor, expertly crafted cupboards with glass-fronted doors and the large wooden table in the centre. There was no sign of Susannah, so I headed into the pantry. I found the pan containing the water gruel, picked it up, placed it on a small table and removed the lid. Just at that moment, Susannah entered the pantry.

'Can I help you, Miss Mercy?' she asked.

My head whipped around. I put my hand up to my mouth.

'Y-Yes, Susannah,' I gasped, my mind racing. 'I've… I've just…' I spluttered before regaining my composure. 'I've just tried some of the gruel in this pan. It tasted stale. Please dispose of what's left immediately and make some more.'

A look of surprise, perhaps even of disbelief, crossed Susannah's face.

'But I only made the gruel yesterday – as you will know, Miss Mercy. I took the master his usual half-pint mug of water gruel last evening. He ate a little while I was with him, but he didn't indicate in any way that there was anything wrong with what he'd eaten.'

'That's rather odd,' I said. 'I don't doubt that what I just tasted was stale. You say that the master "ate a little" yesterday... did he finish the gruel?'

'No, Miss Mercy. He ate about half of the gruel. After that, he told me he wasn't hungry, so I returned to the kitchen with the mug.'

'Then perhaps the master was just being polite – I'll check with him later. In the meantime, please comply with my request.'

'Yes, Miss Mercy. I will do as you say. Once done, I'll leave the newly prepared gruel in the pantry ready for this evening and tomorrow.'

'Thank you, Susannah.' I turned to leave the kitchen, stopping as I reached the door. 'Oh, by the way, how's Alice Eden? She's well on the road to recovery by now, I hope.'

'Yes, Miss Mercy. She's so much better now. Dr Hetherington went to see her. He said he thought she had suffered a bout of colic and prescribed some medication, which seems to have done the trick. She hopes to return to work in two days. I'm going to see her later this afternoon.'

'That's good to hear, Susannah. Give her my best wishes when you do see her.'

With that, I returned to my room, where I heaved a sigh of relief and took my handkerchief and the packet of powder from my sleeve. I hid them beneath my underwear on the top shelf of the linen press, ready to take down to the pantry again, hopefully, the following day.

*

Papa's half-pint mug of gruel was routinely taken up to him for his supper every evening. I waited every day, expecting the powder to work its magic. But it did not. On the contrary, Papa became even more ill-tempered – towards the servants and me equally.

On top of that, he complained of heartburn and intermittent stomach cramps, which aggravated his general demeanour.

I was almost at my wit's end. I couldn't understand why Papa's attitude towards me had shown no improvement – not even if any such improvement had been temporary, like that which had been evident the first time I had administered the powder to him. I needed help and advice.

If only William were here with me!

However, despite my wish, I knew William and I could not be together – for now, at least. The only way I could currently reach out to him was by letter. So, I went up to my room and again put pen to paper.

Dear William,

I hope and trust that you are keeping well.

I am worried and need your help and advice. I have tried to do as you directed in your previous letters to me but to little avail.

The first time I used the powder to clean the earrings in the manner you detailed in your last letter to me, they positively gleamed. However, since then, the powder has not had the same effect. The earrings scarcely shine; they certainly do not gleam.

Perhaps, you might be able to suggest how I might better use the powder in future and so put a smile on my face once more.

Adieu, for now, my dearest. I pray to God to keep us healthy until we can be together again – in true happiness.

Yours affectionately

Mercy

The days passed after I had sent my letter off to William. Oh, how I hated the fact that we were so far apart, hated the delay there would inevitably be between sending a letter and receiving a reply. Oh, how I knew of the pleasures and torments of expectation that I would face until I received William's answer. But finally, the day arrived when Mrs Dawes' maid delivered the reply.

My dearest,

Thank you from the bottom of my heart for your recent letter.

I was saddened to read that the powder did not work as we had hoped.

My greatest wish is that I could be with you now and – yes – to put a smile on your face once more – for when you smile, you light up my heart, dearest Mercy, and divinely deliver my own rich expectation.

Mercy, saying the words "I love you" could never be enough. I need to reach out my arms to hold and protect you – exactly as I will, my dearest love, when we are together once again.

Yours as ever

William

*

Fate intervened just a couple of days before I received William's letter. Susannah was unexpectedly taken ill. She suffered the same heartburn and intermittent stomach cramps that had afflicted Papa and Alice Eden before him. Susannah also experienced bouts of vomiting.

Mr Horton, the apothecary, was sent for. He diagnosed Susannah as also suffering from colic and prescribed various medications for her. He also recommended that she be confined to her bed until she recovered. Susannah protested at first, but I insisted that she follow the recommendation.

With Susannah bedbound, I could take sole responsibility for preparing and delivering Papa's evening gruel until she was well enough to resume that duty. This was an optimal opportunity to administer the powder to Papa without fear of detection.

I took that opportunity the day after receiving William's letter as I took sole charge of the kitchen. I put a large handful of oatmeal into a pan, added one and a quarter teaspoons of salt and then poured a pint of water over it. I then put the pan aside to allow the oatmeal and salt to soak while I went for a walk along the riverbank.

When I returned several hours later, I stirred the contents of the pan before heating them gently until they boiled. I allowed them to cool a little before bringing them to the boil again. I repeated this process two more times before allowing the contents to cool. I then strained the pan's contents through a sieve, half into one pan and half into another. I stirred a quarter of a teaspoon of powder into each pan, together with a little sliced nutmeg. I then covered one of the pans with a cloth and took it into the pantry, ready for Papa's supper the following day.

After that, I returned to the kitchen, added a knob of butter to the liquid in the other pan and stirred the contents briskly until the butter had melted. Then, as a final touch, I heated the pan until it just started to boil again, took it from the heat, gave the mixture a final stir and poured it into Papa's mug before making my way up to his room with it.

I pushed the door open and went in. Papa lay back in his armchair sleeping; the muscles of his face had fallen strangely, and the lines and shadows deepened: he looked ancient.

'Papa,' I called gently. 'I've brought your evening gruel.' There was no immediate response, so I crossed over to Papa and kissed him on his forehead. 'Papa, I've brought your evening gruel,' I repeated.

Papa grunted. He slowly opened his eyes and looked up at me. He sat up in the chair, the flicker of a smile passing his lips. 'Sorry, Mercy. I must have dozed off.'

I handed Papa his mug of gruel. He took the mug from me and took a sip. Then a mouthful. He swallowed and drank some more gruel.

'Ugh!' he cried out, grimacing as he did.

'Is something wrong?' I asked.

'I'm not sure about this gruel,' he replied. 'It feels a little gritty, and my throat suddenly feels on fire.'

'Here, let me look,' I replied. 'I can't think what can be wrong – I've only just made the gruel.'

Papa handed me the mug. My heart was racing. Perhaps I needed to be more careful when I added the powder while preparing the gruel.

I dipped my index finger into the mug, removed it again and rubbed my thumb against it.

'It doesn't feel gritty to me, Papa.' I put my finger in my mouth and brushed my tongue over it. Then I took the finger out of my mouth and swallowed. 'And the gruel does not affect my mouth or throat,' I reported. 'I don't think anything is wrong with the gruel... but would you like me to get you some fresh gruel, just in case?'

'Yes, please, Mercy... if it's not too much trouble,' Papa replied.

I took Papa's mug and hurried down to the kitchen. Once there, I emptied the mug's contents and quickly heated the gruel I had set aside for the following day, adding butter before I did. When I had done this, and as a precautionary measure, I stirred in a nip of sugar I powdered in a mortar. I also added a little rose water. Then I refilled Papa's mug and returned to his room.

'Here, Papa,' I said as I handed him the mug. 'Hopefully, this is better.'

Papa smiled. 'Thank you, dear Mercy.'

He took a sip. Then he swallowed a mouthful. 'That's much better,' he said.

He quickly drank the remaining gruel before handing the mug back to me.

'Not gritty this time, I hope,' I said.

'No, Mercy… as smooth as it usually is.'

'And your throat?'

'It's just fine, Mercy… stop worrying.'

'I'll leave you in peace then, Papa,' I said, feeling like a weight had been lifted off me. 'I'll just tidy things up in the kitchen and then get off to bed.' I leant down and kissed Papa on the cheek. 'Goodnight and God bless you,' I whispered.

TWENTY-TWO

I was up and dressed early. This was partly in case Susannah was still not well enough to return to her duties. In part also, it was to ensure that, if she had returned to work, it would be me, not her, who roused Papa that morning. I needed to ensure that he had suffered no ill effect from the gruel he had drunk the previous evening, especially since he had complained of a burning sensation in his throat after his first few mouthfuls from the first mug I had given to him.

In the event, Susannah was away from the kitchen when I went in. The sole occupants were a by now fully recovered Alice Eden, the scullery maid, who had already laid the breakfast table, and Betty Warfield, the kitchen maid, preparing breakfast. Betty told me Susannah was still indisposed but hoped to be well enough to return to work in a day or two.

As soon as breakfast was ready, I went upstairs and tapped at Papa's door. He had not come down yet, which was somewhat unusual.

'Breakfast's ready, Papa,' I called out and tapped again more loudly, as there had been no response. *He must still be asleep*, I told myself. But when I knocked even louder with no reply, I began to grow anxious and, softly opening the door, I peeped in.

Papa was lying on the bed, and at first glance, I thought he was asleep, but when I drew nearer, I saw that his eyes were open and that he was looking at me intently and, as I thought, imploringly.

'Breakfast's ready, Papa,' I chirped. 'You've overslept. I've knocked on your door three times.'

There was still no reply. Papa lay there silent and speechless, with nothing to show that he was conscious of my presence except the piteous expression of fear and dumb entreaty in his eyes. I was becoming increasingly alarmed. I raised Papa's head and spoke to him repeatedly, begging him to answer me. Finally, when none of my efforts to rouse him were successful, I laid him back gently on the pillow and rushed downstairs into the kitchen.

'The master's unwell,' I called to Betty. 'I'm going to fetch Mr Horton. Go and sit with the master and make sure no harm comes to him until I return.'

I ran to Horton's house and knocked hard on the door.

'Oh, Mr Horton!' I cried as soon as he answered. 'Come back with me! Papa's been taken ill. I can't make out what ails him. He won't move or speak and doesn't seem to take in anything I do.'

Horton went back into the house, appearing moments later with his bag. We hurried back home and up the stairs to Papa's room. Betty stood up as we entered.

'The master's not moved or spoken all the time I've been here,' she reported. 'He just lies there staring upwards, making no sound.'

'We'll take it from here. You go back to the kitchen and attend to your duties.'

With that, Betty left the room. Mr Horton put his bag down by the door, moved over to Papa's bed and began to examine him. I went round to the other side of the bed.

Almost as soon as Horton began his examination, Papa emerged from his apparent trance. When prompted, he slowly recounted to Mr Horton how, throughout the night, he had suffered intermittent pain in his stomach, ongoing nausea without being physically sick and a burning sensation in his mouth and throat. Occasionally, he had also experienced the feeling of floating outside his body, looking down at himself. Throughout, Mr Horton listened attentively to what Papa told him.

When he had finished the examination, Mr Horton stood up, went over to his bag, picked it up and returned to Papa's bed. He sat down with the bag on his lap.

'Just a couple more questions, Mr Grundy,' he said. 'You told me you were not physically sick during the night but experienced stomach pains… did you suffer from diarrhoea?'

'No.'

'Have you eaten anything that could have disagreed with you?'

'Nothing I know of… except perhaps the pea soup I had at dinner. Among other things, it contained herring and anchovies. Perhaps the fish might have been tainted.'

'Perhaps. Well, thank you, Mr Grundy,' replied Horton as he looked down at his bag and opened it. 'On reflection, it seems you have been afflicted by a bout of colic – similar to that suffered by your maids Susannah Gosswell and Alice Eden but a little more severe.' Horton took out a small packet and handed it across to me. 'Here is some powder that should help Mr Grundy,' he continued. 'Give your father one-third of this when I leave. Give him another one-third tonight and the final one-third in the morning. Stir the powder into a glass of water on each occasion. I will return with some more when I call again tomorrow to check on your father.'

With that, Horton closed his bag and stood up. 'I'll take my leave now, Mr Grundy,' he said, looking at Papa. 'I hope you are much better when I return tomorrow morning.'

'I'll see you out, Mr Horton,' I said, standing up before leading him downstairs.

Mr Horton and I descended the stairs and went to the front door. I paused and turned to look at him.

'Do you think that my father is in any danger?' I asked.

'No, I don't think he is in any danger, Miss Grundy,' he replied reassuringly. 'As I said upstairs, I think your father has suffered no more than a bout of colic, but I could be wrong. The medication I have left should do the trick, but if it does not, or if your father takes a turn for the worse between now and when I return tomorrow, I suggest that you send immediately for Dr Hetherington.'

'Thank you, Mr Horton,' I replied before opening the door. 'I'll go back and give my father the first dose of the medication.'

Mr Horton looked at me and smiled. 'Hopefully, all will be well again after you do, Miss Grundy. Until tomorrow then,' he said before leaving me.

'Until tomorrow,' I replied.

I shut the door as soon as Mr Horton left, went into the kitchen, collected a glass of water and a teaspoon and headed back to Papa's room. I opened the door and went in. I put the glass down, picked up the packet of medication and poured an estimated third of the contents into the glass, stirring the water as I did. Once I had done that, I went over to Papa, helped him sit up, returned to the glass and picked it up.

'Here,' I said as I handed the glass to Papa. 'Drink this. Hopefully, it'll do the trick.'

Papa took the glass and emptied the contents. He handed the glass back to me with a grimace and lay back down again. 'That medicine was foul… hopefully a case of the worse the taste, the better the cure.'

'Let's hope so, Papa,' I replied, chuckling, 'for I fear you have a further dose of the medicine you must take this evening and yet another tomorrow morning before Mr Horton returns. Now, would you care for some breakfast? Some hot buttered buns, perhaps?'

'I must confess I don't think I could face anything except a dish of tea and a single slice of toasted bread.'

'Buttered toast?'

'Yes, please, Mercy… but only lightly buttered.'

Papa spent the day in his room – a quiet and restful day, mostly in his bed. At midday, I took his lunch to him – boiled pigeon – which he ate with relish. More importantly, he suffered no ill effects afterwards. As for me, I spent the day busying myself about the house in the morning and in the garden during the afternoon. While in the garden, I cut some flowers, which I took to the churchyard that evening and placed on Mama's grave. As I did, there were the loveliest colours in the sky, and sweeping across the river, a soft and fragrant wind blew my hair about my eyes. All seemed well with the world.

Papa was in good spirits when I took his dinner up to him – even when he took the second dose of medication – but was not desperately hungry. All he wanted was some beef broth with a buttered crust of bread, washed down with a dish of his favourite tea: Bohea.

After Papa had eaten, I cleared away the crockery and tidied up the bedroom generally. Once that was done, I straightened Papa's bed linen. I had almost forgotten how good it felt to be with him – caring for him – we had been at crossed purposes for too long. And I wanted to do more for him.

'Would you like me to read to you, Papa?' I asked.

'I would like that very much, Mercy,' he replied, his eyes sparkling. 'Your uncle, Henry, has sent me a book I haven't started yet… but I should have by now. He's bound to ask me my opinion of it when I see him next. It's in my study… on my desk… James Hervey's *Meditations and Contemplations*.'

'I'll go down and fetch it,' I said eagerly.

I went to the study, found the book and took it upstairs. I drew a chair next to Papa's bed, sat down and began reading. However, before I had finished a second page, Papa had fallen asleep. So, I put the book on the bed and just sat looking at him. He looked so peaceful. But, before I knew it, I also fell asleep.

Papa's voice eventually roused me. I looked up at him, at first through flickering eyes. Then, as he came into focus, I could see him lying there with pitying tenderness in his eyes.

'Poor Mercy,' he said softly. His tender tone and the fatherly love shining so unmissably in his eyes caused me to break down. My lip began to tremble, and, hiding my face in my hands, I burst into tears. 'Don't cry, Mercy. Don't cry,' pleaded Papa with a strange little quiver in his voice. 'I can't bear to see you cry.' He took my hand and squeezed it gently. I raised my face and wiped my eyes.

My thoughts flew to the powder I had given to Papa, more convinced than ever that it was beginning to have a beneficial effect on Papa'.

*

As often seems to be the case in the summer months, when we cannot sleep because there is so little night, I awoke very early. Sunshine was streaming through the open curtains in my bedroom, flooding it with dancing, golden dust. The light rested in soft, yellow shafts upon the wall. Outside, nature had been stimulated by the return of daylight. The revival of stirring life and multitudinous sounds heralded a glorious morning led by a chorus of chattering thrushes seemingly trying to compete with equally vocal blackbirds. In the background, I imagined I heard the persistent tenor of a cuckoo in search of ultimately luckless host parents for a single offspring.

However early it might have been, I could not lie in bed a moment longer; the only thing I could do was get up and go for a walk around the garden. And the day was going to get even better.

Glad of life for the first time in a long while, I returned to the house an hour or so later. To my delight, I was met by Papa as he was about to go into the dining room. He beamed a smile at me; he looked rested and healthier than I had seen him in a long time, and his frame of mind had changed very much for the better.

'There's only so long a man can stay in his bed... especially when he's as hungry as me,' he quipped, taking me by the hand. 'Come, Mercy, let's have breakfast together, assuming you haven't already eaten.'

Papa and I went into the dining room together and sat down. Betty Warfield appeared.

'Where's Susannah?' asked Papa.

'She's still indisposed,' replied Betty.

'Obviously, she doesn't have a constitution as strong as mine.' Papa chuckled. 'Tea, please, Betty.'

He then devoured slices of enriched, fruited spice bread and several caraway-seeded buns, served hot and buttered.

'Steady there, Papa,' I finally chided lightly. 'You mustn't overdo things.'

'Don't fret yourself on my part, Mercy,' he replied with a smile. 'A day of nothing but invalid food has left me near starved... oh, and before you produce any more of that medication I took yesterday, I have no further need of it.'

I laughed.

'As you wish, Papa, but you may have to explain not taking a further dose to Mr Horton when he calls later. In the meantime,

I need to organise today's meals. Do you have any special preferences?'

'I'll go to the Sun for my lunch. I have several people I need to see and, as likely as not, they will be there around noon. For this evening: roast chicken and vegetables, with apple pie and then cheese to follow—'

'And for your supper this evening?' I interrupted.

'Some water gruel, please, Mercy,' Papa replied without any pause for thought.

'I could have some beef broth prepared for you if you'd prefer it.'

'No, I'd rather have a mug of gruel.'

'Your wish, dearest Papa, is my command.'

In the event, Mr Horton's visit was unremarkable. He told Papa that he was now sure that he had suffered no more than a short-lived, albeit severe, bout of colic. He left some further medication. 'In case you need it, Mr Grundy.' After that, Mr Horton left; Papa went to his study; and I headed into the kitchen to prepare Papa's evening gruel.

As I had previously, I divided the gruel equally into two pans. I again stirred powder into each pan but half as much again as I had added previously and a little sliced nutmeg. I then covered one of the pans with a cloth and took it into the pantry, ready for Papa's supper the following day. I left the other in the kitchen, ready for me to make the final preparations before serving it to Papa for his supper and convinced that the larger dose of powder I had added would have even greater efficacy than before.

*

I awoke with a start. Someone was hammering on my bedroom door.

'Miss Mercy! Miss Mercy!' a voice cried out. Seconds later, Susannah burst into the room. 'It's the master. He's been taken ill again.'

I shot up from my bed.

'Susannah, you're back,' I mumbled. 'W-What's happened?'

'Miss Mercy... come quickly. I went to the master's study to ask him what he wanted for breakfast, expecting to find him there. When he wasn't, I went up to his room. As I knocked on his door, I could hear him retching terribly. I opened the door and found him writhing on the floor. There was vomit everywhere, and his nightshirt was soiled and bloody. I ran downstairs to fetch Jarman and Betty, and between us, we changed the master's nightshirt and bed linen and lifted him onto his bed. After that, I came to wake you.'

'But why didn't you come straight to me?'

'I feared that seeing the master in the state he was in when I found him would be too distressing for you, miss.'

'That's nonsense, Susannah – you should have come to me immediately... and you know it.'

'I'm sorry, miss—'

'Never mind that now,' I snapped. 'I must go immediately to the master.'

I rushed to Papa's room and stood in the doorway, horrified by what I saw. Papa was grimacing; his breathing was laboured; and his head twisted left and right on the pillow. I could only imagine the pain he was clearly suffering. But then, I remembered the medication Mr Horton had left.

'Susannah,' I called out, 'run downstairs and bring me a glass of water and a teaspoon.'

Moments later, Susannah returned.

I poured medication into the glass and stirred the contents. I then went over to Papa's bed. 'Help me by lifting the master,' I told Susannah.

As soon as she had manoeuvred Papa sufficiently upright, I put the glass to his lips.

'You must drink some of this,' I pleaded.

Papa sipped a little, which he eventually swallowed after some considerable effort. Then, slowly, he emptied the glass, and Susannah eased him back onto the bed.

'I'll stay here with the master, Susannah. You go and send Jarman for Mr Horton while I do.'

The medication seemed to take effect relatively quickly after Papa had taken it, and he was able to describe what he had experienced during the night.

'Everything was fine after I went to bed,' he said, albeit rather weakly. 'I dozed off… but woke up as the day was breaking with violent pains in my stomach. I tried to sit up. As I did, I vomited all down the front of my nightshirt. Moments later, I suffered near uncontrollable diarrhoea. I was lucky enough to get off the bed before I did, but I still soiled myself. I lay on the floor, unable to move and vomiting sporadically until Susannah entered the room.'

Susannah reappeared while Papa was speaking. She had a jug of hot water with her. She poured some into Papa's washbasin and brought it, some soap and a handcloth over to the bed.

'Thank you, Susannah,' I said. 'I'll see to the master. Please fetch some more hot water, get the basin from the guest room and do what you can to clean up this room.'

While Susannah followed my instructions, I did what I could to wash Papa's face, hands and body. Tears were rolling down my face as I did. Papa was in a terrible state. His hair was matted with sick and his private parts with diarrhoea – some of which was spotted with congealed blood.

I had just finished cleaning Papa and changing his nightshirt when Mr Horton arrived. He took one look at Papa and turned towards me, shaking his head as he did.

'There's nothing I am going to be able to do for your father. You need to send for Dr Hetherington immediately.'

*

It was not until the early evening before Dr Hetherington arrived. I took him upstairs to see Papa, who had continued an improvement that had begun when I gave him the medication I had in the morning.

'Good evening, Mr Grundy,' he said as he entered the room. 'I'm sorry to find you unwell.'

'Good evening, Doctor,' Papa replied, smiling weakly. 'Mercy,' he said, turning to me. 'Please help me sit up.'

I moved towards Papa and helped him as he eased himself up. As he did, I pumped up his pillows and used these to support his back and head. I then sat down on the bed, holding Papa's hand.

Dr Hetherington sat in the chair beside the bed and leant in towards Papa. 'I can see that you are not your usual self, Mr Grundy,' he said. 'I understand that you have severe stomach pains. When did this all flare up, and do you know what triggered it?'

Papa swallowed hard. 'The day before yesterday,' he croaked. 'Mercy brought me my usual mug of gruel for my supper. It seemed a little gritty, and my throat felt on fire after I'd drunk some. I told Mercy of this. She took the mug from me and tested the gruel to see if it was gritty. She also tasted a little. "It doesn't feel gritty to me, Papa," she told me. After that, she made me some fresh gruel, which I drank.'

'And how was the fresh gruel?'

'It was as smooth as it usually was – not at all gritty.'

'And your throat?'

'It was fine at the time – no burning sensation at all.'

'And after that?'

'All seemed to settle initially, and I went to bed at my usual time. However, during the night, I woke with intermittent pain in my stomach. I felt like I was about to vomit, but I wasn't actually sick, and I was now experiencing a burning sensation in my mouth and throat. Occasionally, I felt as if I was floating outside my body, looking down at myself.'

'What happened next?'

'I called for Mr Horton,' I chipped in. 'He thought Papa had experienced a bout of colic and left some medication for him to take. I administered a dose after Mr Horton left another that evening. By the time Mr Horton returned yesterday, Papa was back to his normal self. However, he left some more medication just in case Papa suffered a relapse.'

'Presumably, he did?'

'Yes, Doctor. Things got dramatically worse again last night, after I had taken Papa some more gruel—'

'And how was that gruel?' Dr Hetherington interrupted.

'It seemed fine,' Papa answered before I could say anything. 'There was no grittiness when I drank it and no immediate after-effect. I went to bed shortly afterwards and fell asleep almost immediately.'

'And what happened next?'

'During the night, I was wakened by bad pains in my stomach, but unlike the first time, I was violently sick and suffered bouts of diarrhoea. My mouth and throat felt like they were on fire, and the rest of my body felt like someone was sticking me with needles... both internally and externally... and at the same time. After that, I experienced cold sweats, hiccups, extreme restlessness and anxiety.'

'Have you eaten at all since last night?'

'No.'

'Have you taken any liquid?'

'Not really. I tried to drink some water, but it was excruciating to swallow any, even the smallest amount.'

'Has the diarrhoea continued?'

'No.'

'Have you had any bowel movements since the last bout of diarrhoea?'

'Yes, one – it was excruciating, and, to my consternation, my stools were bloody.'

'Let me look at you,' said Dr Hetherington, who then gave Papa a detailed and careful examination.

Once he had finished, he went over to his bag, took out a packet and handed it to me. 'Hopefully, the powder in this packet will alleviate your father's suffering,' he told me. 'He must be given half the powder mixed in some panada immediately and the other half in panada in the morning.'

Dr Hetherington turned to Papa. 'I am concerned about you, Mr Grundy. For that reason, I suggest that I remain here tonight so that I can be on hand if needed – if that can be arranged.'

'Of course, Doctor,' Papa whispered. 'Mercy will make the necessary arrangements.'

'I'll bid you goodnight, then,' said Dr Hetherington. 'Hopefully, you'll not require my services again tonight.'

'Goodnight, Doctor… I hope so also.'

I went over to the door and opened it.

'The guest room is already made up, Doctor,' I said. 'If you follow me, I'll show you to it. After that, I'll instruct Susannah to make some panada for Papa and bring you hot water and soap to wash with and linen to dry yourself.'

We walked down the landing to the guest room. I opened the door. Dr Hetherington started to enter, then stopped.

'Miss Grundy, as I said, I am concerned about your father. His tongue is swollen, and his throat is inflamed and excoriated. His lips, especially the upper one, are dry and rough and are dotted with angry pimples. The inside of his nostrils is in the same condition. His eyes are a little bloodshot but not unduly so. In any event, this is to be expected in the circumstances. His pulse is rather weak and intermittent, and his breathing is irregular. I also am concerned that brown blotches are breaking out on his body. It all seems odd, and one terrible thought has crossed my mind.' He turned towards me. 'Miss Grundy, has your father any enemies... anyone he might have offended either in the past or recently – servants, clients or anyone else?'

'Not to my knowledge,' I replied. 'Papa has always got on well with everyone and vice versa.'

'Thank you, Miss Grundy,' he replied. 'Tell me, have there ever been any previous attacks like the one your father has been experiencing?'

'No. He is given to occasional attacks of colic or heartburn; nothing like this.'

'I ask these questions, Miss Grundy, because I strongly suspect that your father has been poisoned and doubt that it was by accident.'

'But... that's inconceivable... impossible.' I gasped. 'Who would poison Papa, and why would they wish to do so?'

'Miss Grundy,' he said. 'I want you to think long and hard about whether your father has made an enemy of someone who is now seeking revenge. It is possible that that someone is from outside this house, but I think it is more likely to be someone inside it.'

I felt a cold shiver run through me. I was an obvious suspect. Papa had been taken ill twice. He had fallen sick after eating gruel for his supper on both occasions. On both occasions, I had prepared the gruel. He had suffered no adverse effect from the bread and cheese he had eaten for his supper on the day intervening, and Betty had prepared that.

I felt my brain reel and grow dizzy with horror. But I fought against the faintness which threatened to overcome me and managed to retain possession of my faculties. Then, finally, the instinct present in all living creatures began to manifest itself – the instinct of self-preservation.

I will have to take steps to protect myself.

But, first things first, I had to instruct Susannah to make the panada and take it up to Papa and take hot water and linen to Dr Hetherington.

As soon as I had given Susannah her instructions, I hurried to my room. I collected William's two letters concealed in my escritoire and the box containing what little remained of the love philtre and sat on my bed.

What am I to do? I have to destroy the letters, the box and its contents. The only effective way is to burn them, but the only fire in the house is the one in the kitchen, and servants are working there.

Concluding that I had no choice but to burn the box and letters, I returned to the kitchen and crept through the door. I called out Susannah's name as I did, hoping above all hope that she was upstairs carrying out my instructions. There was no reply. I heaved a sigh of relief, went over to the fire and threw the box containing the powder into the grate. I took the coal scuttle, poured a little coal over the box and placed the letters on top before adding more coal. Having done that, I scurried back towards the kitchen door. Susannah suddenly appeared from the direction of the pantry. Shocked, I gave out an incomprehensible shriek.

'Are you all right, Miss Mercy?' Susannah asked.

'Y-Yes… you nearly scared the life out of me,' I gasped before running out of the kitchen to my room. In my hurry, I forgot all about the pan of gruel I had placed in the pantry the previous afternoon.

*

I sat up with Papa throughout the night. I've never before felt so powerless. In the flickering candlelight, I watched as Papa lay groaning, faintly at first but becoming increasingly loud with each passing hour. He turned his head from side to side with a gentle movement full of agony while constantly opening his mouth as if trying to say something but uttering no words. His shoulders shuddered. He grew as white as the sheets held between his clenched fingers. Lines of sweat streamed down his face. Finally, as dawn broke, he began to vomit blood, and my nostrils filled with the stench of diarrhoea. I uttered a sharp gasp and rose from my chair, terror-stricken.

I rushed to the door of the guest room and knocked loudly.

'Dr Hetherington,' I sobbed, 'I fear that Papa is dying.'

There was a momentary silence before Dr Hetherington responded.

'I'll be with you presently,' he called out just as I was about to knock a second time.

I hurried back to Papa and sat down beside him again. A few minutes later, there was a knock on Papa's door, and Dr Hetherington rushed in. He came over to the bed and pulled back the bedclothes. Then, gently, he passed his hand over Papa's stomach.

Papa let out a loud shriek. He looked vaguely around him, his eyes dilated. His lips were drawn. His limbs convulsed. As I looked over towards him, I could see his whole body covered with brown spots. My heart was racing. I burst into tears. Dr Hetherington looked hard at me; deep lines furrowed his brow.

'May I suggest that you leave me alone with your father? I need to examine him closely, and it might be too distressing for you.'

'B-But... I want to stay.' I sobbed.

'I must insist that you leave us... both for your own sake and your father's.'

Reluctantly, I got up, crossed the room and left, closing the door behind me. I started to walk down the landing and stopped. I turned around and went back to Papa's room. I opened the door and took half a step forward.

'I'll be in the parlour if you need me,' I spluttered.

'Thank you, Miss Grundy. I'll come down to you as soon as I can.'

I went to the parlour and sat in the window seat, staring out into the garden. I didn't know what to think or do. I tried to read but couldn't. I paced around the room aimlessly. Susannah came in occasionally to offer me some refreshments, but I sent her away with a brief "thank you, but no thank you" each time she did. Finally, the parlour door opened, and a very serious-looking Dr Hetherington entered.

'Can someone go to Culham Court and summon your uncle, Henry Stephenson? Your father is grievously ill and wants to make his will.'

'No... no...' I cried out. 'Are you saying that he is dying?'

'I'm doing everything I possibly can, Miss Grundy, but I fear your father will not live for more than a few hours.'

I collapsed onto the window seat. I couldn't think clearly. I couldn't speak. Dr Hetherington crossed the room and rang for Susannah.

'Send someone to Culham Court to fetch Mr Stephenson immediately,' he instructed when Susannah appeared.

'What can I do, Dr Hetherington?' I asked, finally finding my voice again.

'Nothing, I fear, Miss Grundy, other than to pray for your father, perhaps. I suggest you stay in the parlour and wait for your uncle's arrival. In the meantime, please ask your maid to take some hot water to your father's room.'

With that, Dr Hetherington left to return to care for Papa. I felt even more helpless.

Uncle Henry arrived nearly one and a half hours later. Jarman brought him into the parlour, and I led him to Papa's bedroom. I knocked and opened the door. To my surprise, Dr Hetherington stood in front of the doorway, blocking our way.

'I hope you don't mind, Miss Grundy,' he said. 'I think it would be better for the present if Mr Stephenson alone came in to see your father.'

I felt my stomach tightening.

'But… can't I come in as well? I'd like to see my papa… to see how he is.'

'Perhaps after Mr Stephenson has finished his business with your father.'

Filled with acute disappointment but compliant with Dr Hetherington's wishes, I stepped aside to allow Uncle Henry to go past me into the bedroom.

'As you wish, Doctor,' I responded. 'I'll wait in the parlour.'

'It really is for the best, Miss Grundy, I can assure you.'

I turned and started to walk away.

'Oh, Miss Grundy… will you ask the maid, Susannah Gosswell, to come up… and to bring a pot of tea with her when she does?'

I went to the kitchen and instructed Susannah to take tea to Dr Hetherington before returning to the parlour. I couldn't settle. I alternated between pacing around the room and sitting down, either on the window seat or the settee. Finally, I went out of the parlour and into the kitchen, looking for Susannah.

'Can I help you, Miss Mercy?' a voice called out. It was Alice.

'I'm looking for Susannah.'

'She hasn't returned from taking tea up to the master's room,' Alice replied.

A sense of panic began to spread through my body. My heart was racing. *Something's wrong!*

'Y-You mean she's been gone all the time since I came and spoke with her?' My voice died away in uncertain mumbling.

'Yes, miss.'

I felt my jaw drop. For a moment, I stood there speechless before regaining my composure.

'I'll have a pot of tea in the parlour, please, Alice.'

'Of course, Miss Mercy, Bohea or Hyson?'

'Come now, Alice,' I chided. 'I always take Hyson – it's the master who takes Bohea.'

'Of course, miss, I'll bring a pot through shortly.'

There was a knock on the door, and Susannah entered the room.

'The master would like to see you,' she said.

'How is he?'

'He's a little better than he was, but he is very frail. Mr Stephenson and Dr Hetherington are still with him.'

'Thank you, Susannah. I'll go straight up to the master's bedroom.'

I almost ran up the stairs, along the landing, and pushed open the door to Papa's bedroom. I was shocked by what I saw. Papa lay on the bed, his cheeks sunken, his face colourless, his skin appearing transparent. He stretched out his hand towards me.

'Mercy, my dearest daughter,' he whispered. 'Come and sit by me.'

I crossed to Papa's bedside and took his hand. It felt icy. I leant over him and kissed his cheek. That felt icier still. A heavy smell of vomit and diarrhoea pervaded the room. Uncle Henry moved from the chair next to Papa's bed and indicated to me to take his place. I sat down, still holding Papa's hand.

I looked nervously around the room as Uncle Henry joined Dr Hetherington, who was standing opposite me, and then back at Papa.

'Thank God. I am overjoyed to be able to see you again. How are you feeling?' I asked, my voice laced firstly with relief and then with concern.

'Mercy, dearest,' Papa said weakly, 'I am ill, as you undoubtedly see… I don't know how I came to be in this state, but I have my suspicions.' He swallowed with some difficulty. 'I also have questions for you – questions I need you to answer honestly,' he continued, his voice hardening noticeably.

'What questions?' I asked falteringly.

'They concern Dunbar, a man I consider to represent one of the lowest specimens of humanity—'

'William?' I gasped.

'Yes, him.'

By then, I had been rendered almost speechless, my throat dry.

'Have you been in contact with him recently?'

'I haven't seen him for months,' I replied, eventually finding my voice again.

'That's not what I asked – I asked if you had been in contact with him recently,' Papa snapped. 'So, tell me – have you?'

I felt myself being consumed by shame. I lowered my head, looking down at Papa's bed.

'Yes, Papa,' I whispered. 'He sent the linen press that is in my room. I lied when I said it was a present from Mrs Poole. He sent a letter hidden inside it, with a pair of earrings and some powder.'

'Was it white powder?' asked Uncle Henry.

I looked up in surprise. 'Yes,' I replied. 'It was powder he had obtained from a cunning woman in Edinburgh – a love philtre. He told me that if it were administered to Papa without his knowledge, his attitude towards William would improve.'

'Did it ever occur to you that the powder might be poison?' asked Dr Hetherington.

'The thought that it might harm Papa did cross my mind at one point, but I know it isn't poisonous.'

Dr Hetherington looked at me quizzically. 'And how do you know that it isn't?'

'The last time I actually saw William – in London some little while before I received the linen press – he gave me three packets. I put two of these in Papa's tea when I returned to Henley without any ill effects whatsoever. After the linen press arrived, I put some powder in Papa's tea, but it floated on the surface of the tea, so I didn't give it to him at the time—'

'What happened to that tea?'

'I poured it into another dish and refilled Papa's with fresh tea but without putting powder in it as I didn't have any. I assume Susannah poured the tea with the powder in it away when she cleared the dining room.'

'Did you write to Dunbar at about that time?' asked Papa.

'Yes. I told him that the powder he had sent in the linen press didn't dissolve in the tea I had given to you, unlike the original powder. So, he wrote back, telling me to put a pinch of powder in your gruel.'

'And you did that, did you?' asked Uncle Henry.

'Yes, but it didn't seem to work, so I wrote again to William asking for his advice. He wrote back to tell me to increase the amount I gave to Papa. That worked so well that I decided to add even more the next time I put the powder in Papa's gruel.'

'And those would be the two servings of gruel you gave your father before he fell ill?' Dr Hetherington asked.

Suddenly, the enormity of that question hit me. *The powder was poisonous. I had poisoned Papa.*

I fell on my knees beside Papa's bed. 'Papa, dear Papa, forgive me. William has duped me. I swear I will never see or write to him again.'

'Of course, I forgive you, my dear Mercy,' Papa said softly. 'Perhaps at long last, you will see that I have always been right about Dunbar. He is the devil incarnate. Now you must go back to the parlour for fear that you say anything that might prejudice you.'

That was the last time I spoke to or saw Papa.

I was standing by the window in the parlour, looking out into the garden, when Uncle Henry, accompanied by Dr Hetherington, entered. Both were looking stern, neither saying a word at first.

'I'm afraid we have some awful news for you,' Uncle Henry said eventually. 'There's no easy way to say this – sadly, your father died not ten minutes ago.'

Feelings of grief mixed with guilt consumed me. I rushed towards the door. 'Please let me pass. I must go up and see my papa.'

'I'm afraid that that is not possible.'

'Why not?' I replied in a tone which did not betray the hidden anger and indignation I felt instantly.

'We suspect foul play,' said Uncle Henry. 'There will need to be an investigation, and the integrity of all available evidence must be preserved. There will also need to be an inquest. Your father's body will be taken from the house for that purpose immediately. As a precursor to those events, you must hand all your keys to Dr Hetherington. After that, you are to remain here in the parlour with me while your room is searched by Dr Hetherington and until your father's body is taken away under his supervision. After that, you will be confined to your bedroom until further notice.'

With that, Uncle Henry rang for Jarman and instructed him to go immediately to the house of Ned Hardy, the parish clerk, and ask him to come to the house. Once he had done that, he was to go to the home of Dr Nicholson to ask him if Dr Hetherington could carry out an autopsy on Papa's body there the following day and, if so, whether he would assist.

In turn, it was daunting, humiliating and terrifying as I waited in the parlour with Uncle Henry. Throughout, I grieved inconsolably for my papa, sobbing persistently. Uncle Henry sat opposite me, stony-faced and saying nothing. Eventually, Dr Hetherington appeared briefly to both report that he had finished searching my room and take his leave before he left to escort Papa's body to Dr Nicholson's house. Shortly afterwards, Ned arrived and escorted me to my room. Once I had entered, he shut the door, telling me as he did that he would remain on guard outside.

I wasn't sorry that Ned would, in effect, be my gaoler. I had known him for years, and if Papa hadn't intervened to warn him off – according to Papa, Ned had no pedigree and insufficient means – we might have become man and wife.

Once in my room, I went to my escritoire and sat down. I briefly wrestled with my conscience but decided that I had to write to William despite my promise to Papa. The instinct for self-preservation remained strong within me.

Dear William

I have so very little time to write more than just a few lines to you at this time.

It may be a while before I can do so again, but please do not be alarmed if this is the case. I will explain all when I can, my dearest love.

In the meantime, if you reply to this letter, please be careful what you write, just in case your reply goes astray – you know how people can so easily misconstrue things, especially if they are minded to do so.

Yours as ever,

Mercy

Once I had folded and sealed the letter, I opened my bedroom door. 'Ned,' I called out softly.

Ned stood up and turned to face me. 'How may I help you, Mercy?'

'I need this letter posted – would you please ask Papa's clerk to include it with his next outgoing post?'

'Would you prefer me to send it?' Ned asked.

'No, Ned, but thanks for offering. I think sending it out with post from Papa's office would be better.'

Ned pocketed the letter. 'I'm only too sorry things have turned out as they have but, as ever, I'd do anything for you.'

Later that evening, Ned knocked on my door. 'Just to let you know, I gave your letter to your father's clerk. He said he'd send it off for you.'

'I can't thank you enough, Ned,' I replied.

'One other thing, Mercy... I've been asked to go to the churchyard tonight and dig a grave for your father. I'll be leaving shortly and won't be back until mid-morning tomorrow. There will be no one guarding you... if you know what I'm saying.'

As soon as Ned had left, I ran out of the house into the street and headed towards Henley Bridge. I hadn't had time to dress properly and was wearing nothing but a black half-sack. I didn't even have a hoop in my petticoat.

Despite the time, Hart Street was as full of human obstacles as it was at midday. As I hurried through oncoming pedestrians and overtook others heading in the same direction as me, I suddenly heard voices shouting out my name. The next thing I knew was I was in danger of being surrounded. Somehow, though, I pushed my way through an increasing crowd and ran for all I was worth until I reached the Red Lion Inn, seeking refuge. Mrs Dawes came to my aid, shutting the door upon the mob.

I sat down, almost out of breath and terrified. I could hear the mob outside the inn, execrating me vilely. I was a witch, the spawn of the devil and worse. Mrs Dawes came over to me and handed me a glass of wine.

'Here, Mercy, drink this. You look as if you need it,' she said kindly, 'but you can't stay here – it's unsafe. Eventually, someone will smash their way into the inn, and God knows what they would do to you if they got hold of you. So I've sent one of my serving maids to the home of a long-standing friend of my family, Richard Fisher, and asked him to come and collect you from here and take you home. He's a good man – one you can trust.'

I picked up the glass. My hand was trembling so much that I nearly spilt the contents as I tried to drink a little.

'Thank you, Mrs Dawes. I'm sorry to have caused you so much trouble.'

Mrs Dawes smiled at me and gently placed her hand on my shoulder. 'It's no problem – your mama was a good friend to me. It's the least I could do.'

Mrs Dawes remained with me until Richard Fisher drove up to the inn in a post-chaise. He came into the inn, took me by the hand and guided me into the carriage. A variety of missiles ranging from sticks and stones to animal excrement narrowly missed us as we covered the short distance between the inn and the carriage.

I arrived home to be placed into the custody of the sergeant and macebearer to await the outcome of the inquest to be held the following morning.

That day of the inquest dragged on and on. I was confined to my room. The sergeant and the macebearer took turns sitting outside, guarding me. Susannah brought my meals up to me, but I could scarcely eat anything. Finally, Uncle Henry called to see me and tell me that the inquest jury had found that Papa had been poisoned and that I had murdered him.

After Uncle Henry had finished telling me, I stood in front of him, completely stunned. I took a slight step forward before steadying myself again. I looked towards him and then away.

I was in a state of utter despair. I could neither believe nor adequately take in what I had just heard.

'What happens now, uncle?' I whimpered.

Uncle Henry stood and looked agonisingly at me. Then, finally, he lowered his head and fastened his hands behind his back.

'The mayor and coroner will issue a warrant to the constables to convey you to the county gaol in Oxford, where you will be detained until you face trial at the spring assizes. I will arrange for one of my maids to accompany you. I am told she may stay at Oxford and attend to you while you are there.'

I collapsed onto my bed and lay there staring up at the ceiling. Uncle Henry then left the room, shutting the door behind him. I turned over, buried my face in my pillow and burst into tears.

That night, Papa was buried next to Mama. There were just three mourners: Mr Horton, Papa's clerk and Jarman.

The following morning, two constables guided my appointed maid and me into a landau drawn by four horses, and we set out for Oxford. As we travelled, I looked out of the carriage window at the dripping hedgerows we were passing, reflecting with horror on what had happened in recent weeks. A wintry blight seemed to have fallen upon my life – coming days stretched before me in unbroken gloom and dreariness, represented by the cloudy, sunless sky that arched above us and the miserable expanse of saturated meadowlands that lay around.

WILLIAM DUNBAR

TWENTY-THREE

My ambition to possess the fullest of purses – to own enough gold that no castle gate is ever closed to me – was yet to be fulfilled. I still hoped to get my hands on the Grundy fortunes, but those hopes had somewhat dwindled. In any event, the only way I could profit from Grundy in the future per se was by his death, and that prospect seemed to be as far away as ever, judging by the contents of the letters I had received from Mercy.

That said, the arrangement I had entered into with Grundy before I returned had paid dividends. An outlay of 1gn to him and my signature on a piece of paper meant that I did not have to repay debts of some £850 out of my remaining capital, and I had put that money to good effect.

Initially, I lived at my mother's house – a far cry from what I had hoped for or imagined. Still, it eventually proved to be a somewhat advantageous arrangement so far as my finances were concerned. Moreover, it allowed me to cast my net into fresh waters.

My venture involving *The Archer*, whilst disastrous at the time, hadn't put me off the idea of dipping my toe back into the

African and Americas trade. After all, it's not how many times a man gets knocked down that is the measure of him; it's how many times he gets back up again afterwards. Accordingly, I used my family connections – and my mother's hospitality – to become acquainted with one Richard Oswald from Glasgow and, through him, made some small but profitable investments in several ventures in both Glasgow and London in association with him. In addition to these investments, I became a selling agent for planters in the West Indies, who consigned their sugar, cotton and rum to me and I, in turn, sold these in individual lots to achieve the highest possible prices. I also became acquainted with Robert Colquhoun, another Glasgow merchant – an acquaintance that brought further rewards.

It was through Colquhoun that I was able to invest in a small sugar plantation of just over fifty acres in St Kitts. He and I set up our own embryo 'triangular trade' enterprise. We planned to export sugar from my plantation and his much larger one to Glasgow. In return, we would buy Clyde herrings from Alexander Houston and Company and ship those to the West Indies. We also planned to purchase slaves from Oswald, who operated a slave fort on Bunce Island in the estuary of the Sierra Leone River, and transport them to work in the sugar fields in St Kitts.

I had moved to a secure financial footing once more. Mercy had become almost superfluous to my needs. She added too many complications and provided little to no advantage. All I needed from her was news that, finally, Grundy had answered the call to meet his Maker. Meanwhile, I had far more important things to attend to than concern myself with her.

Whilst I was busy developing my new business ventures, I received a message from my brother saying that he needed to meet me without delay. At the time, I was staying in Spittal, just outside Berwick, where I had been in discussions with

Arthur Byram, a boat builder, who was in the process of seeking permission from the Guild of Freemen to set up a shipyard on the Berwick side of the River Tweed. I had been hoping to ship to him oak planks, oak timber, blocks, sails rigging and other materials the town could not supply for carrying on his proposed business.

James and I met in the Old Nag's Head in Berwick. It seemed odd to me that we should, and I was very apprehensive as I entered the inn and sought out James, whom I found sitting alone at a corner table. A glass of whisky was in front of him, and a glass was waiting for me. I sat down.

James raised his glass of whisky towards me. 'Here's to you, brother,' he said with a broad smile and took a sip from the glass.

I picked up my glass and reciprocated. 'And here's to you, James. This is all very strange.'

James looked at me, his face now wearing a troubled look. 'Strange, yes, but necessary, as will become clear.'

'That sounds ominous.'

'It's certainly serious,' James replied. 'Do you still have anything to do with Mercy Grundy of Henley?'

'That's an odd question, James. I haven't seen her since I returned to Scotland – why do you ask?'

'I'll come to that in a moment. You may not have seen her, but have you had any contact with her?'

'We have exchanged one or two letters... oh, and I sent her a linen press.'

'Are you aware that her father is dead?'

Hardly able to conceal my joy, I looked across at my brother. 'Grundy is dead!' I exclaimed. 'When? How?'

'According to an inquest convened in the immediate aftermath of his death, the jury returned a verdict that he had been murdered – poisoned. He died a week or so ago. The jury named his daughter as the most likely perpetrator of the murder. She was arrested and taken to Oxford to await trial at the spring assizes next year.'

'How do you know this?' I asked.

'As you may know, the sheriff depute of Berwickshire is a long-standing acquaintance of mine – and of our father when he was alive. He told me that the mayor of Henley's messenger was sent to Scotland shortly after Miss Grundy's committal for the purpose of apprehending you on suspicion that you were an accessory to the murder. Unfortunately, a letter from Miss Grundy to be left at the Berwick Post House was intercepted before it was sent, so he was despatched here. An application for a warrant for your arrest was made, but it has not yet been granted. This is to allow me time to make contact with you. However, the application will inevitably be granted, so we have little time to get you away from here.'

I sat facing James. Horrified.

'But how do I get away? If the application for a warrant is granted, the messenger will immediately seek to execute it.'

'Leave that to me. Wheels have already been set in motion on that score. Just hold yourself in readiness.'

I felt that, not for the first time, I was about to be knocked down again. All that I had worked for, all that I had achieved since returning to Scotland, was now under threat. But, more frighteningly, my life was under threat. I could be hanged.

They say that the future emerges from the past, and in my case, it seemed that nothing was bleaker than the future, except perhaps the past. As a young man, I dreamt about the future because I had no past, but now I could only contemplate the past because I no longer appeared to have any future.

James arranged for me to meet Alexander Aitken, whom he had hired to take me from Spittal to Glasgow that night. I was to meet Robert Colquhoun in Glasgow two days later and then take a ship bound for St Kitts.

Aitken duly called for me at the Old Nag's Head and, in the chill, quiet hours of the grey dawn, when the sleep of the healthy is soundest and that watchers by sickbeds dread the worst, I stole from my room. I was ready to address myself to the painful task of leaving Scotland and my family, perhaps forever. I noiselessly descended the narrow stairway and went out into the street.

The thought crossed my mind that no runaway schoolboy, no fugitive defaulter, not the most innocent truant that ever slipped away from home under cover of night, ever failed to feel the shame, the hesitation or the remorse that went hand in hand with a stealthy departure of this sort. Aitken led the way as we traversed the silent street, and after a turn here and a turn there, we reached the post road, a track that ran between Berwick and Belford and Holy Island. With a heart beating ever more quickly, I pressed on towards Berwick, too intent upon my purpose to be turned from it now. All the while, I prayed that Aitken and I would meet no one as we went and that no prying eyes would see us.

We were well on our way before there was more than a faint crimson to flush and dapple the pale pearl grey of the sky. Sunrises are more often described than witnessed, at least by those who know how to limn them in word painting. Such as it was, this sunrise came slowly. Some streaks of pink faintly mingled with the sickly grey to the east. The stars disappeared as a confused medley of colours painted the heavens. An undecided gleam of yellow light that seemed to struggle for existence was followed first by a crimson reddening and then a lilac reflex. Next, there was a steady increase of the yellow, modest light as the dawn arrived, and a pale, undecided early autumn day crept into being. As it did, Aitken and I crossed Berwick Bridge and headed down to Town Key, where a fishing boat was waiting to take us to Glasgow.

Once we reached Glasgow, I met with Oswald and, with him, arranged for my passage to St Kitts. There was a ship leaving Glasgow the following evening carrying a cargo of herring. When we reached St Kitts, I would attend to my small plantation while taking up the position of overseer of his.

The plan was that I would join the ship just before it set sail for St Kitts. By then, it would be sitting at anchor near the mouth of the River Clyde. I was to be rowed to it in a boat hired by Aitken. There was, though, one major problem. A fearful thunderstorm broke just as I was about to set off.

I feared it would be impossible for the ship to set off as planned. My luck, though, held up. The storm raced over us, heading inland, doubtless subjecting Glasgow to an unwelcome drenching. My boat left the quayside, and we began the long row out to the ship.

As we did, I could see all the boats' lights that were hung out. It seemed as if the stars had settled down on the face of the Clyde. Wherever I looked, I could see little constellations twinkling far and near till they were lost in faint halos in the distance. It seemed as if I was looking at a city lit up, street after street, on a very dark night. Occasional flashes of sheet lightning in the wake of the thunderstorm lifted the veil of night from the river from time to time and disclosed momentary glimpses of ships lying at anchor as far as I could see and, more significantly, the ship waiting for me.

An hour later, the ship weighed anchor and headed for St Kitts, taking me with it – away from the possibility of a trial and near-certain execution for murder. The fact is that I had a future to look forward to. An uncertain future, perhaps, but it was a future, nevertheless.

MERCY

TWENTY-FOUR

I entered the courtroom, walked like a somnambulist to the dock and stood there staring at the packed courtroom before me. Then, when required to by the clerk of the arraigns, I held up my hand, looking nervously forward as I did. A steady trickle of sweat dribbled down the small of my back. A mixture of nausea, apprehension, uncertainty, misery and terror consumed me. I had been brought before two judges sitting at the Oxford assizes, accused of the murder of Papa. I was on trial for my life.

I was scarcely conscious of what was said as the clerk read out the indictment but was cut to the quick by the allegation made against me. I, having forsaken God and been moved and seduced by the devil, did with malice aforethought contrive and intend to murder my father and then did murder him by poisoning him using white arsenic.

After reading the indictment, the clerk looked at me expressionlessly.

'How do you plead, Mercy Grundy, are you guilty or not guilty of the felony and murder you stand indicted for?'

I swallowed hard. I was blinking almost incessantly. 'Not guilty,' I replied in a half-whisper.

The clerk scarcely allowed a second's pause before firing his next question at me. 'And how will you be tried?'

'By God and my country.' I mumbled the answer I had rehearsed with Samuel Jessop, counsel acting for me.

'May God grant you a good deliverance.'

'Amen to that,' I whispered to myself.

'Cryer, proclaim silence.'

'Oyez, oyez, oyez!' the cryer bellowed. 'My Lordships, the King's justices strictly charge and command all persons gathered here today to maintain silence upon pain of imprisonment.' He then turned to face the jury. 'Oyez! You, good men summoned to serve as jury members in this court, will answer your names when called or suffer a fine.'

The names of each of the twelve members of the jury were called. Each man answered as soon as he was summoned. Once this process was completed, the clerk turned to face me.

'Prisoner at the bar, the men who answered their names will be those who will decide your innocence or your guilt today. If you wish to object to any or all of them acting as a juror in your trial, you must do so before they are sworn in. If you do object, then your objection will be heard.'

I stood in silence as each of the twelve men summoned to serve on the jury was called forward and sworn in. Once they had been, the clerk looked towards the cryer.

'The jurors are all sworn,' he announced. 'Make the proclamation.'

'Oyez, oyez, oyez! If anyone knows of any treasons, murders, felonies or misdemeanours committed or done by the prisoner at the bar, let him come forth immediately and be heard, for the prisoner stands now at the bar upon her deliverance. All persons bound by recognisance to give evidence against her must come forth and give their evidence when required to do so, or they will forfeit their recognisances.'

The clerk then turned to me. 'Mercy Grundy, hold up your hand,' he commanded.

When I meekly complied, he turned to the jury.

'Gentlemen of the jury, look at the prisoner. She, Mercy Grundy, of the parish of Henley-upon-Thames, in the county of Oxford, spinster, daughter of Francis Grundy, late of the same place, gentleman, deceased, stands indicted that she did with malice aforethought contrive and intend to murder the said Francis Grundy and then did murder him by poisoning him with white arsenic. Upon this indictment, she has been arraigned and, upon her arraignment, has pleaded not guilty. She has put herself for her trial upon God and her country, which country you are. Your duty, therefore, is to determine whether she is guilty or not guilty of the felony and murder of which she stands indicted.'

With that, the clerk called upon the Honourable Mr Thomas Bennett, counsel for the Crown, to make his opening address.

Bennett rehearsed events leading up to the death of Papa as he perceived these to be and outlined the evidence the Crown would present before the court in support of their case. Nothing said by him was unexpected except, and much to my relief, he also stated in no uncertain terms that the author and contriver of what had come to pass, William, was not standing before the court alongside me.

Bennett expressed the sincere wish that William was there, stating that I had been ruined and undone by the treacherous flattery and pernicious advice of an abandoned, insidious and repulsive individual. A man who had found the means to inveigle himself into my family home and, whilst there, by false pretences of love, gained my affection.

'"Love" did I call it?' questioned Bennett. 'It doesn't deserve to be called that. If it was the love of anything, it was the love of money in the form of the promise of a dowery of £20,000 and nothing else.'

Bennett concluded, 'We shall now proceed to call our evidence.' He paused before saying, 'I call Dr Anthony Hetherington.'

Dr Hetherington came forward and was sworn in. He readied himself to give his evidence. Bennett briefly consulted his notes and then began to question Hetherington without looking at him at first.

'Dr Hetherington, did you attend Mr Grundy in the period immediately before his death?'

'Yes.'

'Who sent for you to attend upon Mr Grundy?'

'I understand that Miss Grundy sent the family footman, Mr Jarman, to fetch me.'

'Why were you sent for?'

Hetherington cleared his throat. 'Mr Grundy had been taken unwell a few days beforehand and had been seen by Mr Horton, the family apothecary, who diagnosed colic and prescribed medication for that condition. But, unfortunately, he eventually took a turn for the worse, which is why I was sent for.'

'Will you describe Mr Grundy's condition when you were first called to attend to him?'

Hetherington paused, as if trying to recollect before answering. 'He was in bed. His tongue was swollen, and his throat was inflamed and excoriated. His lips, especially the upper one, were dry and rough and dotted with angry pimples. The inside of his nostrils was in the same condition. His eyes were slightly bloodshot – not entirely unexpected in the circumstances. His pulse was rather weak and intermittent, and his breathing was irregular. Brown blotches were breaking out on his body.'

'Did his condition strike you as unusual?'

'Yes. It all seemed very odd, then a terrible thought crossed my mind; Mr Grundy had been poisoned, and not by accident.'

Bennett consulted his notes once more and then looked up at Hetherington. 'What happened next?'

'I stayed overnight. I was awakened during the early hours of the following morning by Miss Grundy, fearful that her father was dying. I went to Mr Grundy's room and examined him further. His condition had worsened dramatically.'

'Did the accused remain in the room?'

'No.'

'Why not?'

'I sent her out. She returned several times and asked to stay with her father, but I wouldn't allow it.'

'Why was that?'

'I was sure by then that Mr Grundy had been poisoned and suspected that Miss Grundy was involved.'

'What did you do then?'

'I went down to the parlour and asked Miss Grundy to send for her uncle, Henry Stephenson, on the pretext that Mr Grundy wanted to write his will. Mr Stephenson was eventually brought to Mr Grundy's room about an hour and a half later. I again prevented Miss Grundy from entering the room. I then asked her to send the maid, Susannah Gosswell, up with a pot of tea.'

'What happened then?'

'I explained to Gosswell that I thought that her master had ingested poison and asked whether she knew of anyone who might have poisoned him. She told Mr Stephenson and me that she had entertained the same suspicion and that certain things had led her to believe Miss Grundy was the culprit.'

'And what were those "certain things"?'

Hetherington paused to clear his throat once again before answering. 'She told us that a while earlier, Miss Grundy had left a dish of tea in the dining room. Gosswell had cleared the dish away and had subsequently permitted the scullery maid, Alice Eden, to drink the tea. Not long afterwards, Eden was taken ill, suffering stomach pains, vomiting and diarrhoea. More recently, Mr Grundy had left half a mug of water gruel uneaten. Gosswell took it to the kitchen, reheated the gruel later and ate it. She was very ill afterwards, also suffering from stomach pains, vomiting and diarrhoea. She could not return to her work for several days afterwards. She believed that both the gruel she had eaten and the tea drunk by Eden had been poisoned. But there was more besides. Gosswell told us that she only returned to work after her illness on the evening I stayed at the Grundy house. I had prescribed some medication for Mr Grundy that was to be taken with some panada. Miss Grundy instructed Gosswell to make the panada and take it to Mr Grundy's room, which she did. However, when Gosswell returned, she saw Miss Grundy throw what looked like a box and some papers onto the kitchen fire. Miss Grundy left the kitchen, and Gosswell, suspecting something untoward, retrieved a box – by now badly burned – and two letters from the fire. She brought those up to Mr Stephenson and me immediately. We found a tiny amount of white powder in a packet in what remained of the box. Whilst somewhat scorched, the two letters were legible. They were from William Dunbar. Gosswell was then sent to ask Miss Grundy to come to Mr Grundy's room.'

'What happened then?'

'Mr Grundy, though gravely ill, told Miss Grundy that he had questions for her – questions he required her to answer honestly. First, he asked her if she had been in contact with William Dunbar recently. After briefly procrastinating, Miss Grundy confessed that Dunbar had sent her a linen press, together with a letter hidden inside it, a pair of earrings and some white powder. Dunbar had obtained the powder from a cunning woman in Edinburgh. Miss Grundy was told that if she gave it to her father without his knowledge, his attitude towards Dunbar would improve. I asked whether it ever occurred to Miss

Grundy that the powder might be poison. She said the thought that it might harm her father crossed her mind at one point, but she knew it wasn't poisonous. She had previously put some powder given to her by Dunbar into her father's tea without any ill effect on him at all. After she received the linen press, she put some of the powder hidden in it in her father's dish of tea, but it had floated on the surface of the tea, so she didn't give it to him at the time. Instead, she poured the tea into another dish and served her father a fresh cup without adding powder.'

'And then?'

'Miss Grundy admitted that she had written to Dunbar to say that the powder he had sent didn't dissolve in the tea. He wrote back, telling her to put a pinch of powder in her father's gruel. Miss Grundy did so, but it didn't seem to work, so she wrote again to Dunbar asking for his advice. He wrote back to tell her to increase the amount she gave to her father. Miss Grundy complied with the instruction and was so convinced of the efficacy of the powder on the first occasion she used it that she decided to add even more powder when she next prepared her father's gruel. I asked if the two servings of gruel that Miss Grundy had given her father before he fell ill contained the extra dosage. At that moment, she fell on my knees and begged her father's forgiveness, saying Dunbar had duped her. She swore never to see or write to him again. Mr Grundy told Miss Grundy that he forgave her. Miss Grundy left the room after that. Mr Grundy died shortly afterwards.'

Bennett paused, seemingly to collect his thoughts. 'Thank you, Dr Hetherington,' he eventually said. 'After Mr Grundy died, did you carry out an autopsy on his body?'

'Yes.'

'When did that take place?'

'On the day after Mr Grundy died.'

'What were your findings?'

'I concluded that Mr Grundy had been poisoned and that it was likely that the poison used to kill him was white arsenic.'

'How did you arrive at that conclusion?'

'The damage to Mr Grundy's internal organs was entirely consistent with that I had seen before – in cases where a person had died due to acute poisoning caused by ingesting white arsenic. I also concluded that Mr Grundy had ingested white arsenic over some time before the two doses that eventually finished him off.'

'Have you since satisfied yourself that white arsenic was used to poison Mr Grundy?'

'Yes. As I have already said, there was a small amount of powder in the packet inside the box Susannah Gosswell handed to Mr Stephenson and me but insufficient to test it. However, several days after Mr Grundy's death, Mr Horton informed me that Gosswell had handed him a pan of gruel she had found in the pantry that she said Miss Grundy had prepared the day before Mr Grundy died. She noticed white sediment stuck to the bottom of the pan. Mr Horton scraped the sediment onto a sheet of paper and handed it to me. I subsequently gave half of the sediment to an experienced chemist in Reading and asked him to test it. I then tested the other half myself. We both reached the same conclusion: that the sediment we tested comprised white arsenic.'

Bennett paused again before he resumed his questioning. 'Thank you, Dr Hetherington, if I may now return to your account of the accused's claim that Dunbar had duped her. Do you believe what she said – that she unwittingly administered poison to her father?'

'At first, I did. However, I now believe that she and Dunbar acted in concert.'

'Oh. Would you tell the court why you believe that to be the case?'

'After Mr Grundy died, I took the box, packet of powder and letters to my home. A little while later, I had occasion to read and study the letters at length. As I did, it struck me that the salutation in both letters did not specifically mention the word "Mercy", yet both contained two instances of the name in the actual body of the letter. I enjoy word games, and as I read and reread the letters, I recalled something Miss Grundy had said to her father about putting powder in his gruel. I then realised that two instructions from Dunbar are evident if you take the initial letter of the words between the two instances where the word "Mercy" appears in each letter. The first is "put pinch in gruel", and the second is "add more". These instructions are consistent with events that followed receipt by Miss Grundy of each letter. For these reasons, I have concluded that if Miss Grundy were an innocent dupe, it would not have been necessary for her to correspond with Dunbar in code. Further, she would not need to attempt to destroy the letters clandestinely the moment it was likely she would be found out.'

'Thank you, Dr Hetherington, I have no further questions for you, but my learned friend counsel for the defence may have.'

I looked around the courtroom wide-eyed. My heart was pounding. I was almost hyperventilating.

Dr Hetherington was subjected to brief but somewhat inconsequential cross-examination by Jessop, after which Mr Horton, Susannah and Alice all gave evidence to confirm the evidence presented by Dr Hetherington. The Crown called two further witnesses: Papa's clerk and Richard Fisher.

Papa's clerk provided evidence that Ned Hardy had given him my letter to William to post, but instead of posting it, he opened it and realised that it was a letter of warning.

In his testimony, Richard Fisher explained to the court that he had been called to the Red Lion Inn to pick me up in a post-chaise to ensure my safety from the angry mob that had followed me there.

In William's absence, the only witnesses that I could call amounted to character witnesses on my behalf. I could only assert that I had no intention of harming, let alone murdering, Papa.

Almost before I knew it, Mr Bennett was making his closing submission. He argued the jury must disregard my assertion that I had not intended to murder Papa – or any notion they may have formed that William had tricked me into poisoning him in all innocence. My letter to William showed we were acting in concert. Where Richard Fisher's evidence had any relevance, Mr Bennet contended that the fact I had left the house was further evidence of my guilt. Why else would I seek to run from the house? Would an innocent person secretly leave her dead father's house at such a time rather than wanting to make proper preparations for his funeral?

By the time he had finished, I knew there was little chance of my escaping the hangman's noose. Sixteen minutes later, there was none.

The courtroom fell silent. The jury had considered their verdict together for less than five minutes and then turned to the court.

'Gentlemen, are you all agreed on your verdict?' asked the clerk of arraigns.

'Yes,' called out all twelve of the jury members.

'Which of you speaks for the others?'

'Our foreman.'

The clerk turned to face me.

'Mercy Grundy, hold up your hand.' Almost instinctively, I did. The clerk turned to face the jury. 'Gentlemen of the jury,' he continued, 'how say you, is Mercy Grundy guilty of the felony and murder of which she stands indicted or not guilty?'

'Guilty,' the foreman replied instantaneously.

'What goods or chattels, lands or tenements, did Mercy Grundy have when she committed the felony and murder, or at any time since then to your knowledge?'

'None,' replied the foreman.

'I will now repeat your findings as these are recorded by the court. You say that Mercy Grundy is guilty of the felony and murder of which she stands indicted. You further say that she had no goods or chattels, lands or tenements when she committed the felony and murder, or at any time since then to your knowledge. So you say all.' He turned back to look at me. 'Mercy Grundy, hold up your hand. You have been indicted of felony and murder. You have subsequently been arraigned and pleaded not guilty to the same indictment. For your trial, you put yourself before God and your country, which country has found you guilty. Have you anything to say as to why the court should not proceed to pass the sentence of death upon you according to law?'

I stared back blankly at the clerk. Dumbfounded. I could not have said anything even if I had wanted to. I took a slight step forward before steadying myself. I looked towards the clerk and then at the two judges. I was in a state of utter despair. I could not adequately take in what I had just heard.

'Oyez!' the clerk cried out. 'My Lords, the King's justices do strictly charge and command all persons present to be silent whilst sentence of death is passing on the prisoner at the bar upon pain of imprisonment.'

Lord Justice Legge looked straight at me, his face expressionless. 'Mercy Grundy, you have been indicted for the murder of your father and for your trial; you have put yourself upon God and your country. But, unfortunately, that country has found you guilty,' he began, his voice almost metronomic. 'You now stand convicted of a crime so dreadful, so horrid in itself, that is repugnant to human nature: the wilful murder of your own father. A father who, by all accounts, was the fondest, the kindest and the most indulgent that lived. That father forgave you in his dying hours – may your heavenly Father do so likewise.' He paused, still looking straight at me. 'It is hard to conceive how anything could induce you to perpetrate an act so shocking, so impossible to comprehend,' he continued. 'One would have thought that your love and respect for your father and the natural softness of your sex might prevent you from considering committing an act so barbarous and so wicked, let alone carrying it out. Your motive for your actions is known only to you. I cannot begin to imagine what it might have been.

'At this bar, we can only make a judgement having heard the evidence produced to us. But do not deceive yourself; remember you are very shortly to be judged in a court much more awful than this, where no subterfuge can avail, no art nor disguise screen you from the scrutiny of the Judge of all hearts. As it is said in the Holy Bible, Daniel, chapter two, verse twenty-two, *He revealeth the deep and secret things, He knoweth what is in the darkness, and the light dwelleth with Him.*

'I urge you to make the best and wisest use of the little time you have left on earth. Try to make your peace with Almighty God, whose justice and mercy are infinite. Nothing now remains but to pronounce the sentence of the law upon you.'

With that, Lord Justice Legge placed a black cap on his head and donned black gloves. I watched him as he did. Transfixed. Trembling uncontrollably.

'The law is that thou shalt return to the place whence thou camest and from thence to a place of execution where thou shalt hang by the neck till the body be dead. Dead. Dead. And the Lord have mercy upon thy soul.'

TWENTY-FIVE

The rumour I had heard was that I was to be executed on the Friday before Easter. Prompted by this, I went up into the rooms above my cell to look at the gallows, which stood outside the castle, opposite the gaol door. Some might say that I was suffering from some form of morbid curiosity by doing so. Perhaps, they were right.

From the vantage point I now had, I looked across Castle Green at a beam that was surprisingly high above the ground, spanning the arms of two trees. I felt a cold shiver run down my spine as I pictured myself dangling from a rope beneath the beam, gasping for breath, my body twitching, my legs thrashing about until I hung there, lifeless, urine running down through my undergarments and onto the ground below. The gawping crowd surrounding the gallows would be watching my death throes with a ghoulish curiosity.

As I stood there, I heard the gaoler call out my name. My body went rigid upon hearing his voice. *They're coming for me already!*

Full of trepidation, I made my way back to my room.

'Has my time now come?' I whispered.

'No, Miss Grundy,' the gaoler replied.

'Then why are you here?'

'There's no easy way to say this. Your time has not come now, but I do bring you grave news,' he said sternly. 'Your execution has been set for Monday morning.'

A feeling of panic spread through my body, and my stomach was tied in knots well before the gaoler had finished speaking. I crossed the room to the writing table, pulled back the chair before it and sat down. I shuffled the chair forward, put my elbows on the table and buried my head between my hands. I began to shake uncontrollably as the gaoler left the room. Now I knew for sure how many days I had left to live: four.

I went to bed at about my usual time on my final night. I tried to sleep but to no avail. All I could picture in my mind's eye was the scaffold, the ladder that I would have to climb, the ladder next to it on which the hangman would stand and the noose that would be dangling, ready to be placed over my head and about my neck. All the time, I wondered whether my death would be mercifully fast or mercilessly slow.

Almost before I knew it, twilight was creeping fast into the cell. I got up from the bed, washed, went to the wardrobe, picked out a black crape sack and dressed. After that, I went over to the writing table beside a window in my cell, sat on the high-backed chair in front of it, took up a quill and sat there poised to begin writing my last words. But no words came to me or rather, none that seemed appropriate. I put the quill down and picked it up again. Still, I could not frame in my mind what I wanted to say.

I put the quill down again, stood up, returned to my bed and lay down, shivering in the chillness of the early morning. My anxiety levels began to increase as time marched on. Exponentially. A myriad of thoughts rushed through my mind, but I couldn't snatch and hold on to any single one, apart from a terror of what was to be.

As I lay there, I drifted into the state of being half-awake, half-asleep. No sooner had I done so than I heard footsteps approaching. I sat bolt upright in bed. Every muscle in my body went rigid momentarily. I held my breath and tried to control myself. There was a knock on the door, and Reverend John Langton, the prison chaplain, entered the room.

He had become my only visitor – a far cry from the first few months I was confined in Oxford Castle. At that time, my imprisonment was more akin to removal to a comfortable retreat rather than the incarceration of a criminal. The maid Uncle Henry had sent to accompany me remained in attendance. My accommodation was one of the best apartments in the keeper's house. I drank tea twice daily. I was free to walk in the garden whenever I wished. My privacy was strictly respected. This all changed when rumours of a plot to break me out of prison reached the authorities in London. Almost at a stroke, the privileges I had been enjoying were stripped from me, and I was removed to the more modest accommodation I now occupied.

As Reverend Langton approached me, I turned and sat on the edge of the bed. The early morning sun had begun to stream directly into the cell, dazzling me. My chest rose and fell with rapid breaths before I gave out a desperate gasp. I said nothing at first, just staring blankly ahead. Then I seemed to gain inner strength. I took in a deep breath.

'Good morning, Reverend,' I said. 'Is it time?'

'I fear so, Mercy,' he replied. 'The sheriff is waiting for us outside, with your counsel, Mr Jessop.'

'I should prepare myself for my end. Will you pray with me, Reverend?' I asked.

'Of course, Mercy,' replied Reverend Langton.

He then knelt beside me and prayed with me.

'Thank you, Reverend,' I said quietly after we had finished reciting the Lord's Prayer.

Reverend Langton crossed the room and opened the door. The sheriff and Samuel Jessop entered. I sighed as the sheriff fastened my arms and hands loosely behind my back with some black paduasoy ribbons he had been carrying. I started to hyperventilate.

'Keep calm! Keep calm!' I whispered to myself before I regained control of my breathing. I turned and looked at the sheriff.

'I will now go out and meet my death as fearlessly as possible.'

As we stepped outside the castle, I caught sight of the crowd that had gathered around the gallows and which stretched back almost as far as I could see. According to the sheriff, some had camped overnight to ensure themselves the best spot. At that moment, some onlookers caught sight of me and immediately began to heckle me, calling me a devil – and worse – but nothing mattered anymore.

We neared my final destination. Terrified, I looked up at the noose waiting for me. Finally, we came to a halt.

Reverend Langton moved round to face me. 'Let us pray,' he said.

I lowered my head. Reverend Langton then recited Psalm 23:

'The Lord is my shepherd; I shall not want.

'He maketh me to lie down in green pastures: he leadeth me beside the still waters.

'He restoreth my soul: he leadeth me in the paths of righteousness for his name's sake.

'Yea, though I walk through the valley of the shadow of death, I will fear no evil: for thou art with me; thy rod and thy staff they comfort me.

'*Thou preparest a table before me in the presence of mine enemies: thou anointest my head with oil; my cup runneth over.*

'*Surely goodness and mercy shall follow me all the days of my life: and I will dwell in the house of the Lord forever.*'

He then looked up at me.

'Mercy Grundy,' he said, 'have you any final words to say to those gathered here this morning?'

'Yes, Reverend,' I answered. I took a deep breath. 'By the mercy of God, through the merits and mediation of Jesus Christ, my most blessed Lord and Saviour,' I said in a trembling voice, looking straight ahead, 'I pray for forgiveness for all my sins. I honestly and sincerely declare with all my being that I neither knew nor believed that the substance that caused the death of my dear papa was harmful or poisonous in any way. I had no intention to hurt and much less intended to destroy him by giving him that substance. I hope and pray that Almighty God, in whose most dreadful and immediate presence I must soon appear, may grant me eternal salvation and mercy. I will die in perfect peace and love for all humanity. I forgive all my enemies, particularly those who have in any manner contributed to or been instrumental in bringing me to the ignominious death I shall soon suffer.'

I briefly looked directly into Reverend Langton's eyes and then lowered my head as he said a final prayer for me.

'Almighty God, we pray to you for Mercy Grundy. May her soul and the souls of all the already departed rest in peace through your infinite mercy.'

'Thank you, Reverend Langton,' I said quietly.

The sheriff approached me, turned me round and undid the ribbons holding my hands behind me. He drew my hands in front of me and bound them again. He placed a large handkerchief over my head.

'When you are ready to meet your Maker, draw the handkerchief down over your eyes,' he said gently.

He turned me back to face the gallows. I felt myself trembling all through my body. I drew a deep, audible breath and, exhaling very slowly, edged towards the gallows ladder.

'*Have mercy upon me, O God, according to thy loving kindness: according unto the multitude of thy tender mercies blot out my transgressions,*' I called out when I reached the foot of the ladder.

Trembling almost uncontrollably, I started to ascend. As I did, I tried desperately to maintain my balance by gripping a rung level with my waist. I placed my right foot on the first rung and then put my left foot alongside. At that moment, I realised that my shoes, with their French pompadour heels, would make it difficult, if not almost impossible, to continue my climb. I very carefully kicked off one shoe and then the other.

I continued my climb, one rung at a time, pausing on each rung as I ascended. But, even with stockinged feet, my ascent was becoming increasingly difficult. I looked across at the hangman when I paused on the fifth rung.

'Sir, must I climb higher? If I do, I fear for my modesty.'

'Please climb a little higher for your own sake. The longer your drop, the more merciful your end.'

I climbed another two steps and stopped again. 'I am afraid I shall fall,' I called across to the hangman.

'One more step,' he called back.

I climbed another step.

'Now turn around,' the hangman ordered.

Trembling almost uncontrollably and fearful all the time that I would slip and fall, I managed to turn around.

The hangman put the noose around my neck and positioned it behind my ear.

I looked up to the heavens. '*Deliver me from blood-guiltiness,*

O God, thou God of my salvation: and my tongue shall sing aloud of thy righteousness,' I cried out in the strongest voice I could muster.

I stood there, composing myself sufficiently before giving the signal to turn me off. Then the atmosphere seemed to grow dark about me all at once, and a horrible chasm of blackness opened at my feet. Wondering vaguely with my last thought what mysterious fate had overtaken me, I sank into that black chasm.

Author's Note

O*ne False Step* reimagines the story of Mary Blandy, who became known as "the fair parricide" and who was hanged on the 6th of April 1752 for poisoning her father. Whilst I have followed the factual matrix of Mary's story to some degree, the book is intended as a work of fiction only.

For those who prefer it, there are four publications I have found that do address the factual matrix of the events leading to Mary Blandy's trial more precisely: *The Arsenic Century: How Victorian Britain was Poisoned at Home, Work, and Play* (James C Whorton, 2011, Oxford University Press, USA); *Trial of Mary Blandy* (edited by William Roughead, published by Wm. Hodge. [Edinburgh], 1914, see also www.gutenberg.org); *Examples of the Interposition of Providence in the Detection and Punishment of Murder* (Henry Fielding, Example XXXIII, 1752, see www. archive.org); and *Miss Mary Blandy's Own Account of the Affair Between Her and Mr Cranstoun* (Mary Blandy, 1752, see www. archive.org and *The Trial of Mary Blandy* [see above]). *The Trial of Mary Blandy* provides a transcript of Mary's trial.

Mary's story was also the subject of a contemporary play: *The Fair Parricide: A Tragedy in Three Acts. Founded on a Late*

Melancholy Event (sometimes attributed to Edward Crane, 1752).

When I was studying for my Bachelor of Laws degree, I was taught that in order for a person to be found guilty of committing a criminal offence, it is necessary to show that s/he has both committed a "guilty act" (the *actus rea*) with a "guilty mind" (the *mens rea*).

It is not disputed that Mary committed the guilty act (i.e. administering arsenic to her father). She admitted as much even before Francis died. But she denied that she acted with a guilty mind – she never meant to harm him.

The jury at Mary's trial decided in a matter of minutes that she did, as did the jury at Mercy's trial in *One False Step*. But could it truly be said that the prosecution had proved beyond reasonable doubt that Mary or, in *One False Step*, Mercy, had committed a guilty act with a guilty mind?